YOU WILL NEVER KNOW

YOU WILL NEVER KNOW

A NOVEL OF SUSPENSE

S. A. PRENTISS

SCARLET
NEW YORK

YOU WILL NEVER KNOW

Scarlet
An Imprint of Penzler Publishers
58 Warren Street
New York, N.Y. 10007

First Scarlet edition

Interior design by Maria Fernandez

Library of Congress Control Number: 2020915869

ISBN: 978-1-61316-192-0

10 9 8 7 6 5 4 3 2 1

Printed in the United States of America
Distributed by W. W. Norton & Company

For my parents

YOU WILL
NEVER KNOW

CHAPTER ONE

The second worst night of Jessica Thornton's life began on Tuesday. After a long day of teller work at Warner Savings Bank, she came home and prepared dinner for her daughter, Emma, and stepson, Craig. With dishes done and put away, she sat down on the living room couch, aching feet up on a footstool, and glanced through the latest course catalog from the Northern Essex Community College in Massachusetts.

The shiny pages with the bright-eyed students and promises of a better life caused something inside her to feel a tingle of desire. Even though her home here with Ted was in both their names, she had always felt like an interloper, not earning enough to do her fair share for their blended family. Her house in Haverhill, with her first husband, Bobby, had felt like a home, even though there had been a lot of fights and bitterness in that little one-story ranch. The house here in Warner was more than a hundred and fifty years old and creaked and settled at all hours of the day; the roof needed repairs, and the oil furnace gasped and groaned during the hard New England winters. But this place had belonged to Ted's family for decades, and she knew he would never leave, never downsize, after his uncle died a couple of years back and left Ted the property.

Even though his real estate business was in deep, deep trouble.

She flipped through the pages some more, glanced over at Emma doing homework on the other side of the room, using the MacBook Pro as easily as if it were a toaster oven. These kids . . . When Jessica was not even ten, her first home computer had been a discarded Apple Macintosh

Classic from Dad's work, and things called the internet and the World Wide Web were just stirring. Jessica had started exploring the world of BBS, AOL, and even software design, learning to take apart hard drives and computer monitors, before a certain boy caught her attention and made her focus on other things.

Her Emma was a star on the school's varsity track team, and Emma's coach had already whispered to her that next year Emma should start thinking about college scholarships. Her girl, having a free ticket to college! Having gotten pregnant with Emma by Bobby during the summer after high school graduation, Jessica had never had the chance to go to college, to expand her knowledge of computers or anything else.

But now it was time for a change.

Jessica went back to the catalog, read the description for getting an associate degree in business management. It said the program "will prepare you to enter the workforce directly in such entry-level positions as supervisors, management or sales trainees, assistant managers, or administrators."

She rubbed the slick pages. After years of plodding along as a bank teller, she now wanted more. Ted owned Warner Real Estate and the real estate market was barely stirring. In the past six months he had sold only an empty storefront lot on Water Street and a condo unit out near the town forest. Three other deals—all homes—had fallen through because the buyers couldn't get financing. Bless Ted, he tried to keep a cheerful outlook about things—"Trust me, hon, the market's ready to rebound"—but this week's news from the famed tony town of Concord, right next to Warner, had really shaken him.

He and a friend had a proposal to subdivide one of the last available empty lots in Concord, and they had gone before the zoning board of appeals to get a variance. Before leaving for the meeting, Ted had kissed her and said, "My bud says it's in the bag, we'll get the variance. Start breaking ground in a month, start selling lots soon after. The income from this project alone will make us fat and happy for years."

But hours later Ted had come home deflated, his usually smiling face somber, and had simply said, "They turned us down."

Now her husband was out with his partner on this deal, Ben Powell, grabbing cheeseburgers and beer at Harry's Place in town, trying to brainstorm another approach. Ted had left a message on the landline's voicemail, the first of two messages. The second message . . . she didn't want to think about it. That one had been deleted almost instantly. It was from the same man who had called here last Friday and left a nearly identical message.

Poor Ted.

Poor her.

Meanwhile, she wasn't going to sit on her butt and wait for the real estate market to get back on track. Oh, it wouldn't pay off for a while, but if she got an associate degree, at least she could be up for a management track at the bank. Earlier today she had briefly talked to the branch manager, Ellen Nickerson, about the bank's scholarship program for employees, and Ellen had promised to help her out.

She turned the page in the catalog, winced at the pain in her right shoulder. This morning she and other tellers at the bank had had to bring in cases of copier paper, boxes of forms and paperwork, and pile them up in a supply closet. Not really the job of a teller, but at Warner Savings, her job description and that of the others always had a clause at the end that said, "Other duties as assigned."

"Mom?" Emma was moving sheets of paper and file folders from one side of the cluttered corner desk to the other. "I can't find my blue folder. Have you seen it?"

Jessica lowered the catalog. "No, I haven't," she said. "Could it be in the kitchen?"

Emma shook her head. She had long, flawless runner's legs, blond hair down to her shoulders, and a sweet face with a little pug nose and perfect white teeth. Jessica was glad to see she was doing better. Two days ago—Sunday—she had stayed in her room all day, curled up in a ball, saying she just felt lousy, something was going on with her stomach and she had cramps, but by Monday she was ready to go back to school, and last night she had even felt well enough to go to a civic awards banquet sponsored by the Warner Chamber of Commerce, where Ted was the master of ceremonies.

"No," Emma said. "I've got my knapsack right here and I didn't open it until now. Oh, damnit . . ."

Jessica said, "Language, young lady."

Emma swiveled in her chair. "Craig and I were leaving school to catch a ride home with Heather and her boyfriend, and we bumped into a couple of kids. Me and Craig dropped our stuff. I bet the folder's with Craig."

"Makes sense."

"Mom . . ." Emma rolled her eyes, biting her lower lip. "Would you mind going up to Craig's room to see if he has it? Do you mind?"

"Nope, not at all," Jessica said, getting off the couch as her daughter turned away. Yet in that simple request, something more than just the reluctance of going up to her stepbrother's bedroom seemed to bother Emma. Jessica had that mother's sense that something was going on with her daughter, weighing on her mind. Just the look on Emma's face—there was more going on there than concern over a missing folder.

Jessica decided not to say anything and walked by her hardworking girl.

After going up the narrow creaking staircase—one of the joys of living in a home built when Lincoln was president—Jessica took a right, knocked on Craig's bedroom door. The upstairs was small and confining, with the main bathroom at the top of the stairs and with Emma's room right across from her stepbrother's.

No answer, which wasn't a surprise.

She knocked again, harder.

Nothing.

Jessica sighed. She didn't want to go back and disappoint Emma, so she opened the door and walked in. The smell of a boy's room struck her. There were clothes on the floor and magazines and an empty pizza box, and there was an unmade bed, posters on the wall for bands she had never heard of. Craig was sitting at a small desk, looking at his computer screen, earbuds in, and—what the hell was on that screen? Could it—

Somehow he sensed she was there, and with one push of a key the computer screen went blank. He turned and slowly blinked twice, as if he were an old turtle that had been surprised. Craig tugged out one earbud and then the other.

"Yeah, Jessica, what is it?"

Three years in and she still wasn't used to him calling her by her first name. Jessica had encouraged him many times to call her Mom but had given up about a year ago. She had tried her best, had even spent a couple of hundred hard-earned dollars on books about blended families. Nothing seemed to work. Some days he was cheerful and upbeat, and other days . . . well, she had heard tales of moody teenage boys, and lucky her, when she had married Ted three years ago, she had gotten one right out of the box.

"Emma's doing homework. She's missing a blue folder. She said you and she bumped into some kids while you were leaving, that you dropped some stuff. Could you have it?"

He shook his head. "Nope."

"Could you look?"

"I don't have to look. I know I don't have it."

"Craig, please," she said, and then he looked at her again, oddly, as if he were seeing her for the very first time in his life.

"Tell me again what Emma said?" he asked.

Jessica felt that by entering this boy's room, she was stepping into a place that held dreams, fantasies, and frustrations she could never understand. "Emma said the two of you bumped into some kids while you were leaving school."

"Bumped," Craig repeated with a smirk on his face. He was tall, gangly, with a rough complexion and a thick thatch of brown hair that was never combed. "The two of us got jumped by our own little group of alt-right clowns—the wrestling team—and they decided to have some

5

fun with us. There was no bump. Just a bunch of elbows and hands flying around, and our stuff dumped on the lawn."

"Craig—"

"I don't have her precious folder." Craig put the earbuds back in and went back to his computer.

But he didn't do anything.

The screen was still blank. Jessica was suddenly nauseated, as if she had just bitten into a crisp-looking apple and tasted soft mush instead. Because of what had been on Craig's monitor when she had opened the door: a shaky video of a young woman's face with an erect penis dangling over her half-open mouth, her eyes closed. Jessica backed out, closed the door, and went back downstairs, stomach still slowly flip-flopping, rehearsing what she would say to her daughter, but Emma beat her to it.

"Found it!" she said, holding up the blue folder. "It must have gotten slipped into this envelope."

"Good girl," Jessica said. "I'm so glad. But Emma . . ."

Emma started tidying up her papers and folders. "Yeah, Mom?"

"Craig said that you weren't bumped into by accident. That it was members of the wrestling team picking on you."

Emma turned, made an exaggerated rise of her eyebrows. "Oh, please, Mom. Craig's a boy, but sometimes he can be such a diva asshole. It was an accident—no big deal. Honest."

Jessica smiled. "Language once more, young lady."

—m—

She spent the rest of the evening watching *Real Housewives*—how could anybody look at those rich, Botoxed, pampered women and call them housewives with a straight face?—and flipping through the thin pages of the *Warner Daily News*. That paper was a half-and-half mixture of advertisements for Warner and local places like Concord and Carlisle and some reprinted press releases.

She checked the time. Shouldn't Ted be home by now?

Jessica next went to the police logs.

"11:12 A.M., Saturday: police dispatched to the town dump and waste transfer station, responding to a call of a fight in progress. Arriving officer reported no fight was involved, just a petition signer and a local resident getting into a heated discussion over a petition to ban plastic shopping bags in town."

"Mom?"

Her head snapped up. "Yes?"

Emma was putting her papers and folders into her blue knapsack. "I'm done. I'm going up to bed."

"Okay, hon, sleep well."

As her daughter got to the bottom of the stairs, Jessica remembered that earlier odd look on Emma's face when she had asked for Jessica's help. She called out, "Emma, you know you can talk to me about anything. Right? Anything at all."

There was a pause. She could sense that Emma was thinking about something. Was she thinking about telling her mom what was really going on behind those bright blue eyes?

Her daughter turned her head, put one foot on the bottom step. "Night, Mom."

—⁂—

When Ted came home, she was startled. Had she dozed off on the couch?

He dropped his soft leather briefcase on the floor by the closet that held his golf clubs and gun locker, pulled off his short leather coat, dropped it on a nearby chair, yawned, and came her way. The sound of him banging the sticky door open had stirred her. Sometimes it took three or four tries to shove the door either closed or open. Jessica checked the time. It was nearly eleven thirty. Had he really been out that long with his business partner?

"Hey," he said, rubbing at the back of his head, smiling. He was five years older than she was, with thick black and gray hair that was always trimmed closely, bright blue eyes, and a ruddy complexion that suggested he spent a lot of time outdoors, which he did, with his golfing, hunting, and fishing. "What's up?"

What's up? Jessica thought. She wondered if she should bring up catching seventeen-year-old Craig looking at porn and thought, *No, Ted's got enough on his shoulders, and what teenage boy doesn't look at porn?*

"Nothing," she said. "Pretty quiet night. The kids are both upstairs. You?"

He shook his head. "Things still don't look good. They look . . . well, they look pretty rough." Another yawn. "But Ben says not to give up. He's got a couple of ideas and I'm going to let him run with it."

"Good."

Ted came over, leaned down and gently kissed her, saw the community college catalog on the couch next to her. "Hey, so you're really going to do it, huh?"

She laughed, gestured to the television screen. It was still on Bravo and its *Real Housewives* franchise, but this one was in Melbourne, not Orange County. "You know it," Jessica said. "If I can get moving better with my career, such as it is, I'll be ready for the day when Bravo starts filming *Real Housewives of Warner*."

Ted smiled, kissed her again. "That's a dream worth going after, hon. Hey, I'm going upstairs to take a shower, then come back down and hit the sack."

He went up the narrow stairs, and she heard Ted's murmuring voice, doors opening and closing, and then it sounded like he went into the bathroom. She picked up the remote, toggled the cable channel guide. Good. This episode was running fifteen minutes over, and then Ted would be done with his shower and they could go to bed together. Tomorrow she'd fill out the paperwork to apply for that associate degree program, get things moving in the right direction.

Ted came running down the stairs, calling out, "Jessica!" The tone of his voice startled her.

"What's wrong?" she asked.

But he went into the kitchen and dining area, then to their bedroom and even their small downstairs bathroom, and her heart started racing. Her mouth was quickly going dry, as if the humidity in their house were suddenly escaping, and she yelled out, "Ted! What's wrong?"

He came into the living room, breathing hard. "Jessica, the kids—Emma, Craig."

"What?"

"Where are they?" Ted asked.

CHAPTER TWO

S ome years back, Jessica had been a bank teller in the dying old mill city of Haverhill, set right up against the New Hampshire border. A widow with an eleven-year-old daughter. One deep and dark secret Jessica had always kept was that she had been on the road to divorcing Bobby Thornton before he died in a drunk-driving accident on I-95 up in York, Maine. Bobby had been a car salesman, flashy and full of himself, but his drinking and anger and the slaps to Jessica's face had gotten worse over the years. While she had shed real tears at his funeral, what she had cried over was the lost opportunity for Bobby to give Emma at least a decade's worth of child support before a trust fund he had set up for her was available for disbursement by Jessica when Emma turned twenty-one, with Emma having rights to the whole thing when she turned thirty.

After his death things had been tight, always tight, with lots of clipped store coupons and ramen noodle dinners for many dreary months, the thought of that trust fund hanging out there like a distant mirage. Oh, there had been a life insurance policy, but Jessica had used most of the money for unexpected bills, like having to buy a used car when the engine crapped out on her Honda and paying for private track lessons and coaching for Emma. Even as a struggling widow, Jessica had been determined to do whatever it took to give her daughter a better life.

Then one Saturday she and other bank employees had been at a charity softball event when she met Ted Donovan. He was working for a nearby real estate agency and was the captain of his group's softball team. He had on shorts and a T-shirt; his legs and arms were tanned and muscular. But it was his smile, and his jokes, and his laughter and gentle teasing, that had attracted her to him.

Ted played that day to have fun, and truth be told, Jessica had dressed to play and get attention as well. She had worn a pair of black Spandex shorts and a light blue sports bra with a center zipper she made sure was lowered some, and Ted had definitely given her a good, pleasant stare when they were introduced.

Later that warm and special day, when both of their teams had been eliminated, he offered to help her use a beer tap to fill up her red plastic drinking cup. The damn thing had been oozing out foam, and he watched her struggle with the hose for a few moments, then softly asked, "Can I help?"

Weeks later, after they had first made love in his condo in Andover, she had said, "You know what really made me want to go out with you?"

Her head was on his chest and one of his hands was gently stroking her hair. "My shiny white teeth?"

She laughed and kissed his chest. "No, silly. It was when you asked to help me with that damn keg, back at the softball game. You didn't charge in and take control. You didn't pull the hose away and try to give me a lesson in how I was doing it wrong. You asked."

His gentle stroking of her hair continued. "I'd like to keep that up, if you don't mind. Asking you before I do things."

She snuggled into his warmth and softness and scent. "Don't mind at all."

And Ted had paused, and then said, his voice lower, "I know it's early, but someday I just might ask you if I could take care of you and your girl, for a long time to come."

Then Jessica had just closed her eyes, and thinking of the disappointment her first marriage had been, she heard a little voice inside that said, *Yes, he just might be the one. He just might.*

Might be the one who could help her with her dreams for Emma.

11

That long-ago moment of peace, satisfaction, and anticipation was now as foreign to Jessica's thoughts as being the first woman to walk on the moon. She knew Ted's emotions, his many strengths and few weaknesses, and she also knew it was impossible for him to tell her a joke without laughing halfway through it.

Now his face was a mixture of surprise, concern, and anger, and there was no humor there.

Whatever drowsiness had been entwined around her mind and muscles was gone. Jessica stood right up, the catalog falling off her lap. "They're not upstairs?"

"No, I checked both their bedrooms and the bathroom, and they're not there."

Jessica got up and went through the dining room to the door leading to the cellar. She flicked on the light, went down the olden wooden stairs, past the small window set into the foundation, and down to the dirt floor. Nothing there except the washing machine and dryer and wooden pallets holding boxes of junk, his and hers.

"Emma! Are you down here? Emma!"

No answer.

She ran back upstairs, and Ted said, "Did they say anything about going out?"

"Christ, no," Jessica said, her neck and chest constricting. "Emma went to bed a couple of hours ago, and Craig . . . he was already in his bedroom. They didn't say anything about going out. And—"

She stopped it right there. For the past three years Emma and Craig had been polite with each other, mostly, but they had kept their lives and their friends separate as stepsiblings. Jessica could imagine either one of them sneaking out of the house on their own, but together? Impossible. Their relationship was not a *Brady Bunch* redux.

Ted started talking, and Jessica brushed past him and ran upstairs to the second floor, calling out, "Emma! Are you hiding?"

At the top of the stairs she ducked into the bathroom and made sure the tub was empty. As she was leaving, she heard Ted opening and closing the downstairs closet door.

What was he doing?

She came out of the bathroom, saw Ted trotting upstairs, and she went to the right, flung open Emma's bedroom door.

"Emma!"

The room was in its typical cluttered state, with an unmade bed and open closet, some clothes on the floor, piles of running shoes. Posters of running greats Gwen Torrence, Sydney Michelle McLaughlin, and the historic Flo-Jo. A handmade poster with dates and grids made by Emma last spring, showing the classes she planned to take over the next two years, her large handwriting stating *Emma's Road to Victory!!!* On a bureau was a cluster of running trophies, ribbons and medals dangling from some of them, and even in this moment of darkness Jessica felt that thrill of knowing that her girl was special, was talented, had a whole future ahead of her.

But where was she?

Jessica even ducked into the small closet, past the gym bags, small hand weights, more running shoes. Nothing.

Ted was standing in Emma's doorway. "Well?" he asked, his face ashen.

"Ted . . . I don't know, I just don't know!"

She brushed by Ted, went into Craig's room. Ted was right behind her. Nothing in the room had changed since she had been in here earlier. It still looked like a typical teenage boy's room—more clothes, more clutter, even smellier.

A typical teenage boy who was gone.

With his attractive younger teenage stepsister.

A teenage boy who a little while ago had been looking at a video on his computer.

"Ted . . ."

The words forming inside her felt heavy and deadly, and she tried to choose them carefully, but seconds were going by and she couldn't wait.

13

She couldn't wait.

"What were you going to say?"

"Ted, I just don't know."

He stepped closer, and she could smell the scent of fear and something else on him, some sickly-sweet odor. "Please, Jessica, what are you thinking?"

What was she thinking? Any other time she wouldn't dare mention it, but no, not tonight, not with her girl gone.

"Damn it, earlier I came into Craig's room and there was something on his computer. A video. There was an erect cock near a woman's face. A young woman who had blond hair. Like Emma. I'm sorry if that upsets you, Ted, but it's the truth. We need to think about that."

His eyes narrowed, and his face flushed even more. He turned and started down the stairs, yelling back up at her, "Christ, Jessica!"

She followed him down, both of their feet slamming hard against the old wood. "I couldn't help it, Ted, how could I? Emma's an attractive girl, and Craig, he's—"

At the bottom of the stairs, Ted whirled and said up to her, "What? A rapist? A kidnapper? A perv? For Christ's sake, he's just a kid!"

Jessica felt the blush of shame for having mentioned it, but how could she avoid it? Ted was protective of his son, that made absolute sense, but Jessica was exactly the same about Emma. And a long-buried memory came back, of Mom in the bathroom, trying to put some sort of makeup on a bruised cheek, saying with a tired voice, "You want to go through life, child, sometimes you have to sacrifice, keep smiling, and keep your mouth shut for your own good."

But this was Emma.

She said, "Ted, I'm sorry, I'm just scared. That's all. I'm sorry."

He looked so angry that he couldn't talk, but Jessica wasn't going to stand there and apologize again. She walked by him and went to the front door, tugged and tugged at it until it squeaked itself free. She stepped onto the granite steps, looked up and down the empty sidewalk, past the other homes on the street, most of which were now unlit so late at night. Ted's leased BMW and her old Sentra were parked side by side in the driveway.

"Emma! Are you out here? Emma!"

Nothing, nothing at all.

Ted was behind her, breathing hard. "Please, get back in the house. Please."

"Emma!"

She allowed him to gently pull her back into the house. The cranky door took two tries before it was successfully closed and Ted said, "Look, I'll go out, see what I can find out and—"

"What do you mean, find out?"

"Jessica, I grew up here, okay? I know the hangouts. The places where kids go. I'll head out for a drive, all right?"

"And what do you think I should do?" she asked, her voice rising. "Just sit here and hope for the best?"

He went to the chair where he had dumped his short leather coat. "Christ, no. Get on the phone. Call Emma's friends, call her track coach. Maybe there's some sort of secret party going on tonight, something like that."

"A party? On a school night? With Craig going, too?"

"Jessica, please, just do it!"

Then he slammed his way out of the house, going to his BMW, and Jessica went to the kitchen, retrieved her iPhone from the charger, started scrolling through her contacts.

She stopped as something heavy seemed to strike the back of her neck.

She had been lightly dozing when Ted had come home, and the sound of him pushing against the old door had woken her. So why hadn't the noise of Emma and Craig leaving done the same?

Her first call was to Emma's cell phone, which went straight to voice-mail. The second went to Craig's, with the same result.

She hesitated and then called Emma again and said, "Emma, it's Mom . . . It's past eleven thirty—where are you? You . . . you know if there's something wrong you can come to me. Honest. Please. Call back soon."

Then she called Craig's number again, and in her growing anger and despair almost left a message as well—*You tell me what you did to my daughter*—but she held back and went on to make other calls.

CHAPTER THREE

After making three more phone calls, Jessica was through, her chest tight, mouth dry, hands shaking.

The first call went to Emma's track coach, John Webber, who also coached two other sport teams at school and who openly lived with his partner, Pete Beaumont. That arrangement had eased a potential problem in Jessica's mind—and that of other mothers—of the creepy coach getting too interested in his female charges.

After Coach Webber, Jessica called the parents of two of Emma's friends, the McAllisters and the Romers, whose daughters were also on the track team. In each case she awakened adults who were grumpy and cautious when they answered the phone but snapped to full consciousness when Jessica explained the situation.

"I'm sorry to bother you, but Emma's gone out and I don't know where she is," Jessica had said to all three. "She didn't leave a note, she isn't answering her cell phone . . . I just wondered if you might have any idea if there's some sort of party or get-together going on tonight with her friends or the track team."

And that had led to being on hold for a while as John Webber checked with other parents whose daughters were on the track team, then later as Barry McAllister interrogated his daughter, Melissa, and even later, when Doris Romer talked to her daughter, Kate.

They could offer nothing, with all three telling her that they would call her if they found anything out and each of them having a tone in their voice of *How in hell do you lose your teenage daughter with no driver's license on a school night?*

—⁂—

Jessica paced back and forth in the old house, floorboards creaking, making sure every light in the house was on. She then took a flashlight and went out to their small backyard, which was bordered at the rear by a tall wooden fence and on either side by shrubbery.

It was starting to rain, and back in the house she called Ted, and damn it to hell, his cell phone went to voicemail.

Enough.

She left the door unlocked and took her car, a wheezing old Nissan Sentra, and drove to the high school, looking at the empty sidewalks in town, slowing down when she saw a couple walking along the side of the road and then speeding up when she saw that neither person was Craig or Emma.

Craig.

She clenched her steering wheel so hard her fingers hurt, replaying the memory of just a few hours ago, seeing the video. She imagined the gangly boy sitting in the chair in his smelly bedroom, jacking off, and then, as his lust built and built, he realized there was a real-life hottie just a few yards away . . .

So what did he do? Peek in on her? Assault her? And if he did that, why hadn't Jessica heard anything?

And damn it, why had she backed down when she had seen that porn on his computer? Why hadn't she said something to Craig? Maybe if she had done that, he would have been shaken up, she would have thrown him off, kept him from doing whatever might have happened.

Not much of a stern stepmother, now, are we? came a nagging interior voice.

The car seemed to shudder around her. Just a few minutes, that's all it had taken for this family to start crumbling, for her to think the worst of her stepson, for her husband to get angry at her.

The windshield wipers were flicking back and forth, back and forth, making everything out there look smeared and smudged, and she drove into the school's parking lot and then carefully maneuvered onto the playing fields near the empty viewing stands. She flicked the car's headlights on high and stepped out, realizing that she hadn't brought a coat.

"Emma!"

Jessica started crying. What was the point of coming here, to the place where Emma was setting records and becoming the envy of track coaches around the state? For years Jessica had enjoyed running with Emma, until that unfortunate event two years back, something she hated to remember, but Jessica never, ever missed a track meet, while Ted could never be bothered to see his accomplished stepdaughter.

"Emma!"

The rain came down more heavily. The fields were sodden.

She got back in her car and drove home.

—◊—

Ted was waiting for her in the empty house and said, "Where the hell have you been?"

She went to the kitchen, tore off a length of paper towel, wiped her face, hair, and hands. "Looking, just like you were. Did you find anything?"

"Christ, of course not," he said. "Why didn't you call me to tell me you were going out?"

She crumpled up the wet paper towel and in a flash of anger that surprised her tossed it at him. "I did, damn it! And it went right to voicemail."

"Oh," Ted said, suddenly remorseful. "Shit, I forgot. I set it to mute when I was at Harry's Place with Ben."

Jessica tore off another piece of towel, blew her nose, and started walking to the telephone hanging on the wall by the cabinets. Ted had insisted they keep a landline in case potential clients found his home phone number from old real estate listings. Refrigerator magnets held up Emma's photocopied track schedules. The sight of those plain sheets of paper nearly made her burst into tears.

Ted asked, "Who are you calling?"

Jessica picked up the receiver. "Who do you think? The police."

Ted shook his head, took the receiver from her hand, put it back into place. "Jessica, no."

Jessica stared at her husband in disbelief. What was going on with him? Didn't Ted see how serious this was?

"What are you talking about?" she said, trying to keep her tone civil. "Our kids are missing. You didn't find anything, I didn't find anything. It's way past midnight. They won't answer their cell phones."

Or can't, a dark part of her suggested, and she shoved that thought away. She took a breath. "I called Emma's track coach and the parents of her two best friends, Melissa and Kate. Nothing. We've got to call the police."

Ted maneuvered himself so he was between the telephone and Jessica. "Just hold on, all right? Just hold on. It's only been a couple of hours. We don't know what's happened yet. Let's just wait a while."

"How long?"

"I don't know, but I know calling now doesn't make sense."

"Ted, I'm sorry, I can't wait," she said, going over to the kitchen counter. "You wait if you want to. I'll use my cell phone if I have to."

And Ted, her love, her husband, the man she wanted to stay with as long they both lived, moved quickly past her, grabbed her purse, and said, "No."

She stood still, staring at this strange man in front of her. He looked ridiculous, holding her purse against his chest. His eyes seemed wide, full of concern, full of . . .

Fear?

Fear of what?

Jessica took a calming breath. "Theodore Alan Donovan, you either tell me what the hell is going on right now or I'm walking out of this house and I'm going to find a telephone and call the police. You can let your son hitchhike to Boston or Providence or stay missing, I really don't care, but I'm going to find my Emma."

He said, "It won't make a difference, not now. They don't investigate unless someone's been missing for more than twenty-four hours."

"That's bullshit," she said. "That's for an adult. Not for two teenagers." Jessica started out of the kitchen. "I'm going out. Don't try to stop me."

"Wait!"

She turned. He slowly put her purse back on the kitchen counter. It almost fell off and he stretched a hand to push it back. It looked sad and almost comical.

"Jessica, with that development in Concord being canceled, I'm in a rough place. Very rough place. The worst since I got my real estate license."

She crossed her arms, trying to squeeze and protect herself, trying to keep Ted from seeing how her hands were shaking, how much she was scared, and how much he was scaring her.

Ted said, "I'm like that guy in the circus, the . . . the wire walker. That's right. The wire walker. Like that guy in the documentary about the World Trade Center's towers. I'm halfway across, there's no net. I've dropped the balancing pole and the wire's starting to fray . . . Jessica, we call the Warner police, the word will get out about our kids being missing. Rightly or wrongly, people will think they've run away from home. And if they both ran away from home, then it must have been because we were bad parents. Jessica, I'm in a pit right now. If people around here think I'm a bad parent, you think they're going to come to me to sell their property? Do you? Something like this will destroy me."

Jessica stared at Ted. She had never seen his face so red, so frightened. It was now so quiet in the kitchen that she could hear the rain hammering the roof of the old house.

She said, "I don't care, Ted. I really don't. If we find the kids and you lose your job and we have to live in a trailer somewhere in Lowell or Lawrence, so what. Getting them back is what counts. Nothing else."

Jessica started to turn and Ted said, "Please, you've got to wait!"

21

She lost it. She couldn't help herself. "My Emma is gone and you want me to wait?"

He stepped forward, fists clenched. "Hey, my boy's gone, too! All you care about is your precious Emma, Emma, Emma. You're so self-centered that—"

"That's not true!" She stood her ground, feeling like she was defending Emma, even with her not here, and she steeled herself for that sudden smack, that sudden blow that had struck her so many times when she had been married to Bobby.

But Ted didn't cross that line. "The hell it isn't true!" he said. "You made three calls, right? Did you ask about Craig? Did you? No, it was all about Emma. My boy's gone too and you didn't care. All you cared about was accusing him of doing something bad, just because he did something every teenage boy with a computer does—look at porn."

"Ted, I called Craig's cell phone."

"And what else did you do? Did you ask me for his contacts so you could call him while I was out looking for both him and your daughter?"

"So this is my fault now?"

They were still arguing when the door shuddered open and a drenched Emma and Craig came in.

It was three A.M.

CHAPTER FOUR

Observed from an iPhone screen being held in the south hallway, first floor of Warner High School, Wednesday morning, 9:05 A.M.:

From Craig: hey
From Emma: what?
Craig: need to see u
Emma: no.
Craig: PLEASE
Emma: why?
Craig: u know why
Craig: still there?
Craig: Emma?
Emma: cafeteria, third period
Craig: K
Emma: K
Craig: u shld know, Randy's pissed about car
Emma: so what
Craig: he's pissed
Emma: its a shitbox. Later
Craig: K
Craig: do u think we'll get caught?
Craig: Emma?
Craig: u there?

CHAPTER FIVE

The next day was rotten, start to finish, and the only way Jessica was able to function at Warner Savings Bank was because she was fortified with three cups of morning coffee instead of her usual one.

Rhonda Monroe gave Jessica a long hard glance once they had both logged in to the bank's computer system. She was twenty years older than Jessica and was her best friend at the bank. Rhonda was still married to her high school sweetheart and had two adult boys, four grandkids, assorted nieces and nephews. She had a sweet smile and her hair was black (with help from her hairdresser) and trimmed short. She always wore out-of-style pantsuits and had been working in this same branch for years, going through at least three takeovers, and seemed content with what she had. Some days Jessica envied her and her simplicity, and she could remember her being distressed only one time, when a previous manager had taken a dislike to her and nearly had her fired.

"Christ on a crutch, Jessica, what happened to you last night?" Rhonda asked. "I'd say you look like death warmed over, but that'd be an insult to death."

Jessica checked her teller area one more time, with forms, pens, and stamps ready, next to three framed photos: one of her and Emma when her daughter was just ten, one of Emma winning a track meet in junior high, and one of her and Ted on their wedding day. She felt chilled, looking at the happy woman in that last photo. That day had been full of delight and promises of the future, but never could she have imagined what had happened last night, with an empty house and a husband who suddenly seemed to gain an equally empty soul.

"Rough night," Jessica said. "One of the roughest I've had in . . . well, a long time, Rhonda."

Since she had arrived at work, rain had started again in downtown Warner. From the rain-swept outside came the sound of a siren as a dark-blue Warner police cruiser raced past the downtown buildings, blue lights flashing, splashing up water from the street.

Rhonda reached over, touched her wrist. "Hon, what happened? Are you okay? Was it something Ted did?"

She shook her head. "No. It was Emma . . . and Craig. Somehow, and I don't know how, they both slipped out of the house last night. Stayed out until three A.M. Drove Ted and me crazy. Didn't leave a note, didn't answer their phones. It was so scary."

"Sweet Jesus," Rhonda said. "What were they up to?"

Jessica turned to Rhonda, the anger from a few hours ago racing once again through her. "That's the thing! Some stupid scavenger-hunt game that they were playing! They just said that they had to go out, that they were sorry, and that it would never happen again. I grilled Emma, Ted did the same to Craig. They wouldn't tell us who ran the hunt, how they learned about it, what they had to do. Finally it got so late we had to send them to bed so at least they could go to school later without falling asleep in class."

Rhonda studied her. "But sweetie . . . I mean, you've told me that the two of them, they don't get along that well. What were they doing out together at that time of the night?"

"That's what doesn't make sense," Jessica said, watching the rain lash the old brick buildings of downtown Warner. "They can barely stand sitting together for dinner at night. I can't believe they'd try to sneak out of the house together. It just doesn't make sense."

One of the two younger tellers, Amber Brooks, went out through the lobby, her young curves swinging and swaying under a lacy white blouse and tight black slacks, and Jessica didn't feel envy, just sorrow, thinking

S. A. PRENTISS

about what kind of future waited for this sweet young girl, now unlocking the main door, who so wanted to meet a Prince Charming to take care of her and her future kids.

Not many princes left, Jessica thought, and then Rhonda said, "You know I'm always here to help. Always."

"Thanks, Rhon," Jessica said.

"I mean, I remember those rough times back—"

"Well, I was happy to help," Jessica said, which was one hundred percent true.

Rhonda asked, "How did your meeting go yesterday with the Ice Queen?"

Even with her exhaustion and cold thoughts of last night, Jessica gave a short laugh at Rhonda's insult. Their branch manager was tall, slim, and always looked hard, as if she had been carved out of marble, and it seemed like she never smiled.

"Not bad," she said. "Ellen confirmed there was a scholarship program, that it was available for certain employees who proved themselves, and said that while she would help where she could, I had to do my part."

Rhonda sounded puzzled. "Like what? You're usually first one in and last one out. Crap, I can't remember the last time you didn't balance your drawer."

"Well, Rhon, there's more than that now. Upper management is looking at how well tellers do in upselling stuff. I need to increase that for her to put in a recommendation."

"Bitch," Rhonda said as the first customers came in, shaking off the rain from their umbrellas and raincoats. One went up to the lobby desk. On the wall was a framed black-and-white photo of Larry Miles, a manager who had died two years ago in a climbing accident up in the White Mountains.

"Bitch squared," Jessica agreed.

Then they both shut up as Ellen Nickerson strode in, tan raincoat belted tight against her waist. She joined the customers in tossing the water off, then she undid the coat belt and came over. Her hair was red,

26

cut short and severe, and she stood just a bit under six feet. Her high heels clicked hard on the lobby surface as she walked. She always wore the latest fashions as declaimed by the Style section of the *New York Times*, but they never softened her hard look.

Jessica held her breath as Ellen came closer.

"Jessica?"

"Yes?"

Something approaching a smile slid across Ellen's severe face. "I made a call to corporate," she said. "Pled your case."

Jessica nodded.

Ellen said, "You do your part, and Warner Savings will do the same."

She turned and headed to her office, and Jessica breathed again, and Rhonda smiled at her and whispered, "Jess, you better start upselling that pretty butt of yours, and quick."

Jessica whispered back, "My boobs, too, if it helps," which resulted in a quick snort of laughter from her friend.

She took a long, deep yawn, tried to feel more awake. Even with everything that had happened in the past ten hours, maybe—just maybe—things were looking up. A Warner fire truck and ambulance roared by, splashing more water along the road.

But Jessica's second miserable day in a row was about to take shape.

—⟨⟩—

With the heavy rains that morning, the foot traffic in the lobby was nearly nonexistent, but the drive-up was busy, with five or six cars in line. At the drive-up window, Percy Prescott was sliding out the drawer to a customer driving a beat-up black Ford Escort. Percy was twenty years old, wore horn-rimmed glasses, and had finely trimmed light brown hair, and he wore the same clothes every day: dark gray slacks, cordovans, and a light green-and-white shirt with a green necktie, highlighting the corporate colors of Warner Savings, as well as his nametag and a bank lapel pin.

"You have a great day now, all right?" he said into the microphone as the drawer slid out, his smiling face bright. Then he flicked off the microphone with a disdainful move of his slight fingers. "And for Christ's sake, the next time you make a deposit, wipe the bills on your ass. They'd smell better than that cologne."

The drawer clattered back and Amber sauntered over, started chatting with Percy. They were young, single, and had gone to Warner High School together. Amber leaned over to point something out to Percy, revealing a tattoo on her lower backside that she claimed was a Chinese character representing the word "courage."

One day, bored and with not much to do, Jessica had sketched the Chinese character and showed it to the owner of the Szechuan Taste restaurant in Warner, and he had laughed and said the character meant "smelly."

Jessica knew she would never tell Amber the truth. She knew how to keep secrets.

—⁓—

About two hours into her morning, luck seemed to appear in front of her—like getting a dollar lottery ticket that was worth a hundred bucks—in the form of an older man taking his time coming up to her window.

"Good morning," she said. "How are you today?"

The man shrugged. "Okay, I guess. Soaked, like every other poor bugger out there. I'd like to cash this, please." He was in his sixties, wearing a rain-soaked dungaree jacket and dirty dark-green chinos, reading glasses that were perched halfway down a prominent nose, and a filthy Red Sox baseball cap, also soaked through.

"This" was a rebate check from Staples, and she recognized the customer—Gus Tremblay. Just to make sure his account was still current, she typed his name into the bank's system and saw his account profile pop up.

Oh my, Jessica thought. Gus dressed like a slob, but that was the uniform for the wealthy in this part of Massachusetts. It just wasn't done to flash one's wealth, especially if your family had lived for decades in Warner or nearby Concord and Lexington, and Gus was certainly keeping that tradition alive. He had more than $35,000 in his checking account and nearly $300,000 in a passbook savings account.

It came to her like a flash of lightning. Upsell Gus right here and now, do a couple more before the end of the week, and then go back to Ellen, tell her that she was on the way to holding up her end of the bargain. Make that scholarship request go through, sign up for the associate degree from Northern Essex, and get running on the path to do her part to help her family, just like Emma was running for her future.

"Hey, ma'am?" Tremblay asked.

"Yes?"

"My money?"

"Yes, right away," Jessica said. She ran the check through the teller terminal, saw again that it was for fifteen dollars, and then took a ten and a five out of her drawer. She slid them over and said, "Mr. Tremblay, I see you have substantial assets here at Warner Savings Bank. Have you ever considered transferring some of those funds to our valued customer money market accounts? Or taking out a home equity loan to make some needed improvements? If you have a moment, I can set up an appointment with our—"

Tremblay took the five and the ten, carefully examined them, and slipped them into a worn leather wallet. "Ma'am, I came here to get my cash. I got my cash. Please don't waste my time."

"But—"

"Jesus, ma'am, you don't goddamn hear well, do you?"

He turned and started walking out, and other customers started coming in, and in a quiet voice so he wouldn't hear, Jessica surprised herself and said aloud, "Have a nice day, Mr. Tremblay. I hope you get hit by a truck."

Then she nearly jumped a foot when Amber, stationed right next to her, started whispering "No, no, no," and her first thought was, *Crap, did she just hear me chew out a customer?*

But in a few seconds she knew it was much worse than that.

Jessica turned and so did Rhonda, and even Percy Prescott at the drive-up looked over. Amber was now sobbing, holding up her iPhone. "I just got a text from my mom! Sam Warner's dead! They found his body over at the Warner Town Forest! Oh, my God! My brother Jack's on the wrestling team with him. Oh, Sam!"

Rhonda said, "Jesus Christ, you mean Sam, Bruce and Donna's kid? The captain of the wrestling team?"

Because Amber was crying, it was hard to make out what she was saying, but Rhonda put a hand on her shoulder and looked over the text.

"Oh, no," she said, "not Sam."

"What happened?" Jessica asked. "Do they say how he died?"

Percy had shouldered his way in to read the text messages on Amber's phone, whistled, and shook his head. "Huh, now it makes sense."

Rhonda said, "What makes sense?"

He started back to his station just as a dark-blue Volvo station wagon stopped in front of the drive-up. "All those sirens from before," Percy explained. "The cruiser and the ambulance. It says Sam was murdered in the town forest."

CHAPTER SIX

Emma Thornton was in the Warner High School cafeteria at 10:41 that Wednesday morning, one minute after it opened for the day, and she found an empty table at the far end, dumped her knapsack, and yawned. Crap, she'd been yawning ever since she had gotten to school, and she hoped she'd be alert enough for that afternoon's track practice. She looked at the other kids coming into the cafeteria, yapping and texting, to see if Craig had shown up.

Nope. Not yet.

This was her study period and she was sorely tempted just to stretch out and plop her head on her knapsack and take a nap. She was sure she'd fall asleep in about sixty seconds, but then one of the noisy teachers who served as cafeteria monitors would come over and ask her if everything was all right and why she was napping, and maybe she'd be sent to see Mrs. Morneau, the school nurse.

Right, and that would mean a phone call or email message to her mom, and after last night—shit, just a few hours ago, right?—Emma didn't want anybody from the school reaching out to Mom.

"Hey." Her goofball stepbrother sat down across from her, dropping his knapsack on the cafeteria table. Emma knew she didn't look so hot after so few hours of sleep, but he looked even worse. His hair resembled a big thicket that could be a nest for a field mouse or a chipmunk or something just as stupid, and knowing Craig, he probably could have a mouse crawl into that hair mess and he'd never know.

Emma said, "What do you want?"

"Like I said, Randy's pissed about his car."

"Did he get paid?"

"Well, yeah—"

"It broke down. It's a shitbox. He should be happy we're not asking for a refund."

Craig looked around and leaned over the light-green cafeteria table. "I still can't believe last night. I mean—"

"Shut up," Emma said quietly. "We both agreed not to talk about this at school, or anywhere else where somebody might hear." She yawned again, put her hand in front of her mouth. Jeez, with track practice this afternoon she'd have to beg a Red Bull from somebody just to make sure she didn't take a wrong turn and end up in Concord or something like that.

"But last night . . ."

"Okay, it didn't go as planned. Shit happens, right?"

"Emma, c'mon, you know your mom and my dad are super pissed."

"They'll get over it," Emma said. "You the smartie, me the best runner—eventually they'll overlook it. That's what parents do. Relax."

Her stepbrother leaned further over the table. Emma saw dirty pores around his nose. "I'm trying to relax," he whispered, "but after last night . . ."

"Keep to the story," she said. "Stop worrying. You keep on worrying and your dad will notice."

"But what happens when—"

"Shut up," Emma said.

He blinked his eyes, sat back, and then said, "One other thing."

"Yeah?"

"You made a promise."

"I did."

"You gonna keep it?"

Emma said, "What do you think?"

His face flushed. "So, when?"

"Never," Emma said. "How does never sound?"

His face grew even redder, the poor slob. "But you promised!"

That last sentence was loud enough so a couple of the closer students turned their heads to see what was going on. Snoops, she thought.

Emma said, "Keep it down, Craig, or I'll change my mind and start talking. And who do you think is going to be believed? The star runner? Or the computer creep who needs to take a shower?"

Emma thought he was going to argue more, but instead he pushed the dark-green knapsack around and unzipped it and then slowly opened it so Emma could see what was inside: the stock of a gun, half wrapped in a white towel, the separated oily-looking metal barrel resting next to it.

"Jesus Christ, Craig, zip it shut!"

He zipped it shut as ordered and said, "Well, what now?"

"Get rid of it. Warner River, down a storm drain, over at Woods Quarry. But get rid of it, you idiot."

He scowled and picked up the knapsack and pushed his way back from the table, making his chair squeak really loudly. He stormed his way out through the nearest double door.

Big deal. He would do what she told him to do.

She yawned again. Christ, where could she get a Red Bull before track practice?

Then a couple of girls at the other end of the cafeteria started screaming and crying, looking at their cell phones, loudly announcing that Sam Warner had been found dead.

Emma wasn't surprised at what they were crying about.

She was just surprised it had taken so long.

CHAPTER SEVEN

T he rest of Jessica's Wednesday went by in a foggy blur as she tried to keep awake and aware by having one more cup of coffee and then a Diet Coke at lunch. Ellen Nickerson spent most of the day in her office. Rhonda and Amber whispered and gossiped during the afternoon, and when the lobby was clear of customers on this rainy day, their voices got louder as they talked about Sam's death. Percy ignored them all and stayed on his stool by the drive-up window.

In the late afternoon Amber took an iPad from her large purse and called up the home page of the *Warner Daily News*, and Jessica was stunned at how quickly the newspaper had uploaded a story onto its digital front page.

Amber read the first two paragraphs aloud as Jessica and Rhonda gathered around her. Percy was content to stay put and play Tetris on his iPhone.

In a quivering voice, Amber read, "'Warner Police and Massachusetts State Police are investigating the apparent homicide of eighteen-year-old Samuel Warner, a senior at Warner High School and the captain of its winning wrestling team. Warner's body was discovered at approximately nine A.M. by two local residents going for a walk along the many trails in the Warner Town Forest. The Middlesex County District Attorney's Office is taking the lead on the investigation. Details of his death and its approximate time have not been released by authorities.'"

Amber wiped her eyes and said, "Oh, God, poor Sam. And his poor family."

Jessica leaned closer and took a better look on the iPad screen, seeing the smiling, cocky face of the young Sam Warner, wearing his letter jacket. Jessica had seen him a few times at the track meets when other student athletes gathered to cheer on their classmates, joined by his family, who had first come to this area nearly four hundred years ago and lent their name to the town.

Rhonda said, "I mean, he was so popular. Who would want to kill him?"

And from the drive-up came the voice of Percy Prescott, whose head was still lowered as he played Tetris. "Take your pick," he said. "The guy was a real dick."

Jessica was shocked at hearing that from Percy, and so were Rhonda and Amber. Amber's face reddened and she said, "How in hell can you say such a rotten thing?"

"Easy." Percy lifted his head, and there was a hard gaze Jessica had never seen before from the usually quiet and cheerful Percy. "I was two years ahead of him in school, and he and his little wrestlers loved to shit on people they thought didn't fit in. They'd fuck with their lockers, knock their books out of their hands in the hallways and in the bathrooms. They were nasty little bastards, they were."

Jessica remembered Craig telling her last night about the wrestling team meeting up with him and Emma just outside the school. *The two of us got jumped by our own little group of alt-right clowns—the wrestling team—and they decided to have fun with us.*

She refused to think anymore about Craig's words.

No, just no.

Emma had said that Craig was exaggerating. That's all. Emma had to be right. Had to be.

A dark-blue Mercedes sedan slowed up and stopped, and Percy pushed the teller drawer out. "Once the cops start investigating, they'll have more suspects than they'll know what to do with," he said.

—◊—

Jessica's shift ended at 4:00 P.M., and as she cashed out and submitted the day's paperwork, she just wanted to go to the ladies' room, empty her bladder of all the caffeine she had drunk, and pick up Emma from track practice. She also planned a serious one-on-one with her daughter to really find out what Emma and her stepbrother had been up to last night.

A scavenger hunt? For real?

Then the day got even crappier.

Waiting in the lobby, pacing back and forth, then quickly coming over to her closed teller station, was Ted. His face was tired, flabby, but there was something scary and pleading in his eyes.

"Hey, what's up?" Jessica asked, going over to her station. Ted hardly ever came to the bank, and never when she was about to leave.

He looked left and then right—where Rhonda and Amber were taking care of customers—and leaned over the counter. "I need to talk to you. Right now."

Something cold seemed to seize her lower legs, freezing her in place. The tone of his voice, the pleading look in his eyes, meant that something was seriously wrong. "I can be home in fifteen minutes or so, Ted, after I pick up Emma from school. Can't it wait until then?"

"No, it can't."

"Ted—"

"We need to talk. Now. It's about the kids."

That last sentence nailed her. *It's about the kids.*

Jessica leaned over the counter and saw that the door to Ellen's office was still closed. "Come along."

It was against bank rules to allow nonbank personnel to come into work areas, but that rule was ignored as much as the one about taking home pens, pencils, and paperclips for personal use. She unlocked the chest-high side door, stepped into the lobby, and led Ted down the short corridor that went past Ellen's office and an office used by one of their ghost employees. The ghosts were young men or women who helped with mortgages, money market accounts, wire transfers, and other bits of complicated banking and who stayed here for three or four months before getting transferred to a bigger branch. No one ever bothered to learn much about them beyond their names.

There was a quick left, past the supply closet—her right shoulder ached again at the memory of moving all those heavy boxes yesterday—and she led her husband into the break room. Thankfully the room was empty. Jessica closed the door. She sat down across from Ted at the small table and held her hands together underneath so he couldn't see them start to tremble.

Never had she seen him so frightened, even including last night.

"What's wrong?" she managed to ask.

He blinked his eyes, shook his head, reached into his coat pocket, and took out an iPhone. "Jessica, I'm sorry, I've been keeping a secret from you for more than a year."

She had a feeling as if she were going into the cellar with the light off, of stepping down and not finding the step. Disoriented, as if she were about to fall into the darkness.

A secret? For more than a year?

"Ted, what secret? You're not making any sense."

He raised a hand, cut her off. "It's about Emma. And Craig." He took a deeper breath. "I'm sorry. I should have checked with you before I did it. I was only going to do it with Craig, but I didn't think that was fair to him. So I did it to Emma at the same time."

Under the break-room table, Jessica clenched her clasped hands into fists. Emma?

"Ted, I don't understand." And right then she hated the tone of her voice. It was that of a confused housewife, a plain old bank teller, a woman who had never gone to college and didn't have the right smarts.

He placed the iPhone on the table, turned it so she could see the screen. "Last spring, when that young girl was kidnapped from Lawrence and it took a month before her body came up in the Merrimack, I decided to do something about it."

She remembered that appalling story and looked down at his iPhone. It was a detailed map of something, showing roads, trails, a stream . . .

Ted asked, "You heard about Sam Warner being found dead?"

"Of course."

"His body was found deep in the Warner Town Forest. I talked to Detective Josephs, a friend of mine from Rotary. He was in a rush and told me Sam had been shot. Preliminary time of death was sometime last night."

The coffee and Coke she had drunk that was still in her stomach was churning and threatening to come out violently, all over this dirty table and Ted's clean suit and tie.

Ted had tears in his eyes. A thick finger tapped the glass screen of the iPhone.

"Hon, last year, after the Lawrence girl story, I secretly put tracking software on both of the kids' phones. It's buried deep in their apps, disguised as some sort of weather station software. I was being paranoid, I know, but teenage kids in these times . . . and it didn't cost much . . ."

She said, "What? And you've kept this secret from me all this time?"

Ted said, "I should have told you. I know. But after I did it, I waited a day. Then another day. A week. Pretty soon so much time had passed I didn't want to bring it up. I never thought . . . Oh, Jesus."

Jessica held her breath, hoping it would calm her stomach, steady her nerves, do something, anything, even block out what her husband was saying.

"Jessica, our kids were in the Warner Town Forest last night. When the cops think Sam Warner was murdered."

CHAPTER EIGHT

There were times in Jessica Thornton's life when she could remember in excruciating detail past experiences, even though she easily forgot daily tasks like going to Hannaford's to pick up some milk and orange juice or swinging by the Warner post office to mail out some bills. She still remembered her first sleepovers with Kristin Young, her neighborhood friend in Haverhill, when she had realized there were families in which Mom and Dad didn't yell at each other after dinner. And that fumbling, painful, yet pleasurable night when she had lost her virginity to Bobby. The time in the hospital in Newburyport when she held the red-faced, squealing little girl and knew for certain that she was instantly in love with her daughter. The night she got the phone call to tell her that Bobby had died in a drunk-driving crash. And the hopeful day she married Ted more than three years ago, filled with desire that her life was finally going to turn around and mean something for her and her girl.

Now, this instant, this time, would join that list of never-to-be-forgotten moments.

"Ted, what do you mean?"

He tapped his finger again on the screen. "See? The red letters *C* and *E*? They mark the locations of Craig's and Emma's cell phones. Last night, for nearly thirty minutes, they were here." Another tap of the finger. "This is a stream in the middle of the town forest. And this is where a wooden footbridge is. And that's where Detective Josephs told me they found the body of Sam Warner."

Ted drew his hand back and Jessica saw it quiver. "For God's sake, what do we do now?" he said.

Jessica wished at that moment that somebody, anybody—even Ellen Nickerson, the Ice Queen—would come in and break this mood, this terror, the cold feelings running up and down her back. Good Lord, even a bank robbery would be a wonderful gift at this moment.

"But last night, when we were looking for them, why didn't you see them on your iPhone?"

"I couldn't access the program because the damn software was being updated or something. Jessica, what do we do?"

That question just hung in the dead air of her bank's break room. Ted, who had all the answers, who thought he knew everything, was coming to her for help.

It was a dizzying change.

"We need to talk to them again," Jessica finally said. "Last night they both told us that they were out on some sort of scavenger hunt. That it started around eleven. That they lost track of the time. We need to ask them again. We need to make sure what went on."

Ted rubbed at his face. "Jesus, Jessica. Okay, let's get them both together later tonight and we'll talk it out."

Jessica said, "Okay."

"I mean, I don't want to think of what this might mean, you know? If this . . ."

Jessica made a point of looking up at the break-room clock. She didn't want to keep talking; she didn't want to see where this conversation might lead. She just knew she had to get out of this room.

"Ted, I need to get going. I'm picking up Emma after track practice. I'm sorry. When does Craig get home?"

"Don't you know?"

"No, I'm sorry, I don't."

Ted said, "Sometime after four thirty, I think."

Jessica said, "When I pick up Emma, we'll head home. Then we can talk to them both and see what we can find out."

40

Ted nodded, looked up at the clock. "All right. But Jessica, don't talk to Emma beforehand, okay?"

That last comment concerned her. "What?"

Ted said, "You shouldn't tell Emma about the tracking software. I won't tell Craig either. It'll be better if we talk to Craig and her together, so we can see how they both react. You see what I mean?"

Jessica said, "Okay, that does make sense."

Ted looked again at the clock. "Christ, I gotta go, too. We'll see what we can learn later." He stood up, let out a big sigh, and shook his head. "There has to be a simple explanation, you know? A real good one. Maybe something to do with that scavenger hunt. Otherwise . . . I mean, I felt like passing out when I saw where they had been last night."

Jessica stood up, rubbed at her bare arms. "I don't even want to think about it."

He came around the break-room table and opened his arms, and Jessica slid against him, accepting the tight hug. He kissed her cheek and said, "I know things haven't been great these past few months, hon, but we can get through this. As a family. If we just stick together. Okay?"

She hugged him back, her voice choking, and said, "Absolutely. We need to stick together. As a family. And you're right. There has to be an explanation."

—⁂—

Back in her work area, Ted slipped into the lobby and turned and gave her a wave. Jessica waved back. From her teller station Amber said, "Jessica, your hubby is so sweet, stopping by like that. I hope someday my hubby will do the same thing."

"I know—I am lucky, aren't I?" Jessica replied, almost saying, *And you should hope your future hubby never, ever has to break news like Ted just did.*

As she went to get her purse from under her teller station, the branch's telephone rang. Rhonda picked up.

"Hey, Jessica, there's a phone call for you."

She said, "Do you know who it is?"

Rhonda shook her head. "It's a guy, that's all."

Jessica slung her purse over her sore shoulder and went to the end of the teller area, where a phone was set up on the wall, next to the printer and fax machine for the tellers. She picked up.

"Hello?"

A man's voice came at her quickly, and she recognized it from the phone message she had deleted yesterday and from the message also erased last Friday. "Mrs. Thornton, please don't hang up. Please. If you hang up, it'll make it hard for you and your daughter. I really don't want that to happen."

She squeezed the black receiver hard. "Go on."

Jessica could hear the relief in the man's voice. "Thank you. And I mean it, thank you."

"Could you hurry up, please? I have an appointment I'm about to miss."

"Certainly," he said. "My name is Gary Talbot. I'm a private investigator from Portland. I've been hired to look into the circumstances surrounding the death of your first husband, Robert Thornton."

The way Talbot said the name, she was sure he was mistaken. Robert Thornton? Nobody ever called him that. He was always Bobby Thornton, Bobby the Trusted One, seen in newspaper ads, heard in radio spots, and also spotted late at night on some of the more obscure cable channels in the area, trying to sell cars, like some odd creature from those old Mutual of Omaha television shows.

"What circumstances?" she asked. "I'm sorry, I don't understand. My husband, Bobby"—she put a choking sound in her voice—"he died in a car accident on I-95, just outside York. Several years ago. The state police and the York police both said he was drunk and struck a deer, went off the road and hit a tree."

Talbot said, "Well, that's what the reports say, and the medical examiner's paperwork states the same thing. But I've been asked to look into this further."

"Who asked you?"

"That's confidential, Mrs. Thornton."

Jessica made a quick turn and saw that the three other tellers—Rhonda, Amber, and Percy—were all working very, very hard to pretend that they weren't listening.

"Mr. Talbot," she said, "if you want my cooperation, you need to tell me who hired you. Or I won't say a word."

There was silence, and then Percy's drive-up drawer clattered out, and Talbot said, "Well, you're going to learn eventually. I was hired by Grace Thornton."

Grace? Who the hell was Grace Thornton? Jessica then recalled the name and the face it was attached to. A teenage girl, Bobby's youngest sister, who always sat away from everyone else at family events, from Thanksgiving to Christmas, and who always looked at Jessica with pure, unadulterated hatred. She loved her older brother and hated Jessica for marrying him.

Grace . . . she must have been seventeen or so when Bobby died. Now she was in her twenties, and like a dish best served cold, she was coming after the woman she thought had taken her brother away. But why? Why now?

"Grace?" she asked. "Grace Thornton? Bobby's younger sister?"

"That's right."

"But . . ." Jessica closed her eyes. Took a deep breath, tried to keep her legs still. She wanted so much to hang up on this man, ignore him like she had ignored his two earlier messages. And she remembered what the private investigator had said earlier: *If you hang up, it'll make it hard for you and your daughter.*

She couldn't let that happen.

"All right," she said. "I'll talk to you. I . . . I promise I'll call you tomorrow. Perhaps we could set up a time to talk face-to-face? I don't feel comfortable talking like this over the phone."

"Certainly, Mrs. Thornton," he said. "That sounds quite reasonable."

He slowly gave her his phone number, and with a spare pen nearby Jessica scribbled it down on a torn deposit slip. She read the number back to him, and then she asked, "Mr. Talbot, I'm sorry to ask you this, but why did Grace Thornton hire you? What on earth is she looking for?"

"Oh," he said, and he proceeded to reply, voice lowered, as if he were ashamed to pass on such news. "Mrs. Thornton, Grace doesn't think your husband's death was an accident."

CHAPTER NINE

A steady breeze was coming over the playing fields of Warner High School, and Jessica stood by herself, enjoying the buffeting sensation from the wind. The rain had finally stopped.

But the words still rattled around in her mind. *Mrs. Thornton, Grace doesn't think your husband's death was an accident.*

Grace. Sour, moody, and ill-tempered Grace. In the years Jessica had known Bobby, from high school to marriage to his shocking death, never once had she seen that girl smile. Or laugh.

Not once.

And why was she hiring a private investigator now? What was prompting her? What demons were driving her to bring up the horrid accusation that Bobby's death wasn't an accident?

The wind felt good, pushing on her face. She leaned slightly into it, hands in her pockets, looking over the playing fields and the stands and the squat and wide two-story brick building that was Warner High School.

A few students nearby were wearing sports or running gear, and all had small black ribbons pinned to their shirts. Standing alone with a clipboard and a stopwatch in his hands was the girls' track team coach, John Webber. He was easily over six feet tall, wearing spotless khaki slacks, sneakers, and a blue sweatshirt that had WARNER on the back in simple white letters. He was completely bald. He spotted Jessica and she went over to him.

"John," Jessica said, "I'm sorry again for calling you so late."

He said, "You weren't the first parent to do so and you won't be the last. No worries. I'm just glad it worked out." He paused. "You want to talk about tough phone calls, think about the poor detective who had to call Sam Warner's parents."

Jessica shivered. "God, I don't even want to think about it. I mean, Ted and I were furious at Emma and Craig last night, but at least they came back home safe."

"It was some sort of scavenger hunt, wasn't it?" John asked.

"That's what Emma and her stepbrother said. Just the two of them. If it weren't for track and Craig's computer club membership, they'd both be grounded for a month. As it is, Ted and I are still thinking about the appropriate punishment."

Webber checked his stopwatch. "Emma should be coming in first. No surprise there."

Jessica folded her arms, feeling once again the pride she experienced when her daughter was praised in public. "If so, it's because of your coaching."

"Hardly," he said quietly. "She's got incredible talent, and, more importantly, she has the discipline as well. She's in varsity right now, but I don't see why she can't go to statewide competition later this year. And if she can keep her focus for the next two years, Jessica, she'll be able to write her own ticket to any one of a half-dozen colleges."

Jessica hugged herself. A few raindrops came down from the gray clouds overhead.

"That's what I'm hoping," she said. "Keeping her safe, keeping her focused—sometimes it feels like a full-time job, especially at her age."

Her coach said, "Here she comes."

From the other end of the grassy field, near a line of woods, a runner emerged from a trail, running fast and gracefully, and Jessica's heart raced with joy to see Emma running so freely. Emma had on her usual running shoes, white socks, dark-blue shorts, and a loose WARNER TRACK T-shirt, also blue, and her blond hair was pulled back in a simple ponytail that bounced with each hammering step. Like the other students, she had a black ribbon pinned on her shirt.

Jessica was so entranced by Emma's racing form that she couldn't move. She remembered being taught some Greek mythology back in school, about a goddess named Atalanta, who could outrace every suitor and did so to protect her virtue and to honor the gods. But one sly man had gotten three golden apples from another goddess, and in his footrace with her he had tossed them aside to slow down a curious Atalanta so he could win the race and marry her.

But there were no golden apples out here, nothing to halt Emma from winning yet another race, even if this one was just a regular after-school practice, and when Emma ran past two orange plastic cones set up on the field, Webber clicked the stopwatch and grunted with satisfaction.

"Your girl—boy, can she run."

Jessica waved and Emma saw her and waved back, but she didn't come over. Instead she slowly moved around in circles, slim hands on her slim hips, cooling down. Jessica didn't feel insulted or overlooked. It was Emma being Emma, getting her job done.

One, and then two and then three other members of her track team emerged from the woods, racing to Emma and the orange cones, and Emma stood aside, clapping her hands, shouting encouragement to her teammates.

Webber said quietly, "That's why she's a winner, why she'll go far. She's not a diva—she supports her teammates. She's got that special spark. Keep it going, Mrs. Thornton. Keep it going."

The delight Jessica felt at those words overwhelmed any thoughts of her girl's absence last night with Craig, the murder of a classmate, the news of the tracking device Ted had put on their phones, and that disturbing call from Maine. None of that mattered at this moment. It was seeing that happy, glowing, and energetic daughter of hers go to the stands, retrieve a small knapsack, and come over to her mother—that's what counted.

—⁓—

Inside the Sentra, Jessica turned on the engine while Emma took a long swallow of Gatorade. Emma waved her free hand in front of her face and said, "God, Mom, I smell gross. Can we leave already?"

"Just a sec, hon," Jessica said, not wanting to say what was on her mind: that she loved the aroma of her girl once she was off the running field. There was nothing gross about it. It was the scent of dedication, of exertion, of hard work, of finding one's own path and not depending on a boyfriend or husband or any other male out there to take care of you.

But Jessica knew she had to bring up a difficult subject and then delayed it for a moment by touching the black square of cloth pinned to Emma's shirt. "What's this about?"

Emma glanced over. "Oh. That. It was the student council's idea. A mourning symbol, for Sam Warner. Poor guy. I hear his parents are really freaking out. They're even talking about having a memorial service for him tomorrow night, at the common."

"Did he have any brothers or sisters?"

Emma took another slug of the Gatorade. "Nope. Only child. Mom, can we get moving? I really need to take a shower."

"A single child." Jessica's throat tightened as she imagined losing Emma after getting her to high school, after seeing her grow from infant to toddler to little girl, now ready to blossom into adulthood. She found it hard to swallow, find her voice. "Em?"

"Yeah?"

"We need to talk about last night."

"Oh, Mom, please. We already went over it. Me and Craig, we went out on a scavenger hunt, that's all. We had to go around town and pick up some stuff, and it started raining, and Craig got us lost. That's all that happened. I'm sorry I put you and Ted through that. Honest."

"And who was running the scavenger hunt?"

She shrugged. "I don't know. Maybe Craig knows. We both got printed notes in our lockers, saying to go out last night and pick up some stuff. Like somebody's lawn gnome. Or a porch mailbox. Or a bicycle. The notes weren't signed. It was . . . it was stupid, all right?'

"So why did you do it?"

Emma shook her head. "Some of the kids in school . . . they're smart, they're rich. They go to places. Parties. Road trips. Stuff that other kids don't know about. It's stupid, okay, but it's important. Sometimes they like to invite others to go along, using that scavenger hunt. And I wanted to do it. I mean, Mom . . . I'm sort of related to Craig, and he's a real loser most times. A drag. Doing this scavenger hunt might have helped me in school, even if I had to go out with him at the same time."

That caused a memory of Jessica's own days in high school to stab her. Trying to fit in, trying to dress right on a poor budget. Bringing in last night's leftovers as lunch in a Tupperware container while the other, happier, better-dressed and better-groomed classmates got their hot lunch from the cafeteria. Sitting by herself, maybe playing solitaire or spades with a couple of other losers like herself, seeing with jealousy the tables with the laughing and confident classmates who had it all figured out and mapped out for them, with the help of their rich and connected parents.

"Tell me, how in the world did you and Craig sneak out without waking me up?"

Emma smiled and then quickly dialed it back, as if she didn't want to piss off her mother. "Craig thought it out. We used the small window in the basement foundation. Earlier he had oiled up the hinges so it wouldn't squeak and it could move easier. We just snuck downstairs, squeezed out that window, and walked into town."

Jessica bit her lower lip to prevent herself from smiling. That sounded like something she would have done, back in the day.

"Mom . . ."

"One more thing," Jessica said. "I promise. And then we'll leave."

The rain was now coming down harder, and Jessica left the wipers off. It made everything out there look blurry and obscured and made her feel like she was hidden with her daughter, sharing secrets and confidences.

"Emma, just so you know. In case your stepfather brings it up or something. And I need to know this, just between us two, about your cell phones last night."

49

Her daughter said, "What about our cell phones?"

"Well, it's, uh . . . well, it's like this. Your cell phones. Your stepfather is a suspicious sort. He might . . . well, he might be able to contact the cell-phone company. Check their records. I know there's something the cell-phone companies have that they can tell where a phone might be because their service towers can track it."

Emma kept quiet and Jessica went on. "So if you and Craig weren't in town last night and went someplace you shouldn't have, the cell-phone company might know that and tell your stepdad."

Her daughter shook her head in exasperation. "Mom, I told you that last night, didn't I?"

"Told us what?"

"That was part of the scavenger hunt," Emma explained. "The rules were, you had to take your phone with you, put it in a plastic bag, and put it under a bush over by the Minuteman Monument in the park. That way you couldn't cheat by looking up people's addresses or by texting your friends to help you."

"And the phones were there when you got back?"

Jessica's own iPhone started chiming. She ignored it.

Emma said, "Of course they were. Why wouldn't they be?"

Jessica's chest lightened up and she found she could take a nice long, deep breath. It all made sense. Everything was just fine.

The cell phones had been out of Emma and Craig's possession. Whoever had picked them up, well, they had gone to the town forest. Maybe she and Ted should report that to the police—she would talk to him about it later, when they got home—but right now the disgusting thoughts and suspicions that Ted had mentioned could be put away.

She looked at her phone. Ted was calling. She let it go to voicemail.

Jessica turned on the wipers, put the Sentra into reverse. "Let's get you home to a nice warm shower."

Emma said, "About time, Mom."

"And what we talked about, the phones, keep it just between us, okay?"

Emma didn't say a word. She was busy retrieving her iPhone from her knapsack.

But seeing her girl running . . . Lots of memories came back, and Jessica said, "You know, hon, I really miss running with you. It's been more than two years. Why can't—"

Emma had her iPhone in her hands and was busily working the screen. "Oh, Mom, not now, okay?"

Okay, Jessica thought. She backed the Sentra out and headed home.

—⁂—

The ride home took about ten minutes, and Emma's fingers and thumbs were texting away madly, her head lowered. Jessica had the radio station on low, but she really felt like cranking up the volume and singing along with whatever oldie the local station was playing, because she felt so free and relieved. Her daughter was safe, was fine, and would continue to be safe and fine for the future.

As for her former sister-in-law Grace, well, she would deal with that silly crank tomorrow, when she called back the private detective.

A private dick! The thought of that made her snicker, and Emma looked up from her cell phone. "Mom, what's so funny?"

"Oh, something that just came to me."

"What was it?"

"It was nothing," Jessica said.

"Mom . . ."

When she got home, Ted's dark-blue BMW was in the driveway, and parked on the street, right in front of the old house, was a black Chevrolet sedan. A client? God, she thought, that'd be great, get everyone's mind off last night and the screaming that had taken place early this morning, when Emma and Craig had finally returned.

Jessica suddenly yawned. God, she was so very, very tired.

The rain had drifted off to drizzle, and before Jessica could get her door open, Emma had grabbed her knapsack—after tossing the empty

Gatorade bottle onto the rear seat—and raced inside, going past Ted, who had opened the door.

Jessica stepped out and went around the rear of the Sentra and up the stone steps, and Ted, his face almost the color of the steps, opened the door wider.

Standing next to him was a young man wearing a dark-gray two-piece suit, white shirt, and blue necktie. His face was slightly round, he had a pug nose, and his brown hair was closely trimmed. In his left hand he had a soft leather briefcase. In his other he held out something small with a gold shield in the center, and Jessica couldn't look at it, could only hear the man's strong voice.

"Mrs. Thornton?" he asked. "Detective Doug Rafferty. Warner Police Department. I need to talk to you and your husband about your children."

CHAPTER TEN

There was a flash of movement as Emma went upstairs to the safety of her bedroom, and Jessica was glad to see her daughter retreat. A moment passed, and now she was on a couch, sitting next to Ted, with no memory of how she had gotten there. The police officer—no, a detective, which was much worse, meaning that he already had suspicions that had brought him here—sat in a nearby chair. He took out a small notebook and pen from his jacket. His leather briefcase was at his feet.

Jessica's hand was now in Ted's, and he squeezed it gently, and Jessica was surprised at how reassuring it felt.

"Mr. Donovan, Mrs. Thornton, I—"

Ted held up his free hand. "Please, let's not be so formal. Ted and Jessica, okay?"

A slight nod. "Sure, that's fine."

Ted said, "Can we get you something to drink? Water? Coffee?"

"No, I'm fine," the detective said. "But I'd like to get one thing out of the way. You're married, but Mrs. Thornton, you kept your maiden name?"

She said, "No, that's the name of my first husband. Who's deceased. When Ted and I got married, it just seemed easier to leave everything the way it was."

"Got it."

Ted said, "Again, we want to help. Anything you need."

"That's good to hear," Rafferty said. He slowly flipped his notebook open, and Jessica tried to keep her breathing slow and even. She didn't want to show this man any fear, any concern. He was a slim, okay-looking guy, but his presence overwhelmed the living room. He was the Man, the Law, and in those hands flipping open the notebook was the power to wreck this family.

If there was anything there.

If.

He looked up. "I'm working the Sam Warner case."

Jessica said, "That's so awful. How are his parents doing?"

"As poorly as you would expect," he said, his voice low and surprisingly bland. "What I'm doing now is getting some background information, trying to fill in some blanks, get an idea of Sam's life beyond just being a high school senior and being active in sports."

"Our children," Ted said. "You said you had questions about them. Why is that?"

Rafferty's face seemed to flush. "Well, I guess I was getting ahead of myself. I misspoke when I said children. I just want to talk to you about one of your kids, not both of them."

Oh, God, Jessica thought. What if it's Emma? What if he was here because of her girl? Had the police found out more about where the two of them had been last night, despite what Emma had said about the cell phones?

Fifty-fifty.

Half and half.

Up and down.

Craig and Emma.

Rafferty said, "Ted and Jessica, I have some questions about your son. Craig."

Jessica squeezed Ted's hand and Ted squeezed back, but inside Jessica was joyful, something she dared not tell her husband. It wasn't Emma!

Rafferty looked down again at his notebook. "Ted, what can you tell me about the relationship your son had with Sam?"

"Craig?" Ted asked, surprised. "Craig and Sam Warner? I don't think they had any kind of relationship at all."

"Are you sure?"

"Positive. They didn't move in the same circles."

Rafferty flipped a page. "That's interesting."

"Why?"

"Because I talked to Mary Casey, the guidance counselor at Warner High School. She said that Craig came to visit her four times after incidents with Sam. Incidents of bullying."

Jessica turned to Ted. Bullying?

"Ah, well, I don't know anything about that," Ted said.

"Ma'am? You?"

Jessica spoke clearly. "This is the first I've heard of it."

"I see," the detective said. "Well, those instances were also reported to Assistant Principal Bob Hale. He's responsible for disciplinary action at the high school. Do you know Mr. Hale?"

Jessica said, "No, I don't."

Ted paused. "Slightly. I guess."

"And you don't know about these incidents being reported to Mr. Hale?"

"No," Ted said.

Rafferty nodded, bent over, and took a file folder from his briefcase. "Well, that's odd," he said. "Perhaps you could help me narrow something down. You see, I have here a copy of a letter from Mr. Hale sent to you, Mr. Donovan—"

Jessica stiffened at hearing the detective stop saying "Ted."

"—outlining the bullying incidents that had occurred and informing you that disciplinary action would be taken against Sam Warner. Mr. Donovan? Do you recall this letter?"

Silence. Rafferty leaned over and passed across the sheet of paper. He said, "You'll see, Mr. Donovan, that your signature appears at the bottom of the letter. Is that in fact your signature? Acknowledging that you in fact received this letter and read it?"

Ted kept quiet, but Jessica shifted her view. She skipped reading the bland bureaucratic prose from the assistant principal and saw Ted's familiar scrawl at the bottom of the sheet. And he had never told her!

"Ah, yes, it does appear so," Ted said, taking his hand away from Jessica's, holding the sheet with both hands. The paper trembled slightly.

"Are you sure?" Rafferty asked. "Could it have been forged? Could your son have written your signature in?" The detective attempted a smile. "I have to admit I did something similar when I was in high school, forging my mother's signature on my report card the semester I flunked Spanish."

"No," Ted said, his voice sounding slightly defeated. "That's my signature."

He passed the paper over and Jessica saw it tremble some more. What in God's name had Ted done? What was he hiding? Was he hiding anything else? Ted?

"I see," Rafferty said, taking the paper back, gently replacing it in his folder. "I wonder if—"

Ted spoke quickly. "I'm sorry. I'm remembering it now. I mean, this has been a very, very busy few months for me. Lots of papers pass through. I now remember Craig asking me to sign something—he did it one morning just as I was leaving to go to work. I thought it was a permission slip or something like that for a school trip. I . . . I had no idea it was something that serious."

Rafferty glanced again at his little notebook. Jessica's heart went *thump-thump*. Her stepson was getting caught up with a prominent high school senior, captain of the wrestling team and a murder victim. Official records of bullying and fights. Nothing she had ever heard from either Craig or Ted.

Or even Emma. Did Emma know about the bullying her stepbrother had suffered? And if so, why hadn't she told her mother?

"I see," Rafferty said. "Well, that's certainly reasonable. Now, like I said, I'm just gathering information, collecting facts at this point. It's like one big jigsaw puzzle and I'm starting with the easiest parts, the borders. Do you know what I mean?"

Ted didn't say anything, but Jessica said, "Absolutely, yes. That does make sense."

"Thank you, Jessica," Rafferty said. "The question I have is that your son, Craig . . . he had some unpleasant encounters with Sam over the past year. A couple involved some physical altercations. Now, I'm not making any accusations or casting doubt. But I need to know this. Just for the record. Where was Craig last night?"

Not quite believing what the detective had just said, Jessica quickly replied, "You mean the night when Sam was murdered?"

"Like I said, last night," Rafferty said. "Could you tell me where Craig was?"

Ted spoke right up. "He was here, all night."

"Never left the house?"

"No," Ted said. "He never left the house."

Jessica's mouth went dry. This was serious, this was dangerous. This was police business. *Ted had just lied to the police detective.* She realized what Ted was doing, protecting his son. But what should she do? This was much more than the thought of Ted lying to her—that was . . . hell, that was what happened in some marriages. Sometimes husbands and wives kept secrets from each other. That was the way of the world. But lying to a police detective?

What should she do?

Rafferty said, "Jessica?"

"Absolutely," she said. "Craig was here all night. Didn't leave the house once."

Rafferty scribbled something in his notebook. "Very well, that's quite helpful."

But what about the cell phones, she thought, what about the cell phones?

Not now. Later.

Rafferty asked a few more questions—Did they know anyone who had a serious grudge against Sam Warner? Could they ask Craig and Emma if they knew someone like that? Since Ted and Jessica worked in the community, had they heard any rumors about Sam and his wrestling teammates? Then he flipped the notebook shut and smiled at them both.

Jessica was so relieved she almost sat back against the couch. He stood up, extended his hand, and both she and Ted reached over to give his hand a shake. She found his hand firm and dry.

"Well, I guess that's that," he said. "I appreciate you taking the time to talk to me."

Ted said, "Glad to help. Honest."

Rafferty produced two business cards, crisp and firm, with raised lettering. "If either of you, or Craig or Emma, can think of anything to do with Sam and his activities, anything at all, please call me. At any time. And even if it's something you think is small or not worth telling me, please tell me. You can reach me at any time via the Warner police dispatch."

Jessica took the card in her hand while Ted examined it and placed it down on the coffee table. "Can I see you to the door, Detective?"

He bent down, picked up his leather case. "Certainly."

Ted and Rafferty walked to the front door and the detective said, "There may come a time when I might want to talk to Craig or Emma. Would that be a problem?"

Jessica was going to say no, not at all, and was surprised at how quickly Ted replied. "Well, Detective Rafferty, we'll have to think about that carefully. And perhaps consult with our family attorney. They're both minors, and sometimes they think they know things when they really don't. If you do make a request, we'll certainly consider it."

"I see," Rafferty said.

Ted's voice suddenly got stronger. "And just to make things clear, so there's no misunderstanding, I don't want you or anyone in the Warner Police Department talking to either Craig or Emma without us being present."

Jessica was shocked at the tone of Ted's voice and was also surprised at how calmly the detective took Ted's words. He just said, "I fully understand, Mr. Donovan."

He reached the door and tried to pull it open. It was stuck. He tried again. Still stuck.

Ted stepped over and said, "Yeah, this door is a real pain. Let me help you out. You need to pull and lift at the same time."

Her husband did just that and the door squeaked open. Rafferty nodded in appreciation and said, "Oh, before I forget—Mr. Donovan, like I said before, I'm just checking off the boxes and filling in the blanks. So please don't take offense."

By the solemn way the detective was talking and the way he saved the best for last, she had an idea of what Rafferty was about to ask, and sure enough, that's exactly the question he posed to her husband.

"Mr. Donovan, could you tell me where you were last night?"

Jessica waited for Ted to speak, and it was strange: even though she was a couple of feet away from him, she was sure she could feel a shake or tremble go through him when he answered. A simple second passed and Jessica felt the world would now be divided between *then* and *now*, all because of what Ted was about to say next.

"Last night? Heck, I was here all night, Detective. Right with Jessica on the couch. Reading the paper and watching one of those *Real Housewives* reality shows."

He swiveled his head to Jessica, smiling widely and confidently, as if he were about to close a deal on a prime piece of business property in downtown Concord. "I forget, hon, which one were we watching? Orange County? Beverly Hills?"

Jessica was looking at Ted and didn't dare to shift her look over to the detective. The man was a cop, a pro. She had no doubt he could look right at her and determine that she was lying.

Still on the couch, she thought for a terrifying moment that she couldn't speak, and then the words came out. "It was the New York housewives, followed by the ones from Australia."

Ted laughed. "Detective, there you go. I mean, I can't tell which one is which. It's all about these rich housewives screaming at each other and spending their husbands' money."

Rafferty said, "So I've been told. Thanks for your help. Contact me if anything comes up, all right?"

Ted said, "You can count on it," and closed the door.

CHAPTER ELEVEN

There was a knock on Emma's bedroom door right after the shouting started, and before she could say anything Craig barged in. She was sitting up on her bed, legs stretched out, shoes off, checking her iPhone before taking a shower. Despite how tired she was after last night's outing, she had still done well at practice.

As always.

"They're fighting downstairs," he said, sitting down on a chair by her cluttered desk.

"Yeah, thanks. I didn't notice."

He just sat there, breathing hard. "They're fighting about the cop who just came by. About what they said to him."

"And what was that?"

"I don't know. But I heard both of our names mentioned."

"Doesn't mean anything."

"What the hell. Emma, why do you think the detective came here? For the hell of it?"

Emma said, "Calm down. Jesus. Okay. He was here. He was doing his job."

"But—"

She lowered her voice, scooted closer to Craig. "That thing you were going to dump . . ."

"What thing?"

60

It was times like this when Emma couldn't figure out whether her stepbrother was being dense or was being a pain in the ass. Maybe both.

"What was in your knapsack," she said. "From my study period this morning. You dumped it, right?"

"Shit, yes," he said.

"Where?"

"Someplace safe."

"Not safe, Craig. It has to be someplace where it won't be found."

Craig didn't say anything, and Emma didn't like that.

"Craig?"

"It's gone, okay?"

Downstairs the shouting was still going on. Emma didn't have many memories of her real dad, who had gotten himself killed in a traffic accident after his car hit a deer up in Maine, but one thing was sure—she didn't have any memories of him screaming like that.

"You done?" Emma asked.

"Yeah."

She swung off the bed, sitting up. "Okay, don't freak out."

"Huh?" Craig kept on rubbing his hands up and down on his jeans.

"It's like this. I think your dad knows someone at Verizon, someone who can track our phones from the local cell towers."

"Oh, suck."

"Yeah."

"How do you know?"

"My mom told me when she picked me up from practice. She said there was a chance your dad could check with somebody from the cell-phone company, track our movements last night."

"Emma, we are so screwed."

"Jesus, Craig, cut it out," Emma said. "I got it all figured out."

"What?"

She smirked at her older and supposedly smarter stepbrother. "I told Mom that as part of the scavenger hunt last night we had to put our phones in plastic bags and leave them underneath a bush at the town common."

61

"Really?" Craig asked, hope now in his voice.

"Yep," she said, pleased with herself. "I told Mom that whoever ran the scavenger hunt didn't want us using our phones to use Google Maps, and she bought it."

Craig ran both hands through his thick hair. "Really?"

"Yeah, really." Emma's iPhone was chiming away as her friends from school were sending her Snapchats or texts. She ignored them. "So that's the story, okay? We hid the phones in plastic bags, we couldn't use them, and we got lost."

"And we still don't know who sent us on the scavenger hunt."

"That's right. And maybe whoever sent us on the scavenger hunt, maybe they went into the woods last night. Not us."

Her dopey stepbrother was sitting there looking like a lost puppy. Emma loved puppies and had asked for one each Christmas, but she never got one. She smartened up three years ago and stopped asking.

But Craig looked so much like a dog that Emma couldn't help herself. She touched his right cheek for a moment and said, "We stick to the story, we back each other up, and we'll be okay. Got it?"

He clasped his hands tightly together in his lap. "Yeah. Got it."

The shouting downstairs seemed to ease up, which meant she had one more thing to do.

"Craig?"

His eyes lit up and, speaking of Christmas, he looked like how he might have looked ten or so years ago, coming downstairs to check out the wrapped presents underneath the twinkling Christmas tree.

"Get the hell out, okay? I need to take a shower."

And like the good puppy he was, Craig got up and left her room.

Still, a few minutes later, when she did take her shower, Emma made sure that the bathroom door was locked.

Emma had always liked puppies, but they could never be trusted.

CHAPTER TWELVE

Jessica had two urges roaring through her, one to hit her husband and the other to storm out of the house, but whatever cool and logical part of her still existed managed to keep both urges under control.

She found herself walking around the living room in a large oval, seeing the furniture, knowing most of it was originally Ted's, wondering if he and his ex-wife, Amanda—now living in California—had laughed and giggled and loved while choosing these pieces. For some reason that irrational thought made her even angrier, and again she felt like an interloper. And with what Ted had just done a few minutes ago with the detective, she felt like an outsider, someone tossed into the middle of a dramatic play without knowing her lines.

The community college catalog she had been reading with such enthusiasm and excitement was now discarded on the couch, the colorful cover and happy students mocking her.

How can you even dream of such a thing? a voice echoed within her. *You're a nobody. A housewife with a high school diploma, working as a bank teller. Nothing more than a human ATM. Even your own daughter won't run with you anymore. A foolish failure.*

Aloud she said, "For Christ's sake, what the hell were you thinking, telling Detective Rafferty that you were here all night? Damn it, Ted, it's one thing to lie to protect our kids, but you didn't even warn me of what you were going to say!" She turned to him. "Why? Why did you lie like that?"

Ted was sitting in his favorite chair, watching her pace around the living room. His face was mottled, the tone and volume of his voice matching hers, syllable for syllable.

"I couldn't say I was out with Ben Powell," Ted said, his fists clenched. "I couldn't."

Jessica stopped. "Why the hell not?"

Ted looked like he was struggling to talk, and something dark pierced her as she thought, *Another woman.* Was that it? Had Ted been out with someone else?

He shook his head. "Because."

"Because? What's this, sixth grade? Cough it up, Ted. Now."

His face flushed more, and she couldn't believe it—were there tears in his eyes? Then he unclenched his fists and sat back against the chair, all of his limbs and his chest and torso loose and relaxed, as if the muscles and tendons inside had all suddenly turned into mush.

"Because we weren't alone, that's why," he said.

Oh, shit, she thought.

"Who was she?"

He violently shook his head. "It wasn't a she. It was a he."

"Who?"

A hesitation, and then he said, "Gus Spinelli. From Boston."

"Who the hell is Gus Spinelli?"

"An . . . investor," Ted said.

"So why couldn't you have said that?"

Ted didn't answer.

It came to her. "Boston? Let me guess. The North End, right? Where what's left of the Mafia tends to hang out."

Ted said, "It's not like that, it's just that—"

"What?" she asked. "If it's not like that, what's it like?"

Ted shifted in his chair as if it were no longer his favorite piece of furniture, as if when this painful conversation was over he would never, ever sit in it again.

"Gus Spinelli is a guy who's got money," Ted said. "All right? He's been friends off and on with Ben Powell since they grew up in the same neighborhood. And some of Gus's money . . . it comes from different places. It can't be reported. But he lends it out—he invests it in projects he thinks can make him some money."

Jessica folded her arms. It helped focus her on not reaching and slapping her husband. "Money laundering."

"Investing," Ted said.

"Ted, stop being so goddamn insulting. I've been in banking all my life. I know what laundering is and what it's about."

"Well, that's your problem," he shot back.

"What problem is that?"

Now Ted looked like the pouty young boy who can't keep himself from talking back to Mom or Dad. "You've worked all your life in banking. You've developed skills. Good for you. If Warner Savings were to close tomorrow, you could pick up and get a job with Citizens Bank, TD Bank, or any other bank in the state. You've got the experience, you've got the background." He took a breath. "When I'm selling a home or a piece of property, I'm selling myself. Don't you get it? Buying real estate is one of the biggest things people do in their lives, and they need to trust their realtor, need to know he's on the up-and-up. So if I were to tell that detective that I was out last night with Ben and some guy from the North End with big bucks who has a rap sheet for some assaults and loan sharking, I can tell you what would happen."

"Ted—"

He talked right over her, holding up his fingers in a row to emphasize his points. "One, no matter how professional that detective is, the word would get out. He'd have to check my alibi, go to the restaurant, talk to Ben Powell, and people would start talking. That's a given." He paused, went on. "Two, I could kiss that Concord development goodbye once those bowtie-and-sensible-shoe-wearing zoning board members thought that Ben and I had anything approaching dirty money." Another finger. "Third, my real estate business here in Warner would fold up. I'd be finished in another month. Heck, I might even be investigated by the Board of Registration, get my license pulled. And fourth"—four fingers were now up in the air—"I would have pissed off Gus Spinelli, because our meet was supposed to be confidential. And trust me, you don't want to go through life having pissed off a guy like Gus Spinelli."

Jessica unfolded her arms, wiped at her eyes, and said quietly, "What did he offer you, this Gus Spinelli?"

"Some additional financing through a relative of his, nice and clean. We get that financing, we go back to the Concord zoning board showing that we've got the financial resources to proceed, and then we can start breaking ground in a month, start selling lots in two months."

She wiped at her eyes again. "What's the interest rate?"

Ted looked defiant.

"Ted . . . the interest rate."

"Fifteen."

"Jesus Christ," she exploded. "Fifteen? Christ, the highest we can charge for a business loan is under five percent, and you went with fifteen?"

"We had no choice," he said, and he surprised her by not raising his voice, not arguing, not putting up a fight. It looked like he had just given up. "We had no choice," he repeated. "You know how tight things are, how stretched we are. Nobody would front us the money, Jessica. Nobody. Gus was our last option."

Seeing his defeated look and hearing the tone of his voice changed something inside her. Now she wasn't so angry. Now she was feeling sorry for her husband.

"Okay," she said. "What next for you, him, and Ben?"

Ted tried to smile. "Good things. Ben liked what he had to say. We should have the money we need in a couple of days."

"All right, but listen to me, Ted. You're going to pay him back as quickly as possible. These guys, they love to get their hooks into you, they love to milk you dry. Don't let that happen. I won't allow it to happen to you and our family. Pay him off, say goodbye, and just make that development work, all right?"

He nodded. "Jessica, I promise. I so promise."

She was exhausted and felt like walking a few steps into their bedroom and just collapsing. But there was one more thing to do.

"Let's get the kids down and talk to them, all right? We need to tell them what we told the detective. They need to know we're protecting them. And we need to know exactly what they were doing last night."

Ted looked as relieved as someone being told that a physics final exam had been rescheduled for next week.

"That makes sense," he said, getting up from the chair. "I'll go fetch them."

—⁊⁊⁊—

Five minutes later Jessica and Ted were standing in front of their respective children as they sat on the couch together. She couldn't remember the last time they had talked to their kids like this, interrogating them, demanding to know what they had done. Over the past years, in an unspoken but mutual understanding, Ted had taken care of Craig's problems while she had done the same for her Emma.

Ted started. "Look, we had the police in here a while ago, all right? The detective was asking questions about Sam Warner and about you two."

No, Jessica thought, *that's not right.* She wasn't about to allow Ted to bring Emma into this.

"Ah, actually," she said, interrupting Ted, "Detective Rafferty was most interested in you, Craig."

"What?" he said, sitting hunched over, his hands on his knees. "Me?"

Ted gave Jessica a quick, angry glance and then returned his eyes to Craig, and Jessica didn't care. So what? It was Ted's problem, it was Craig's, and it certainly wasn't hers or Emma's.

"That's right, son. Apparently you went to the counselor when Sam bullied you."

Craig sat back against the couch. "Wasn't bullying."

Jessica said, "Craig, the detective said there were four instances of Sam and you getting into a fight."

"Wasn't a fight either."

Ted said, "So what was it?"

The boy folded his arms, looked up at his father. "You know all about it, Dad. You had to sign that paper."

"But tell us again, so your stepmother can hear it."

"It wasn't bullying!"

"Craig, knock it off," Ted said. "Tell your stepmother."

It was rare to hear Craig talk back to his father like this, and Jessica wondered what was going on in the boy's mind. Craig glanced at Emma for a moment, as if he were hoping that she would say something or intervene in some way, but Emma kept her mouth shut. She had the slightly pleased look of someone who was not in trouble. The look was similar to what was on her face during award ceremonies, when she was waiting to step up and get what was hers. Contented pleasure.

Craig said, "It was dumb stuff, that's all. Knocking books out of my hand, bumping into me hard in the hallway, stuff like that."

Jessica didn't want to say a word, but she felt like she had to do her part as a mom in this crisis. She didn't want Ted to accuse her later of letting him be the bad cop in this meeting.

"Then why did the guidance counselor and the assistant principal get involved?" she asked.

Craig shifted his arms around as if he were trying to squeeze something hard, and he said, "Because some teachers and aides that didn't know enough to mind their own business had seen it and whined about it."

"So you didn't whine about it?" his father asked.

"Dad, crap, no," he said. "What's the point? Sam—nobody crossed Sam. Nobody. I wasn't gonna do anything like that."

Emma kept on looking pleased with herself, and even though she was Jessica's daughter, Jessica didn't like the smug look. What did her daughter know, and why wasn't she saying anything?

Ted turned to her. "Jessica?"

Her turn now. "We need to make sure we know exactly what you two were up to last night. Emma?"

Even with being put on the spot, Emma still looked self-assured, smug, as if she were prepping to race against a runner from junior high.

"It was a scavenger hunt," she said. "Okay? Just like we told you this morning. We both got invites, secret invites, to go out last night."

"Both of you?"

Craig said, "That's right. Both of us."

Ted said, "And do you know who sent them?"

"No," Emma said.

"No," Craig said.

"All right, then," Ted said, and he looked at Jessica, gave her a look as if to say, *Okay, here we go.*

"Where were your phones last night?"

Emma looked puzzled. Craig said, "What?"

"Your phones—did you keep them with you last night?"

Emma still looked puzzled, and then Craig shook his head. "Um, no. We didn't."

Jessica nearly had to sit down from relief. It was true, what Emma had said. Neither she nor Craig had been in possession of their iPhones.

"Go on," Ted said.

"Uh, the rules of the scavenger hunt said that we had to leave our cell phones behind. So we couldn't use Google Maps. So Emma and I, we, uh, took some plastic bags—"

A relieved voice inside Jessica started saying, *Yes, yes, yes . . .*

Emma broke in. "That's right. We wrapped the phones in the plastic bags, then put them under a bush near the Minuteman statue on the town common. Then we went out and got turned around, and the rain started . . "

Jessica could sense Ted relaxing as well. Maybe this frightening little thing was about to wrap up.

Then Ted surprised them all. "Where're the notes?" he asked.

Craig whipped his head around and looked at Emma.

What? Jessica thought. *What is going on?*

Emma said, "What notes?"

"The notes you got about the scavenger hunt. About what you were both hunting for. Where you had to go. Where are they?"

Craig started to talk. "I think mine is back at—"

Emma interrupted. "We destroyed them."

"Really?" Ted asked. "Why? Why didn't you keep them?"

There was the briefest of pauses, and Emma said, "There were rules. Whoever runs the scavenger hunt, they don't want other people to know what's in it. So we had to throw away the notes when we were done. That way other teams couldn't have an advantage if they started at a different time."

Jessica said, "Okay, we get it. Ted? Anything else?"

Ted stared at his son and said, "Just this. I . . . I mean, Jessica and I, we've gone out on a very, very big limb for the both of you. The detective who was here a while ago asked us if you were both home last night with us, and we said yes. Do you understand?"

Craig just nodded, but Emma said, "Yes, we do understand."

"And if you kids find out any more about who was running this scavenger hunt, you've got to tell us. That could be a lead that might help the police. If somebody took your phones and went to the town forest and . . . well, you understand, right?"

Jessica followed up on Ted's lead. "We trust you both. We . . . we're a family. A blended family, but a family nonetheless. We both believe in both of you, and we don't want either one of you to get into trouble. We both believe you don't have anything to hide, and that's why we told the police what we did. I hope you both appreciate that."

Emma said, "Gosh, yes, we do."

Craig said, "Oh, yeah. We appreciate it."

"Good," Ted said. "Jessica, we done here?"

Jessica said, "Yes, we are."

—⁂—

Later that Wednesday night, after a quiet and strained dinner of reheated homemade beef stew and rolls, she was in bed with Ted, her back to him, breathing softly, staring out the window at a nearby streetlight.

"Hon, you still awake?"

She hesitated before answering. What now?

"Still awake."

"I think it went well. Don't you?"

She automatically replied, "I guess so."

"That story, though, about the scavenger hunt. I find it hard to believe, you know?"

Out in the distance a train rumbled along the old B&M tracks north of Warner. She couldn't remember who now owned them. There came the mournful sound of a horn as the train reached a crossing.

Jessica quietly said, "I do, too. But I don't want to ask them any more about it, all right? Can we just drop it for now?"

Ted didn't answer, and for a moment she thought he had drifted off. Then he said, "You're right. I can't believe our kids would be involved in something like what happened to Sam Warner."

It was as if Ted couldn't say the word "murdering" or "killing," she thought.

He went on. "So we'll drop it. Leave it be, hope the police get an early break in the case. As for what went on last night, it'll be our family secret. How does that sound? A secret we'll keep forever."

She reached around, grasped his fingers as the mournful train horn sounded again.

"Yes," she said. "A forever secret."

—⁊⁊—

Jessica woke up. She had been dreaming about an earthquake, and she listened to another train rumble along a set of tracks closer to the house. Since the house was so old, trains on the near tracks caused it to shake.

She looked over at the clock, saw it was 2:10 in the morning, just as the louder train horn sounded.

She was thirsty. She swung out of bed, paused. Ted was breathing softly and deeply, and she had a flash of memory, of how her first husband, Bobby Thornton, had snored and coughed during the night, forcing her onto the living room couch when she couldn't sleep. Ted wasn't perfect, by God, but at least he never snored.

Jessica went out to the kitchen, found a glass in the sink, rinsed it out, and took a satisfying swallow of water. It tasted good, cleared her throat. She put the glass back in the sink and it slipped from her fingers at the last moment, hit the sink hard, and nearly shattered. The noise scared her.

She wanted to go back to bed, but there was something in the back of her mind, something that made her go to the staircase.

When she got upstairs, she saw a light on in Craig's room. With the age of the house, sometimes it settled, and the old doors would pop open. She remembered the first few months here, when Emma was convinced ghosts were haunting the place because closed doors would open on their own.

At this time of the night Jessica felt that fear of the unknown, of thinking maybe Emma was right. Maybe this old house *was* haunted.

Craig's door was open about a foot.

Jessica moved quietly over, peered in.

Her stepson was sprawled out on the bed, one long leg dangling over one side. He was wearing checked underwear and a gray T-shirt that had ridden up, exposing his back, and one arm was over his face. His breathing was as slow and as regular as his dad's. There were no lights on in his room save the screensaver on his computer, just a jumble of shifting, oozing lines of green and red.

Jessica thought about the secrets that computer held, especially the source of that porn video.

Any other mother or stepmother might have sneaked in and unfrozen the computer to see what could be found, but she wasn't any other mother or stepmother. She backed out and went over to Emma's door.

72

It was closed.

She waited a bit and then turned the doorknob and took a look in. The first thing she noticed was the scent of her girl, the scent of her running shoes and clothes. Any other mother would have found the scent disgusting, but she wasn't any other mother. Jessica took a step in. She found the scent relaxing, reassuring.

Her girl was huddled underneath the covers. A nightlight was on, bright enough to illuminate her trophies, medals, and ribbons, her posters of female track stars, and her homemade chart outlining her bright future. A memory ached inside Jessica as she recalled the times after Bobby's death when they would share a bed because Emma had such scary nightmares and because Jessica . . . well, she found the presence and scent of her daughter reassuring when her husband was gone.

Not that she missed him that much. No, it was just the emptiness of his not being there and the cold, cold feeling that she couldn't rely on Bobby for Emma's immediate future.

She thought of what Ted had said earlier. Secrets. Family secrets.

One secret was that private investigator calling from Portland, checking up on Grace's belief that her brother had been murdered. Whatever was going to happen with this investigator was going to be a secret she would never, ever tell Ted.

For a brief moment she was tempted to crawl into bed with her daughter once more, to be reassured and comforted, but instead she walked out and gently closed the door behind her.

CHAPTER THIRTEEN

Emma waited until she heard the door click as her mother closed it and then slowly lifted her head from underneath the covers to make sure.

Yep, Mom was gone.

What Mom and stepdad Ted didn't realize was that climbing the stairs caused so many creaks and groans that it was easy to know when one of them was coming up to the second floor. When Emma had caught the usual sounds a few moments ago, she had ducked under the covers to make sure Mom didn't see anything.

She hadn't.

Good.

Emma went back to her iPhone, where she was carrying on two conversations at the same time with other girls on the track team, Kate Romer and Melissa McAllister.

> Kate: are u still in trouble with yr parents?
> Emma: just a bit. tomorrow shld be better
> Melissa: cant believe Sam W is dead
> Emma: i know
> Kate: what were u and C doing out late?
> Emma: NOYB lol
> Melissa: who'd want to kill Sam?

Emma: dunno
Melissa: poor Sam. such a sweetie. you feeling ok after Sat?

Emma paused at that last message, fingers and thumbs hovering over the iPhone's keyboard. *He was a fucking creep,* is what she wanted to type. Instead she wrote

yeah I know

followed by a frownie face, and then

I'm feeling better
Kate: r u going to Sam memorial?

Again she paused, fingers over the keyboard. It was warm and safe under the covers, the iPhone light giving everything in here a soft, sweet glow. Times like this she wished she could stay under the covers forever and not think of anything, anything at all. Just her and her iPhone and her friends. That's all she needed.

Back to the keyboard, answering Kate's message.

I guess

Then her iPhone pinged again. A third person was now texting her. "Shit," she whispered.

It was Craig, just across the hallway.

Craig: Emma u up?
"Shut up and go back to sleep," she whispered.
Craig: Emma I'm scared

She switched the phone off, stuck it under her pillow, and rolled over, the covers still enveloping her, still protecting her.

Before the Warner Savings Bank opened its front door that Thursday morning, branch manager Ellen Nickerson had a quick employee meeting in the lobby. Included in the meeting were the two young ghost employees, who had emerged from their small offices like young bear cubs emerging into the light for the first time in their lives. And overlooking it all was that framed photo of Larry Miles, dead in that climbing accident, smiling forever.

"There's going to be a public memorial service tonight at the town common, celebrating the life of young Sam Warner, beginning at six P.M.," Ellen said, looking at an email printout. "Warner Savings Bank is a prominent member of the business community, and I expect everyone to attend. Any questions?"

Jessica had one question but didn't want to be the brave one by asking it, but Percy Prescott decided to step up and risk Ellen's wrath.

"If attendance is mandatory, will we be compensated?" he asked.

Amber looked at him in shock, and Jessica thought, *Well, there you go.* Amber was still mourning the popular and athletic student she had once known, teammate of her younger brother, and Percy was going to have none of it. Even Rhonda seemed taken aback by Percy's directness.

"No," Ellen said. "You won't."

Percy pressed on, his arms folded in front of him. "Then how can you order us to be there?"

Ellen stared back at the young teller. "Because if you don't go, it'll be noted in your performance review later this year. Do you understand, Percy?"

He just nodded and muttered something, and Ellen checked her watch and said, "Okay, people, let's get to work."

At her midmorning break, Jessica ducked outside and went to the parking lot at the rear, where she made two quick calls.

The first one went well.

"Talbot Investigations," came a woman's voice.

"Is Gary Talbot in?"

"May I ask who's calling?"

After identifying herself, she was put through and said, "Mr. Talbot, I was wondering—"

"Please, no need to be formal. Gary."

She listened to the murmur of traffic going in and out of Warner, wondered if any one of those vehicles contained a woman juggling as many problems as she was.

"Gary, thanks," she said. "I know I said I was going to call back today to set up an appointment, but something's come up."

"Oh?" came the suspicious reply.

"Yes," she said. "I'm not sure if you've seen the news or not, but a violent crime has taken place in Warner. A teenage boy from Warner High School was found murdered the other day."

"Oh," Talbot said again, but this time there was sympathy in his tone.

"You see, this young boy and his family . . . well, we were very close to them, and things are just a horrible, horrible mess. In fact, there's going to be a memorial service for him tonight and I've volunteered to help out, and the wake will be coming soon, and the funeral, and—"

"Mrs. Thornton, please, I understand," he said. "You do what you have to do. I understand, and I'm sure I can make my client understand as well."

"That's very gracious of you," she said. "Thanks so much. I think I'll be free in a day or two, and I promise we'll set up an interview."

"That sounds fine, Mrs. Thornton," he said. "My condolences."

"I appreciate that."

The next phone call didn't go as well. She called Ted and it went straight through to voicemail, and then she called his office and her call was answered by Paula Fawkes, the office manager.

"Oh, hey, Jessica, nope, he's in conference right now with a couple of clients. Can I help you?"

Jessica checked the time on her iPhone, saw that she had exactly ninety seconds left to get back to work.

"I was hoping Ted had time for lunch."

Paula said, "Oh, Jessica, he's busy, but I'll make sure he gets your message. Okay?"

"Okay," Jessica said, "I appreciate—"

Paula had signed off.

What was that about?

Jessica went back to the lobby. A car honking its horn up by the common nearly made her yelp.

—◊—

About one hundred fifteen miles to the northeast, in Portland, Gary Talbot leaned back in his office chair and looked out the near window to the city's harbor. The window was smeared with dirt and seagull droppings, but the building's owners refused to get them cleaned and he didn't have the spare cash to have the job done himself. The woman who pretended to be his secretary was in some cubicle somewhere else in the city, being a receptionist for him and a half-dozen other small companies that needed to appear to be doing well.

Gary wasn't doing well. He was doing okay, but with his credit card balances increasing each month and the rent going up in two months, okay wasn't going to cut it. His office was small, with light gray filing cabinets with good locks and a framed certificate listing his official license as a private investigator in the state of Maine.

Nowhere on any of the walls was there any mention of his previous career as a Maine state trooper.

At his elbow were his computer monitor, a stack of paperwork, and a telephone. A few minutes ago he had gotten off the phone with Jessica Thornton of Warner, Massachusetts. It had been an excellent call, even though the woman couldn't possibly know why he considered it excellent. For Gary it meant the bait had been taken, and even if she had delayed the meeting, so what? Jessica Thornton was ready to meet with him, which was a success, no matter how you looked at it.

Funny thing, his client, Grace Thornton, had left just a few minutes ago. Talk about coincidences. She was a bitter young woman who basically needed someone to bitch to, and Gary was okay with that, letting her bitch to him for a nice rate of a hundred bucks an hour. For some reason she was obsessed with her older brother and his untimely death and was convinced that her evil sister-in-law—ha-ha-ha—had been involved.

So what?

But still, the weird young lady's suspicions about her brother's death didn't seem unfounded. Even though he wasn't about to admit it to her.

—⁓—

Two weeks earlier Gary had gotten a heads-up phone call from an old trooper friend of his, Sarah Sundance, who was now working for the York County Attorney General's Office.

"Gary, I hope you'll forgive me, but I've just tossed a case your way."

He rubbed at his forehead with his free hand. "Sarah, my checking account just forgave you. What's the problem?"

"I have a woman who's been haunting us for months, wanting us to reopen a case involving her brother. He got killed in a drunk-driving accident a few years back."

"So what's her problem?"

Sarah laughed. "She thinks our previous employer screwed the pooch and didn't do a good job investigating the accident."

He found a yellow pad, started scribbling. "What's her name?"

"Grace Thornton."

"Her brother?"

"Bobby Thornton."

Gary paused in his scribbling. "Why does that name sound familiar?"

"Because he ran a car dealership in northeast Massachusetts," she said. "Ran a bunch of late-night TV commercials on cable."

"Oh, yeah, now it comes back," Gary said. "Was there another car involved in the accident?"

"Nope, single car," she said. "Leased from his dealership. Was going to some retirement dinner in York up on I-95, struck a deer, went off the road, and slammed into a tree trunk. Dead at the scene."

"So what's her problem?"

Sarah said, "Okay, this is when it gets out there. Grace is convinced that her brother was murdered and that her sister-in-law had something to do with it."

"How? Did she bribe a deer to commit suicide by standing in the middle of the highway just as he was driving by?"

Sarah laughed. "No. I'll let her tell you herself. She's tried two other PIs and hasn't gotten anywhere."

"You think I can do any better?"

"Gary, you can do anything better than most," she said. "Don't get pissy at me, all right? I wanted to toss you some business. You don't like it, you don't have to do it."

He paused for a moment, took the phone, and rapped the end of it twice on his forehead.

Moron.

Then he went back to talking to Sarah. "You're the best, thanks," he said. "What's her contact info?"

Sarah gave him Grace Thornton's landline number, cell number, home address, and email address. Gary read the information back and Sarah said, "Look, I'm late for a meeting. Hope this helps."

"Thanks," Gary said.

"And remember, what happened on that traffic stop wasn't your fault. Okay? No matter what anyone says."

A burning sensation started in his gut, and he felt again as if he were outside on that November night, standing at the side of the road on I-295 north of Falmouth, making a traffic stop that would end with the crippling of a young man and the death of his beloved career in the Maine State Police.

"Thanks, Sarah, I appreciate that."

He hung up as quickly as he could, then reached out to Grace Thornton, and twenty-four hours later she was in his office.

Gary always liked to size up his potential clients within sixty seconds of having them in his office, and the first word he thought of when Grace came in was "tight." Not that she wore tight clothes. Far from it. She had on a shapeless gray jacket and floppy black slacks, and her dark brown hair was cut in a bob—blob?—and she wasn't wearing makeup. But her eyes were alight with a fire that meant she was either on a special mission or just crazed.

"I need your help," was the first thing she said, dropping a thick folder on his desk.

And for the next forty minutes Grace Thornton went into a practiced spiel about how her beloved brother had died in a single-car accident on the night of July 12 on I-95 in York—a stretch of road Gary knew quite well from his previous career—and how, despite the official report saying that her brother had died from an accident caused by drunk driving, first hitting a deer then a tree, she was convinced that his wife, Jessica, was responsible. After his death it came to light that his entire estate had been left in trust for young Emma Thornton, administered by Jessica Thornton, said trust not being available to Emma until she turned twenty-one, to be disbursed by her mother. The entire trust would be available to Emma when she turned thirty, whereupon she wouldn't need her mother to write checks from the trust fund.

Grace leaned over at this point, tapping a finger on the thick file. "Please don't laugh at me. I can't stand having people laugh at me. And I know I don't have direct evidence. It isn't there. But there's enough circumstantial evidence that I'm sure clearly connects Jessica to my brother's death."

Gary just nodded. "All right."

"Will you take on my case?"

Of course, was his first thought. His bank account and overdue rent payment for this office demanded nothing else.

"Before I give you my decision," he said, "I need to know one thing. What's your goal?"

"Excuse me?"

He said, "I'm sorry to say this, Miss Thornton—"

"Please—Grace."

"Grace, I'm sorry to say this, but even if I manage to find some connection between your brother's death and his wife's actions, I doubt we'll find enough to bring it to the state police or the attorney general's office."

"That's all right," she said, folding her arms, pursing her thin lips. "Just to put that bitch in her place will be enough."

"I see."

She glanced around his small office and said, "Excuse me, could you tell me where the restroom is?"

"Hold on," he said. He opened the desk drawer and took out a key attached to a block of wood, which had been lying next to his snub-nosed .38 Smith & Wesson revolver—you never knew when some nutcase, or at least an angry male nutcase, was going to storm in here. Gary handed the key over to her. "Go out the door, take a right. It's at the end of the hallway."

Grace frowned, and he said, "It's all right, honest. The building owners keep it nice and clean." Unlike the windows, he thought.

"All right," she said, and when she left, he leaned back, rubbed his eyes. What was that expression? She brightened a room whenever she left it.

Yeah. True.

He brought his chair forward. The funny thing was, after nearly an hour of her blabbing at him, Grace was right to be suspicious. Nothing solid, nothing you could ever take to the attorney general or the state police. But enough to badger this Jessica Thornton and maybe squeeze something out of her as well. A nasty thought, a bad thought, but his supply of good thoughts had drained since he had been forced out of the Maine State Police.

He waited.

The thick file was in front of him. He pulled it over, started flipping through it. He found stuff that made sense. Copies of little news briefs listing the accident and Bobby Thornton's death. Copies of the accident report. Photographs of the accident scene. Autopsy report.

Ugh, he thought. Imagine going through an autopsy report for your older brother. Gary was an only child, but his skin crawled at the thought of doing that for a close relative.

He dug deeper into the files. Weather reports. Copies of advertisements placed in the *Portland Press Herald* and the *York County Coast Star,* looking for witnesses to the accident. Damn, the woman had even gotten copies of the maintenance records from the Maine DOT for that stretch of highway!

From a distance he heard the restroom's toilet flush.

One last thing. Folded-up paper. He had time to unfold it, saw . . . It was the trust paperwork. But attached to it were a number of printouts from various websites, and he gave them all a speedy glance, seeing instantly what Grace was up to.

He folded the papers, returned them to the folder, and pushed it back across to its original position on the desk.

The door opened and Grace Thornton came in and sat down heavily in the chair.

"You were right," she said. "The place was nice and clean."

"Good."

Grace said, "I need a decision, and I need it now. Will you take on my case?"

"Yes, I will."

Something that appeared to be a smile creased her face. "Thank you."

He explained his rate, what he would do and where he would go, and she quickly signed the contract for his services.

Gary motioned to the thick file. "I'd like to have you leave that, if you don't mind. I need to see what work you've done so I can start by knowing what's what."

That odd expression on her face faltered. She took the thick folder off the desk and placed it in her lap, as if she were placing it in quarantine.

"I'll get the paperwork copied and sent over to you."

He decided to have a little fun. "You can leave it here."

"No, I'll have copies made."

"Grace, I'm a professional, and—"

Her voice grew sharp. "I said I'd make a copy!" Then she seemed to realize that she had gone too far, and she tried to smile again. "I'm sorry," she said. "You can tell I'm . . . passionate. I've spent more than a year researching this. It's taken a lot of effort, a lot of setbacks." She patted her rough hands on the cardboard. "I can't stand not having this nearby. I'll make a copy of everything, get it to you straightaway."

He nodded. "That will be fine."

She gathered up her folder, went to the door, and turned and said, "Thank you. Thank you for taking on my case."

Gary said, "You're welcome."

Thinking, *Crazy lady, I know what you've got in there, and this is* my *case. Not yours.*

—⁓—

Now Gary Thornton opened the thick folder of accident and weather reports that had been couriered to him nearly two weeks ago. He was not surprised to see that the internet printouts that had been attached to Bobby Thornton's trust paperwork and that provided a roadmap to Grace Thornton's future plans were missing.

He had been counting on it.

CHAPTER FOURTEEN

I t was crowded at the Warner town common, which surprised Jessica. She knew Sam Warner had been popular in high school—even if Percy Prescott was bitter over his treatment by Sam and his teammates—but there were at least two hundred men, women, and students crowded around the circular bandstand that during the summer months hosted the Warner High School's jazz band every Wednesday night.

Greeting folks walking into the grounds of the oval-shaped common were groups of two and three high school varsity cheerleaders, handing out packets of matches and long thin candles with a piece of round cardboard slipped halfway up. Standing by themselves, heads down, feet not moving, were a crowd of young boys in blue-and-white wrestling jackets: Sam's teammates, here to support and mourn their teammate and captain.

She made her way toward the bandstand, octagon-shaped, with a roof supported by a set of pillars. Jessica nodded and whispered hello to a number of parents and bank customers she recognized. She looked around, wanting to see if Ted had shown up. He had promised to meet her by the bandstand at 5:45 P.M., and Jessica checked her iPhone: it was 5:51. Where was Ted?

Up on the bandstand was a minister, standing with his arms around a couple who looked tired and shrunken.

Something seized in Jessica's throat. Sam's parents.

To lose a child to an accident—a drowning, an accidental drug or alcohol overdose, a car accident—that burden could kill a mother or father. But to have your child, your love, your life, murdered?

Jessica couldn't look at Sam's parents anymore.

Near them was a coatrack holding what looked to be Sam's wrestling jacket, as well as a sound system and the principal of Warner High School, Michael Glynn, who was looking down at a folded-over piece of paper. A few feet away was a large photo, mounted on cardboard and held up by an easel, that showed Sam in his tight blue spandex wrestling singlet with a white *W* on the chest, standing in some gym, a round gold medal hanging from a red, white, and blue ribbon around his neck. Sam had his arms folded; his biceps were clearly defined, and he had a cocky grin that said that even at his age everything was safe, everything was planned, and his bright future was preordained.

Until a gunshot had cut him down in the town forest two nights ago.

Jessica checked her iPhone again. It was 5:59 P.M. Where was Ted? She called up the keyboard and texted a quick message:

at the common where are u?

"Hey, Jessica."

She looked up from her iPhone. Rhonda was standing there, hands in her jacket.

"Hey, Rhon," she said. A few yards away she saw Ellen Nickerson talking to one of the two ghost employees standing next to her. Ralph. Was that his name? And she thought, *What difference does it make? In a month he'll be off at another branch, on a track for upper management, just like we were dreaming about. But we're stuck here and he's heading out. Lucky boy.*

Amber Brooks was on the other side, wiping at her eyes, talking and sobbing with two other young women, probably classmates from the time when Amber was in high school.

But no sign of Percy Prescott. Big surprise.

"Some turnout," Rhonda said. "I doubt you or I will get such crowds when we have our funeral."

"I don't think we'll be in a position to complain."

It was good to have Rhonda next to her.

But Ted . . .

"How are the kids? Still in jail?"

That phrase startled her. In jail? What was that all about? Did Rhonda know something about the police visit yesterday?

Jessica took a breath. *Overreacting,* she thought. In jail. Rhonda was just gently teasing about whatever punishment she and Ted had given the kids.

"Not yet," she said. "But Ted and I are working on the appropriate punishment."

Rhonda said, "Really? Didn't know you two were such softies. Heck, if I had pulled a stunt like that when I was their age, I wouldn't have been able to sit down for a week."

Jessica gently nudged her friend. "Even with that extra padding you carry around down there?"

Rhonda nudged her back. "If you weren't my best friend, I'd be pissed off at that. But still, remember the last time we were at something like this?"

"Yeah, that memorial service for Larry Miles. Though I have to admit, I wasn't sad at the time."

"Neither was I." Rhonda reached over and briefly rubbed Jessica's back with affection before going on. "Yeah, for some reason he hated me, right from the start. I still don't know why. Maybe I reminded him of his mother, or a schoolteacher. And I knew he was doing everything to get me fired, just when my family needed my job the most. Even with you and the others sticking up for me."

"I didn't understand it either, but it was still awful when he had that climbing accident. Even jerks like him don't deserve to die like that, up in the air, your crampons falling apart."

It seemed Rhonda was going to reply when there were whispers of "It's time, it's time," and little flares of light popped up as people around

Jessica started lighting their candles. She did the same. Rhonda had trouble with her candle, so Jessica lit it for her.

"Thanks, hon," Rhonda said. "You know, it's such a pretty sight. Too bad we're all here because of such sad news."

Jessica thought, yes, Rhonda was right. It *was* a pretty sight, the people on the common, all residents of this small Massachusetts town, coming out to mourn the death of one of their sons. Even with the number of people crowded around the bandstand, there was just the slightest murmur of voices. The traffic going around the common seemed to have slowed in recognition of what was going on on this stretch of grass where hundreds of years earlier the farmers and merchants of Warner had first drilled to defend their people and land.

"Poor Bruce, poor Donna," Rhonda whispered.

Who? Jessica thought, and then she was briefly ashamed. Bruce and Donna Warner, up there on display in the bandstand, ready to do their part in their son's memorial.

"I can't believe they're here," Jessica whispered back. "If I lost Emma that way, I wouldn't be able to leave my bed for a month."

"Or Craig, I'm sure."

Jessica spoke quickly. "Yes, of course, Craig as well."

The minister went up to the microphone, tapped at it a few times, blew into it, and his voice echoed across the common. "My friends, my parishioners, my neighbors, I'm Reverend Earl Wessex of the Episcopal Christ Church of Warner," he said, his voice low and soothing. "This is a night of sorrow, of remembrance, of mourning, but also it's a night for our shocked and stunned community to come together. Please, let us bow our heads, no matter your creed, and join together in the Lord's Prayer."

The voices of the crowd murmured the familiar words: "Our Father, which art in heaven, hallowed be thy name. Thy kingdom come. Thy will be done, on earth as it is in heaven . . ."

The candle above Jessica's hand flickered, making her skin look like old parchment, and as the prayer was slowly recited, Jessica looked away from the bandstand and observed the crowd around her. More familiar faces.

Ellen Nickerson was still standing with the ghost employees, holding court, the two young men next to her, ensuring that she was taking note of their attendance.

Amber Brooks had her head buried in her hands and was quietly sobbing as her friends flanked her, gently rubbing her shoulders. And—

There was Emma.

It was odd, but seeing her out here, Jessica gave a shudder of relief. Her girl was holding a candle in one hand, her other hand blocking the wind to keep the flame alive, the light making *her* hand looking delicate and translucent. She was with a tiny knot of her fellow runners, and Jessica knew she might be making things up, but it seemed as if the other girls were gathered around her as her friends and supporters, as if Emma were the leader.

And Craig? She couldn't see Craig.

Damn it, she still didn't see Ted. Should she text him again?

Principal Michael Glynn went up to the microphone, rustled his paper, coughed, and said, "My fellow residents of Warner, and friends of Sam, and his family, I think it's appropriate to read this tonight." He held up the paper and started reading. "This is from A. E. Housman, written back in 1896. 'To an Athlete Dying Young.'" The stanzas came out of the sound system, echoing across the town common.

> *The time you won your town the race,*
> *We chaired you through the market-place;*
> *Man and boy stood cheering by,*
> *And home we brought you shoulder-high.*

Listening to Principal Glynn's firm voice and hearing the stanzas, Jessica had a memory of an English class back in high school, Mrs. Simpson reading the poem and leading a discussion afterward about how this poem had been published and passed along during the First World War, when so many young Englishmen were being slaughtered in France. Back then—paying more attention to Bobby Thornton sitting in the rear, leaning back in his chair, grinning at her—she thought Mrs. Simpson had been exaggerating. But not now. Not tonight.

Sobs and wails broke out as the words written long ago came over the sound system and the young athlete posed forever up on the bandstand, the polished surface of the mounted photo flickering from all the candlelight around it. And poor Bruce and Donna Warner, clasped together in mutual mourning and grief, were no longer a separate entity, no longer Mom and Dad, but now one unit, forever known as Grieving Parents.

> *Now you will not swell the rout*
> *Of lads that wore their honours out,*
> *Runners whom renown outran*
> *And the name died before the man.*

More sobs and cries.

Then, a . . . giggle? A muffled laugh?

She couldn't see anything nearby, but Jessica noticed some folks turning. She stood on tiptoe and saw Percy Prescott standing near a row of shrubbery at the other side of the common, with another young man next to him. The young man had a paper bag in his left hand, brought it up, and took a sip of something, then passed it over to Percy. Percy took a good-sized slug and then whispered something to his friend, and the friend burst out laughing and then covered his mouth. A few sharp whispers from folks standing nearby shut them up but didn't hide the pleased smiles on their faces.

Rhonda asked, "What's going on?"

"Percy and a friend seem to be enjoying themselves," Jessica said.

"Oh, no," Rhonda said.

"Oh, yes," Jessica said.

"But on a night like this . . ."

Jessica said, "I guess it just goes to show you it takes all kinds."

Rhonda's candle then flickered out, and Jessica leaned over and relit it. Wax had puddled on the round slip of cardboard.

Principal Glynn stopped talking and then—

A touch of her right elbow.

"Mrs. Thornton? A moment?"

She quickly turned, her hands suddenly going cold.

It was Detective Doug Rafferty.

In the warm light of the candles his face looked open and friendly, but Jessica didn't want to move. But she also didn't want Rhonda to hear.

"Sure," she said. She took a few steps, thinking, *What's going on, what's going on, what's going on,* and she stopped and tried to gauge what was happening behind that calm and smooth police detective's face, but nothing was obvious.

"Sorry to bother you," he said. "I was here at the service and I saw you and thought I'd save a phone call."

"Makes sense," she said, the words just coming automatically.

Jessica took a few steps more. Up on the bandstand Principal Glynn was still talking.

Detective Rafferty said, "I was hoping I could talk with you tomorrow."

"About . . ."

"Mrs. Thornton, you know what I'm investigating. Please."

Now she felt guilty, under pressure, the calm eyes of the detective holding her still, like a predator seizing its prey with only its look, like a snake before a field mouse.

"Okay," she said. "I'll see what time works for Ted."

"I'm sorry, maybe I didn't make myself clear," Rafferty said. "I meant I wanted to talk to you alone, without your husband."

"But—"

Rafferty said, "Something's come up in our investigation and it would be best for all of us if we could speak face-to-face. It would be extremely helpful."

The words seemed to come out automatically again. "All right then. Tomorrow."

"Good," he said. "What would be a good time?"

"Ah . . ." She imagined going to Ellen Nickerson and saying, *Excuse me, Ellen, do you mind if I take some time off at about eleven* A.M.*? The police are investigating the murder of Sam Warner and they want to talk to me. You okay with that?*

"Lunch?" she said.

"Excuse me?"

"I have forty-five minutes for lunch," she said, thinking desperately whether this would work. "I could walk over and meet you at the station."

"Sure," he said. "That would be fine. Would noon work?"

Her usual lunch break was from eleven forty-five to twelve thirty. All right, no lunch tomorrow. Jessica couldn't see how she would have an appetite anyway.

"That would be great, Detective," she said.

"Very good, Mrs. Thornton, I'll see you tomorrow."

At the bandstand Principal Glynn was finished, and he gestured to Bruce and Donna Warner. Bruce took a half step forward, stopped, and looked at his wife with anguish. She shook her head and he leaned over, whispering something, and the sound system was sensitive enough to pick up her cracked voice saying, "No . . . no . . . I can't."

He touched his wife on the cheek and ambled forward, then stood there, looking at the microphone as if it were some magical instrument from the future dropped in front of him and he couldn't puzzle out its workings. Bruce was about the same age as Ted, with a closely trimmed black beard, an open and smiling face, and he worked at a medical device company somewhere in Littleton, making a ton of money. Donna didn't have to work and let everyone in the PTA know how pleased she was with her lot in life.

Jessica had a savage punch of a nasty thought traveling through her, that German phrase about reveling in the misfortune of others, and she wondered how pleased Donna would be at the next PTA meeting. She was horrified at the thought and hoped the detective standing next to her couldn't sense her feeling.

Bruce finally got to the microphone. "Ah . . . thank you, thank you all. Aah, at some point Donna and I, we plan to set up a scholarship in the memory of our Sam . . ."

He stopped. Looked down. A long weeping whimper escaped as he clasped the microphone stand with both hands. Bruce took one hand off the stand, wiped his face and eyes, and stared out at the silent crowd. "Please . . . anybody here, if you know anything, please talk to the police. I . . . please find out who did this to our boy."

He started sobbing, and Principal Glynn fumbled and switched off the sound system, and the Reverend Wessex went over and embraced both parents. Jessica couldn't look anymore. Detective Rafferty was still there.

"You see what my job is now, don't you, Mrs. Thornton?" he said. "Tomorrow at noon. My office."

Rafferty started to move away in the crowd, and she said, "Detective?"

He said, "Yes, Mrs. Thornton?"

"Can you tell me what this is about?" Then she corrected herself, "I mean, as part of the investigation into Sam's murder, can you tell me more?"

The detective gave her a sweet and understanding smile. "No," he said, and then he moved among the other mourners and was gone.

―ɯ―

Jessica didn't want to go back to Rhonda and explain what had just happened. Her candle had flickered out, but she didn't care. Then she spotted Ted talking to someone familiar, and she saw it was Paula Fawkes, the office manager at Warner Realty. Paula was short and on the curvy side—as Rhonda had once said, after Paula had made a deposit at the bank, "She's about fifteen pounds overweight, but it looks good on her"—and her blond mane was always elaborately styled and coiffed. Jessica had never really warmed up to Paula, and the feeling was mutual, and—

Paula laughed, and Ted laughed, and then she touched Ted's shoulder. Ted walked away and came over to Jessica.

"Hey, sorry I'm late," he said. "Had to catch up with some things at the office."

"That's okay," Jessica said quietly. "I understand." *I always understand,* she thought.

He gave her a clumsy hug, and as the wind shifted, a scent came to her.

"What a terrible, terrible night," Ted said.

The scent tickled her memory.

"I can't believe how strong Bruce and Donna are," he said.

Now the memory came to her.

"Can you believe being here after knowing your son was murdered the other night?"

The scent. The same scent Ted had on him the night he came home late, the same night the kids went missing.

The scent from Paula Fawkes.

And, like her job at the bank, where the numbers never, ever lied, Jessica knew.

She knew.

CHAPTER FIFTEEN

Ted Donovan stepped out of the shower, dried himself off with a thick light-green towel, and then looked at himself in the mirror, pinching the thick rolls along each hip. Damn. He would have to start paying attention to these lumps of fat if Paula Fawkes were going to continue seeing him.

He tossed the towel to the floor, picked up his robe. Okay, "seeing him." That was a weaselly way of saying having an affair. Though, truth be told, it wasn't much of an affair, not that he was complaining. It had started two months ago, when they were both working late and she was wearing this too-tight white blouse. She had come over to his desk with a new real estate listing, and as she leaned over the desk, one of the buttons had popped loose, revealing a fine lacy bra and gorgeous fleshy cleavage. He had stared at those delicious curves for about two seconds too long before Paula had said, "You like what you see?"

"A lot," he had replied.

With a teasing voice she had said, "Then do something about it."

And he had done so, right then and there, on his desk, with the tiny sane part of his mind screaming at him, *You fool, you're married and so is she, and her husband is in Afghanistan in the army.* But once he got his hands on those curves . . . Forget it.

After a few minutes of recovery—unheard of at his age until then—he had sat down on his office chair and she had straddled him and they had gone at it again.

He pulled the robe tight, amused and slightly embarrassed that the memory of that and of what had happened earlier tonight, making him late for that sobfest on the town common—when Paula had grabbed him by the necktie, dragged him into the small break room at the rear of the office, and got down on her knees—was stirring him again.

He ran a comb through his hair, not bothering to worry about where this was going, only knowing that the guilt about cheating on Jessica was overwhelmed by the hot sex he was getting from Paula. His wife was sexy in her own way, but to be brutally frank, she had let herself go over the past several months. Not in terms of gaining weight or not bothering with hairstyle or makeup, but just in her general appearance. She wore the same black slacks to work every day, with a number of blouses that she rotated depending on the day or the season, and on weekends or days off she liked to lounge around in sweats or old T-shirts. Okay, that wouldn't be a problem, and he hated to admit this like a horny teenage boy, but since they had gotten married, the lingerie, the lacy bras and panties, had been either tossed in the back of her bureau drawers or thrown away.

But Paula . . . Sure, she was a bit heavy, much heavier than Jessica, but she carried the weight well, and God, what she loved to wear underneath her office clothes—lots of lacy stuff, tight panties, thongs—it drove him crazy, and now he couldn't quite believe he had her for his own.

Okay, he thought, heading out of the steamy bathroom, he was sharing her with Captain Antonio Fawkes, but Antonio was in Kabul and she was here, and he was gone for another eight months, and Ted wasn't going to worry about that right now. That problem would be dealt with once the time came.

Ted got out of the bathroom, saw that the door to Emma's room was closed but the door to Craig's was open.

This other problem, right before him, couldn't wait.

He went to Craig's door, knocked, and said, "Hey, bud, can I come in?"

There was a grunt and Ted walked into Craig's room. He was impressed by how clean the boy kept it, compared to the shithole his own bedroom had been back when he was Craig's age. Jessica always complained about how cluttered it was, but she really, really didn't know boys now, did she? Craig was in bed, wearing gray shorts and a Warner T-shirt, and he was sitting up reading one of those Batman graphic novels that seemed so popular nowadays.

Ted pulled the chair away from Craig's small desk and sat down. "Time for a chat?"

Craig lowered the graphic novel. "I guess so."

Ted said, "I didn't see you at the town common. Were you there?"

"No," Craig said. "I was over at Mark Borman's house."

"Doing what?"

"Just hanging, that's all."

"Don't you think you should have been at the common?"

"Why?"

"Because Sam was a fellow student, that's why. To show respect."

Craig rolled his eyes. "Dad, Sam was an asshole."

"Craig . . ."

"Sorry, okay, Sam was a jerk. You know how he and the other members of the wrestling team treated me and lots of others—like Percy, the guy who works at Jessica's bank."

"Mom's bank," Ted said.

"Dad, Mom is in California. Jessica isn't my mom. She never will be."

Ted didn't want to restart this old argument. His first wife, Amanda, said she had "grown" in her marriage and was now living in a lesbian pottery co-op in California. Ted always hated remembering and talking about Amanda. Now he said, "Still, it would have been good for you to show up. Make you look like the better man, the bigger man. Do you understand?"

Craig kept quiet and Ted added, "I was pushed around and bullied when I was your age. I didn't really get my shit together until I started working, until I started making deals. You know what I found out, Craig? When you get older, the people who tormented you in high school, they end up as losers. I saw it myself."

Craig scratched his nose. Ted went on. "But you know I've got your back. Always. No matter what."

His son just nodded. Ted continued, "Now, the police are going to be looking into Sam's murder thoroughly, and the reason that detective was in here yesterday was because of the bullying you experienced from Sam."

"It wasn't bullying."

Ted held up a hand. "Okay, I hear you, bud, but according to the police and the school, it was bullying. The police are going to be looking into other things as well, like that scavenger hunt you and Emma did."

Craig's eyes flicked back to the graphic novel, as if his entire life, his hopes and dreams, none of that mattered except for his father leaving him alone so he could go back to his Batman comic.

Ted went on. "I'm sure the police are going to find out about that scavenger hunt. Word gets around. It'd be helpful for you and Emma to be proactive, to come up with the names of the students who sent you the invitations."

"I told you, we don't have the invitations anymore," Craig said. "We tossed them."

Ted stared at his son and said, "Craig, listen to me, and listen to me very, very carefully. If the police are investigating, we want them to widen their search. We don't want them coming back to you for any reason, any reason at all. Okay? We don't need them poking around you and our family."

He was surprised at what Craig said next: "You mean you, right, Dad?"

His skin felt much warmer, like a sunlamp had just switched on. "What do you mean by that?"

"Nothing."

"Craig . . ."

"I hear things," Craig said. "I see things."

"Like what?"

"Like your business isn't great. Might go bankrupt."

"Who told you—" Ted caught himself. "Forget that. I'm not going bankrupt. But again, listen to what I'm saying. We don't want the police focused on you, or me, or anyone else in the family. If other people were out there on the night of Sam's murder, as part of this ridiculous scavenger hunt, then I need to know about it. Got it? Some names, that's all."

Craig shifted his long legs and said, "Okay, Dad. I'll do it."

Ted nodded, got up, and patted his boy's knee. "Good. Do that and we can get all this behind us. And Craig?"

"Yeah?"

Ted was stunned at how quickly his eyes filled and his voice choked. "I will always protect you. I swear to God. Don't you ever forget that. You're my son, I love you, and I'll be with you until the end."

His words seemed to slip past his boy's defenses. Craig wiped at his eyes and picked up his graphic novel, and Ted turned and left, wiping at his eyes as well.

—⋘—

Downstairs in their bedroom, Ted crawled into bed, thinking Jessica was asleep, but she moved around and said in a soft voice, "Everything okay?"

Holy shit, how to answer that question? His business was on the cliff edge of diving into bankruptcy, the murder of Sam Warner was like a bomb tossed into their family, he was having an affair with his office manager, and . . .

"Things are fine," he said.

Then a sliver of ice dipped into his throat when she said, "Is there anything you'd like to tell me?"

Almost on automatic, he said, "No, not at all. Things are okay." He reached over and touched her shoulder. "Things okay with you?"

"Sure."

As an afterthought, he added, "Anything you'd like to tell me, hon?"

Her answer was brief, quick, and to the point. "No."

—⋘—

During her morning break the next day, Friday, Jessica went out to the rear parking lot. The morning had passed by in a long, shadowy daze. Rhonda had done her best to talk to her about last night's memorial at the town common, and she had just answered with "Yes," "No," or "Uh-huh." Rhonda had noticed her mood and had left her pretty much alone. The other two tellers, Amber and Percy, stayed away from each other during the morning. Amber's face was still swollen from last night's weeping, and Percy had a sly little smile on his face, as if he had been at Gillette Stadium at the fifty-yard line to personally see the Patriots win another Super Bowl.

It was a fine crisp morning and Jessica's hands were cold as she took her iPhone out of her slacks pocket.

What now?

It was hard to believe, even to imagine, that the next several minutes were going to determine her life's future and that of her marriage. Jessica took a long breath. She could recall only a few times when she had thought, *This is it, things are going to change, there is no going back.* The night after graduation when the stick from the pregnancy kit in her bedroom made a line. The day her father died of a heart attack in the backyard as he was dragging heavy broken pine branches from a winter storm, and how her mother laughed and cried when she realized that her tormentor was now gone. That night years later when she walked out of an ICU unit at Mass General, having watched her mom gasp out the last few minutes of life, now knowing she was terribly alone. The phone call from the Maine State Police telling her that Bobby was dead.

All of those moments had come at her hard and fast. Now it was time for another moment.

She switched on her iPhone, flipped through the directory, called up a familiar name and number, and tagged it. Jessica stared at the line of parked cars in the small lot, wondering whom the vehicles belonged to, if they had problems like hers, if they were waiting on something that would change their lives forever.

The phone rang once and was answered. "Harry's Place, Sue speaking."

"Hey, Sue," she said, trying to keep her voice upbeat and cheerful. "Jessica Thornton here. Is Brad around?"

"Hold on," the young woman said, and there was a *clunk-clunk* as the phone was put down and voices in the distance, and then it was picked up and a familiar male voice came on the line.

"Hey, Jessica, how's it going?"

"Not bad," she said. She and Ted had often stopped at Harry's Place when they were a bit more flush. It served pub food, nothing fancy, but it was a nice place to relax and have a craft cheeseburger and homemade fries, drink a local brew, and watch the Red Sox or Patriots play.

"Glad to hear it," Brad said. He was the son of Harry Blair, the original owner of the place. "How's Ted doing? Business picking up?"

"Oh, you know how real estate is, always up and down," Jessica said. "But I think things are really turning around for him."

Brad said, "Hey, that's good to know. Ted's one of the best guys I know."

"You're not the first to say that," she said, "but I'm afraid he's forgetful. He called me this morning, said he can't find his wallet."

"Okay."

"So he asked me to call you to see if he left it at your place two nights ago."

"Really?" Brad asked.

"That's right. He said he was there having dinner with a couple of business associates. He's pretty sure he left his wallet behind in one of the booths. Could you check that out?"

The line went quiet, so quiet she could hear the bar's TV set in the background.

"Brad?"

He cleared his throat. "Jessica, are you sure he was here two nights ago?"

The air suddenly got chillier, as if a thick cloud had suddenly obscured the sun, even though the sky was a clear, crisp blue. "Yes, of course I'm sure."

"Ah . . . well, he wasn't here, Jessica. Maybe he made a mistake."

She strained to make her voice light and lacking any concern at all. "Oh, maybe it was my mistake. It's been pretty busy at the bank the past few days. I'll call Ted and see if I can find out where he really was."

"That sounds good, Jessica, and hey, we're starting a new brunch this Sunday. Maybe you and Ted and the kids could stop by."

"Thanks Brad, I'll keep that in mind."

She disconnected the call and put the phone back into her slacks.

Jessica closed her eyes for just a moment. She felt like she had entered a zone, a new place, a new territory, one she wasn't familiar with. What to do now? What options? Choices? What were the rules?

She wiped at her eyes, surprised to see that her hand was trembling. Took a deep breath. She had to get back to work.

—m—

Just after signing off, locking her drawer, and putting up her NEXT TELLER PLEASE sign, Jessica took a moment and dug through her purse to find her black folding wallet. She opened it up and flipped through the little plastic sleeves, looking at photos of Emma growing up, her face getting cuter with each passing year, her body in gymnastics tights and soccer uniforms until she was in junior high, when she found that running was what she was destined for. Even in these days of the cloud and iPhones and photo hosting services, Jessica liked printing out new photos, trimming them, and putting them in her wallet.

She flipped through some more, as if she were in some miniature time machine, until she got to her favorite photo of her mother, taken on a family trip to Hampton Beach at least twenty years ago. Mom had on a one-piece black bathing suit and a wide straw hat to protect her fair skin, and she was smiling at the camera. One of Jessica's aunts had taken the photo, and Jessica had carefully trimmed away Dad so only Mom was there, smiling forever.

Poor Mom. Unlike her granddaughter, she had had no talent for running, no talent for getting away. She had been a hairdresser who had barely gotten through high school and loved reading Harlequin Romances. She was fierce in defending her daughter, and now, looking at that smiling photo, Jessica once again saw the darkness and depth in her mother's eyes.

Your men will always disappoint you, she had told Jessica once, after another late night when Dad had come home drunk. *Prepare yourself for that, honey, that your men will always disappoint you. Remember that always—you can survive that way. But never tell them how they disappoint you. They should never know.*

Jessica closed the wallet. She had made a mistake with Bobby Thornton, sticking with him as a teen bride—such a cliche!—but she had been seduced by his promises that eventually the dealership would thrive, would bring in lots of money, so he could really take care of her and Emma. Then he had died, and the insurance money, which she had used to pay for coaches and additional training for Emma and other expenses, was long gone.

Oh, how right Mom had been about Bobby. And Jessica had had some dreams as well. She ran track in high school—not as well as Emma—but Dad had worked for Hewlett-Packard, and for a while, fascinated with computers, she had dreamed of a high-tech career after college.

That career never happened. Emma happened, and then Bobby got himself killed, and she was alone for a few long and empty years until the day of that softball game. And with Ted, she had thought she had found a man who would eventually prove her mother wrong. But Mom, dead for so many years, had been right once again.

She closed her purse, checked the time, said, "Later, Rhonda," and walked out of the bank.

—∽—

The Warner police station was less than a ten-minute walk from the bank. It was part of a brick-and-white-clapboard building that held the town hall, the town offices, the fire station on one side, and the police station on the other. It was on the other side of the town common from where last night's ceremony had been held.

At the entrance to the police station, Jessica halted for a moment. It just seemed so absurd, so unreal, that she would be going in there to talk to a police detective about a murder and the investigation that had apparently caught up with something connected to her family.

To the rear of the building was a small parking lot, with blue-and-white police cruisers and cars that she assumed belonged to the department workers. The building looked so simple and plain, but for some reason it looked like a haunted house to Jessica. At some point she had read an article or book about haunted houses, and one theory was that the apparitions people saw in these houses were those of deceased men or women who had left behind some sort of energy trace from some bloody, powerful event.

Now she thought of all the violent tales that must have been heard in the rooms of this building. The people arrested for crimes, from burglary to rape to murder, being interrogated and processed. The trembling victims of assaults, who had to report what had happened to them through tears or sore jaws. Or parents who were ushered into a small office to be told that their love, their child, their gift, was now dead.

Jessica took a breath, went to the door, walked in. One more ghost story, ready to be told.

CHAPTER SIXTEEN

She was in a small lobby with two light-orange plastic chairs to the left and a heavy gray metal door in front of her. A sign on the door warned that ALL CONVERSATIONS BEYOND THIS POINT MAY BE RECORDED, and there was a bulletin board with various town notices and flyers about two lost cats. Another sign said VISITORS NEED TO SIGN IN. There was also a display cabinet with old police memorabilia.

To the left was a glassed-in area with an opening at the bottom to slide paperwork back and forth. An older woman got up from her desk and came over, and Jessica said, "I have an appointment with Detective Rafferty."

"Just a moment," the woman said, and she went back to her desk, made a call, nodded, and then came over again, holding a lanyard with a green-and-white plastic badge that said VISITOR. "He'll be here in a sec," the woman said, pushing the lanyard through the opening.

Jessica slid the lanyard over her neck just as the door opened and Detective Rafferty stepped in, holding the door open with one hand.

"Mrs. Thornton? Thanks for coming by."

She walked in, and, smiling, he said, "This way."

Jessica followed the detective down a tiled hallway, past an open door that said BCI—AUTHORIZED PERSONNEL ONLY, then to some head-high cubicles. He ushered her into one that had RAFFERTY on a nameplate.

"Not so luxurious, is it?" he said, his voice almost apologetic. "We're one of the richest towns in eastern Massachusetts, and each year when the chief makes a budget request for a bigger building . . . Well, enough about that."

Jessica was surprised at how small his work area was. It was a third of the size of Ellen's office. There was his chair and the one she was sitting on, a cluttered desk, a metal wall shelf filled with binders and files, and a computer. Rafferty's suit jacket was hanging from the metal edge of the cubicle, and he had on black shoes, gray slacks, a white shirt, and a plain blue necktie. At his belt were a gold detective's badge and a holstered pistol.

She was scared around guns, even though Ted was an avid hunter.

"What does BCI mean?" she asked.

"Oh," he said, picking up a file folder and turning the swivel chair around so he was facing her. "Bureau of Criminal Investigation. Pretty pompous-sounding, isn't it?"

She sensed he was trying to put her at ease, but she sat there with her purse in her lap, clenched with both hands. This was huge, something big, something scary, but the detective with the short brown hair, pug nose, and slightly round face didn't seem that dangerous or intimidating.

Among the clutter on his desk was a small framed photo showing an attractive dark-haired woman with two very young girls in formal wear standing to each side of her. A dad with two daughters. A detective, looking into a murder.

Remember that, she thought. *Remember that point only.*

And also remember that he wanted to talk to her alone, without Ted, without her husband. Which probably meant that this young man was going to set some traps, some contradictions, and she had to be on point.

A bank teller versus a police detective.

Detective Rafferty moved again in his chair. "Thanks for coming in on your lunch break. I appreciate it. I'll try to get you out of here as soon as possible."

"Thank you."

He flipped a sheet of paper. "What happens in an investigation like this, you've got a lot of threads drawn out, about the victim, about his last hours, where he was, who he saw, and then you backtrack a day, and then another day. And you also talk to the family, his friends, even folks he didn't get along with. And you try to connect these threads together, have some sort of clear picture emerge about what happened."

"I understand."

"You do? Well, that's nice . . . It was good to see the turnout last night at the town common, wasn't it? All those people gathered together, offering a memorial to young Sam Warner. Very touching."

"It certainly was," Jessica said, wondering where the detective was going with this.

"What's interesting, as past investigations have shown, is that during an event like that, you know what happens?"

Jessica shook her head.

"Most times—heck, almost all times—the murderer is there in the crowd, taking it all in. There are two schools of thought on this. One is that the murderer gets off on seeing the reaction, standing with family and friends, keeping his or her secret under wraps. The other is that the murderer is feeling guilty and tries to address that guilt by taking part in a community mourning process. Interesting, isn't it, that last night, the murderer was in that crowd? Too bad we just didn't know who he was."

She just nodded. She was feeling warm. The purse felt heavy.

Then he abruptly changed direction. Trap number one.

"Mrs. Thornton, did you know there was a party Saturday night at Sam Warner's house?"

"A party? No. I had no idea."

"Huh."

Rafferty kept quiet for a few seconds, and it came to her, like a lightning flash from way off, that he was playing with her, trying to get her to say something incriminating.

She waited.

"Do you know where your daughter was Saturday night?"

Jessica's mouth was drying out. Now she knew.

"She was out studying with a friend."

"What was the friend's name?"

"Bertie Woods."

"Is Bertie male or female?"

"Female. Her name is Roberta, but everyone calls her Bertie."

"So that's where your daughter was Saturday night. Studying with Bertie."

"Yes."

"Huh."

Rafferty was staring at the sheet of paper, then looked up. "That party—we don't have all the details, but something happened that night. It was at Sam Warner's house, but his parents were away. There were about twenty or thirty students there, some even from Concord and Carlisle. There was shouting, yelling, maybe even a fight that took place outside the house. We've managed to get a list of most everyone who was there."

She tried to swallow. Couldn't.

"It looks like Emma Thornton's name is on that list."

She just wouldn't say anything at the moment, thinking, *Emma, Emma, Emma, how could you?* A bit of her knew that there would come a time when her perfect running girl, as part of growing up, would start lying to her, keeping things quiet, not revealing secrets or concerns. But now? Here? While Jessica was being interviewed by a police detective?

"Well," she managed to say, "I guess that wouldn't be the first time a daughter lied to her mother."

That made Rafferty smile, and he gestured to the framed photo on the desk. "I know. And that's what my wife, Lara, and I are scared of. That when our girls get older, they'll turn into teenagers and make our lives hell for several years." The smile faded away. "But getting back to your daughter . . ."

Please, no, she thought.

"You didn't know she was at that party?"

"No."

"Did you have any indication that she was at the party?"

Something came to her and she said, "Sunday."

"What about Sunday?"

"She said she wasn't feeling well. That her stomach was upset. She spent the entire day in her room, curled up on her bed."

He nodded. "She's fifteen, right? Sure. Might have been her very first hangover. Poor girl. Did she go to school on Monday?"

"Yes, she said she felt better."

"But she said nothing about Sam Warner."

"Not a word."

"Were they friends?"

"No, they weren't," she quickly said. "I mean, she knew Sam, everyone knew Sam. And I know that sometimes Sam and his teammates would come to practice or meets to cheer on the track team. That's what they did. But I'm positive she and he didn't spend any time together."

"Uh-huh," he said.

"Wait a minute."

"Yes?"

"You . . . you said something like 'It looks like Emma is on that list.' What did you mean? Is she or isn't she?"

He smiled. "So far I have one witness who thinks your daughter was there but isn't certain. Other students . . . they didn't see her. So right now I'm putting her down as a definite maybe."

Emma, she thought. *All right, maybe you weren't there after all.* Officially.

Rafferty went on. "But Craig . . ."

"My stepson."

"Right," he said. "According to school records, he's had some encounters with Sam at school."

"I didn't know about that," she said. "Ted . . . my husband for some reason kept that a secret from me. I only learned about it when you brought it up."

"Really?"

"That's right."

"But that's not what he said when I visited your home."

"Excuse me?"

He flipped through a few sheets of paper and said, "Ted said that he signed the report from the school about the bullying incidents but he didn't know what he was signing. So you're saying he knew and was hiding it from you."

"No."

"But that's what you just said."

"I made a mistake," she said, thinking, *Damn, fell into a trap.* "I don't know what Ted knew about the bullying Craig received. All I'm certain of is that I didn't know."

"I see. All right, then. Now, speaking of your husband . . ."

"Yes?"

He scratched his left ear. "Just to clarify what we're looking at for the timeline, Sam Warner's body was found Wednesday morning. Preliminary investigations indicate that he was murdered sometime Tuesday evening. And although it hasn't been in the paper yet, we do have someone who was in the town forest that night who said he heard a gunshot."

"Oh," Jessica said.

Rafferty kept quiet again.

Those damn pauses. She wanted to look at her watch but didn't want to give Rafferty the satisfaction of knowing that he was making her feel very, very uncomfortable. So she stayed still.

"Your husband is devoted to his son, isn't he?"

"Of course. Any father would be."

"Yes, I'm sure," he said.

Another pause.

A phone was ringing somewhere, once-twice-thrice, and Jessica thought, *Pick it up—will someone pick up that damn phone already.*

Rafferty took a pen, moved it around in his fingers. "If we can go back just a bit, you said your husband had been lying to you."

"I didn't say that."

"In a manner of speaking, I'd say you did."

"I just said I thought he was keeping secrets, that's all."

"Secrets. All right, then."

He went back to another folder, ran his finger down the page as if he were looking for something. "I just need to refresh my memory about something."

"Sure."

"When I talked to the both of you yesterday, I asked about the whereabouts of your children. You said they were upstairs while you were watching a reality television show, the one about housewives."

"Yes."

"Are you sure they were upstairs?"

"Positive."

"How do you know?"

Jessica said, "After dinner Craig went straight upstairs. Emma stayed downstairs for a while, doing homework, and then she went upstairs, sometime around nine or nine thirty."

Rafferty played with the pen for a moment. "And you're sure they stayed up there."

A lump was growing in her throat. She was lying—God, was she ever so lying to this police detective.

"Yes."

"How? Couldn't they have sneaked out while no one was watching?"

Now Jessica was really experiencing that sensation of being in a hole and digging yourself—and it—deeper.

"No," she said. "You've been in our living room. The stairway is just off to the right, near the kitchen. Trust me, detective, with me sitting on the couch, I would see if anyone was coming down to go out."

"You and your husband."

"What?"

"You and your husband," Rafferty said. "You said, 'with me sitting on the couch.' Didn't you mean to say that?"

"Well, I—"

"He was there watching television with you, correct? That's what you said in your statement. That's what your husband told me yesterday. That he had been home that night, along with you and your stepson and daughter."

Jessica felt like she was going to slide off this chair in front of this detective.

"But maybe he wasn't on the couch, right? I mean, you could have been saying 'with me sitting on the couch' because your husband was sitting elsewhere in the room."

With her voice wavering just a bit, Jessica said, "I suppose that's true."

"I see."

Rafferty again peered at the papers in the folder. Jessica decided that after this day she would never, ever eat lunch again, so she wouldn't have any cue to remind her of this hideous day.

"But ma'am, the funny thing is, when Mr. Donovan was telling me where he was that night, the night we think Sam Warner was murdered, he said . . . Hold on, yes, he said, 'Heck, I was here all night, Detective. Right here with Jessica on the couch.'" The detective sat up straighter and stared hard at her. "Which was it, Mrs. Thornton? You said he wasn't on the couch, and he said he was."

She didn't say anything.

"Who's wrong? You or your husband?"

She couldn't say anything.

"It was only two nights ago," Rafferty went on. "If a week had passed, I could see how the two of you could be in disagreement. But less than two full days . . ."

She wasn't going to say anything else to this man, ever.

"Mrs. Thornton, where was your husband that night?"

The odor that had been on his body. His lying about being at Harry's Place. And now she remembered the sounds of the door opening and closing and the closet opening and closing. Lying about the bullying, and most certainly lying about where he had been.

And having an affair with that bitch Paula Fawkes.

"I don't know," she said, and it felt like a chunk of her had just torn apart and was drifting away.

This was now. The past was no longer relevant.

"Mrs. Thornton?"

"I don't know where Ted was that night."

"I see." From the tone in his voice, Jessica knew Detective Rafferty was pleased that his hunt was now making progress, that a scent had come to him. "Are you sure?"

"Positive."

"Out with friends, coworkers?"

His . . . God, what word should she use? Girlfriend, mistress, lover?

"I don't know."

"Again, are you sure?"

She just nodded.

He stared at her, pen in his hand, still resting on his desk.

"Where do you think he was?"

"I don't know."

Muffled voices off in the distance at this place of law and order, guilt and innocence, and confessions, always confessions.

Rafferty lowered his voice, made it softer. "This is very, very difficult. I know from experience. And I commend you for your bravery. Because in the end we need to get justice for Sam Warner."

Jessica still couldn't speak.

"So I need to ask you this. And I apologize in advance for putting you in this position."

She nodded.

Rafferty let out a bit of a breath. "Is there anything you can tell me, anything at all, that could possibly assist me in this investigation? Anything related to your husband's . . . absence?"

His voice sounded so odd that she had a hard time now recognizing it. She waited. Remembered Ted last night, standing next to Paula Fawkes. How she had touched him, and how he had touched her in return. Smiling at each other with the confidence of lovers.

A fury started within Jessica as she recalled the closeness of the two of them, being so open and blatant with their affection, with Jessica just feet away, watching her humiliation unfold live in front of all those people on the common. Ted had hurt her so much.

"There is one thing."

"What's that, Mrs. Thornton?"

"Ah, I was upstairs, getting ready for bed"—*Liar!*—"and I heard the door to the house open and close. You know how hard it is to open and close."

"I remember."

"Well, there was something else Ted did."

"What's that?"

"He opened and closed the closet door."

Rafferty tilted his head. "And why did that get your attention? Couldn't he have been putting a coat away?"

"No," Jessica said. "Ted only puts his coat away during the winter. Times like now, he just drops his coat off in the entryway, on a chair."

"I see. So why do you think he was opening the closet?"

"Because of what's in the closet. I think . . . I think he might have been putting something away."

Rafferty narrowed his eyes. "Like what?"

"In the closet, Ted keeps something."

"Which is?"

"A locked gun cabinet."

"That's very interesting."

Jessica felt her head move in an automatic nod.

The detective said, "What weapons does he keep in that cabinet?"

"A rifle. And a shotgun."

Rafferty slowly nodded. "Mrs. Thornton, I can't tell you how helpful you've been."

CHAPTER SEVENTEEN

The rest of Friday went by in a dull blur, and at one point Jessica couldn't imagine why she was so hungry, until she remembered that her lunch break had been taken up almost entirely by the interview with Detective Rafferty. She barely remembered walking back to Warner Savings, and when she walked into the familiar lobby and saw the faces of the customers and her coworkers, she felt as if she were going into some sort of safe harbor.

As she cashed checks, received deposits, helped customers with questions about their mortgages or money market accounts, she kept thinking about what she had just done at the police station with Detective Rafferty. She had betrayed her husband to the police.

With no evidence, no real hard proof of anything, she was sure she had just pushed Ted into the top tier of suspects in the death of Sam Warner. Rafferty had kept his composure during the interview, but something had changed in his eyes when she had told him about the gun cabinet and the sound of doors opening and closing.

And there were Ted's lies, saying he had been at home that Tuesday night when in fact he was out with . . . Well, not with his partner, Ben Powell. That was for certain. So he had been someplace else, and because of the scent she had detected on him on Tuesday night and last night, she was certain he had been with Paula Fawkes, his office manager.

All right, then. Ted had betrayed her. She was just repaying the favor.

A young girl came in, shepherded by her proud mother, and an old-fashioned passbook was slid across the counter, along with four single dollar bills and a filled-out deposit slip in shaky printing.

Despite everything, Jessica smiled at the young girl, who could barely see over the counter. "Good job," she said. She ran the slip and passbook through, passed it over to the girl, grabbed a lime-green lollipop from the jar, passed it over.

Her mother smiled, took the lollipop, and said, "What do you say, Pammy?"

Pammy looked serious. "I like grape."

Her mother look horrified, but Jessica said, "No problem." She took the lime-green treat back, replaced it with a grape one, and to young Pammy she said, "Never be afraid to ask for what you really, really want, okay?"

But that piece of advice went right by both the girl and her mother, and as they sauntered out of the lobby, that voice came back to her:

She had betrayed her husband to the police.

Then another voice spoke up in her mind, one tinged with the syllables of her own mother. *So what? If there's betrayal, he went first.*

Which was true!

Ted had been the first to betray her. Ted, lying about where he was, lying about a meeting to get necessary financing and then sleeping with his office manager.

Sleeping. The word sounded so bland, so innocent, so quiet. No, they weren't sleeping together, they were—

"Jessica?"

She looked up from her counter. Ellen Nickerson was standing outside. "Got a minute?"

Rhonda gave her a sideways glance, a look of *Hey, be careful out there.*

"Sure," Jessica said.

She locked her cash drawer, logged off the computer, put up the NEXT TELLER PLEASE sign, and went out to the lobby.

Ellen ushered her into the office, closed the door, and sat down. Her face was heavily made up, her hair and face looked sharp enough to cut paper, and today she had on a gray-and-black pants-and-jacket ensemble that seemed to cause the office's temperature to drop ten degrees. The office was spare, clean, and ordered. No personal photos, no souvenirs, no knickknacks.

Quite a contrast to her predecessor, Larry Miles, who had loved the outdoors and who had piled up snowshoes, cross-country skis, and climbing gear in the corners of the office. He had liked to post photos of himself skating on the frozen Walden Pond or climbing Mount Washington in February or skiing at Wildcat.

Ellen looked like she was collecting herself to speak.

And Jessica recalled one of the last times she had talked to Larry, here in this same office, when he had said, "Jessica, I need your help. Rhonda's a drag on this branch, she's too old and set in her ways, and if you help me get rid of her, I won't forget it."

And she remembered her answer back then: "I won't betray a friend."

And she hadn't. Oh, she certainly hadn't.

Ellen folded her hands in front of her. "Jessica, I'm sorry, but there's no way to make this sound better."

And she knew. Her chance for a better life was over.

"Why?" Jessica asked.

Ellen let out a small sigh. "The latest financials came in, and cutbacks are being made, no hesitation. The scholarship program was first on the list."

After her earlier visit with the police, Jessica had nothing much to say.

"I'm quite sorry," Ellen said. There seemed to be genuine feeling behind her words.

"Thank you," Jessica said. She started to get up and Ellen made a slight motion with a finger. Jessica sat back down.

Ellen said, "The other matter I talked about on Tuesday."

She didn't even want to think that far back.

Ellen added, "About your performance."

"Oh."

Her manager sat back against her chair. "Jessica, with the cutbacks coming down from corporate, there's also an emphasis on personal performance."

"I see."

"Before today I could let some things slide. But no longer."

It was hard to believe, but right now Jessica wished she was back at the police station. There, all she had had to defend was her daughter. Here, she had to defend herself and her job.

Ellen said, "It's like this, Jessica. Corporate now thinks, more than ever, that balancing one's drawer and not taking sick time is just doing your job. The bank has other factors to consider. There's an algorithm—pretty complicated—that takes into account each teller's upsales. You know what I mean, right?"

Jessica just nodded. She knew where this was going, like the time you go into the kitchen and smell something smoky and sharp, and right then there's no excuse, there's no hope, there's no nothing except that the meal you've planned for and worked on is ruined.

"Yes," Jessica quietly said. "New credit cards. CDs. Home-equity loans. Other products. Just like you said on Tuesday."

"Jessica, those products are what makes a bank branch like this one profitable," Ellen said. "Upselling to our customers is part of your job."

"But I know most of my customers," Jessica said, realizing how sickly her voice had become. "They're barely scraping by. They don't have any spare funds to waste on—"

Ellen's eyes narrowed, and Jessica instantly knew she had made a big mistake. At Warner Savings, none of their products were a waste. Ellen was the branch manager but was also a company woman through and through.

Ellen unclasped her hands and tapped a finger on the screen of her computer monitor. "Each month we track upselling for each teller. For the last three months you've been dead last, and by a wide margin."

Jessica kept quiet, not wanting to get deeper into the hole she had just fallen into.

Ellen went on. "This branch is one of the least profitable in this region. That's why I was brought in here, to turn it around. Now, with this new corporate directive, I have to put it plainly to you, Jessica. If we don't see a significant and quick improvement in your upsales, we'll have to ask you to leave. We're bringing in a new girl next week who will be making a lot less money than you. And if we need to let somebody go in the near future, well, it won't be a difficult choice."

Jessica flashed back to that depressing moment when she had tried to upsell to Gus Tremblay. Gus had been a longtime customer of hers, had plenty of disposable income, and yet she hadn't been able to upsell to the tight bastard.

"I understand," she said. "All right if I get back to work?"

"Yes."

She took down her sign and Rhonda said, "What's up with the Ice Queen? Did she ask you to help her with the stick that's up her ass?"

Jessica looked out to the empty lobby. No upselling opportunities visible.

"I wish," she said. "That I wouldn't mind."

Rhonda rearranged some of the stamps on her counter. "Oh, hon, was it that bad?"

"Oh, yes, it was that bad," she said. "The scholarship program—it's gone."

"Damn, hon."

"And another thing," Jessica said, face warm at the memory of what had just been told to her. "Ellen says if I don't increase my upsales, I'm out. Just like that."

"Shit."

"Yeah," Jessica said, nearly numb from her long day. "That about covers it."

Rhonda reached over, gently grasped her hand, gave it a squeeze. "If there's anything I can do . . ."

Jessica squeezed her friend's hand back. "Well, you've got lots of relatives. Any chance you could convince them to line up in the lobby tomorrow so I can start selling them credit cards or home equity loans they don't need?"

And in a moment Rhonda was hugging her, and, embarrassed, Jessica squeezed her back and gently pulled away. "I'll be fine, honest. I'll be fine."

Rhonda dabbed at an eye. "You know, if you told me you were going home and were going to hide out in your bathroom for a day, I'd understand it."

That phrase jolted a memory for her, something Rhonda couldn't have known, but Jessica had seen something like that before, when her drunk dad had cornered Mom in the bathroom for some vague insult and Mom had barricaded the door. Dad had smashed the door with a hammer before breaking in, and then he had screeched and stumbled back when Mom had sprayed his face with deodorant. "I'm tired of hiding!" Mom had shouted. "I'm not going to hide anymore!"

And an uneasy truce had developed, one that had lasted until Dad had dropped dead in the backyard, tugging those snow-covered branches, the day she had stayed home from school and Mom had had to go to work. An odd, cold day, having a living dad in the morning and a dead one in the afternoon.

"No," she said, her voice sounding stronger than she could have hoped. "I'm not going to hide. Not at all."

"Good girl," Rhonda said.

More minutes slurred by, until her late-afternoon break came up and she stepped outside once again to the rear parking lot and made a quick phone call.

"Mr. Talbot?" she asked when the phone was answered. "This is Jessica Thornton."

The private investigator from Maine said, "Yes, of course. Mrs. Thornton. How are you?"

"Lousy," she said, knowing she was speaking the truth. "Are you available to meet me tomorrow to go over what's going on with my former sister-in-law?"

"Hold on," he said, and in a moment he came back and said, "Yes, my morning is free."

"I'll see you, but only if you can drive down here. Perhaps we could get a cup of coffee or something, to talk. I want to find out what Grace's problem is, take care of it straightaway."

"Do you have a place in mind?"

"Yes," she said. "Not fancy, but it'll be easy for you to find. The Exit 5 Truck Stop on Route 128, in Avon."

"How does ten thirty tomorrow morning sound?"

"Sounds fine. I'll be there."

He attempted a laugh. "Do you have the day off tomorrow, then?"

"No," she said, disconnecting the call.

—⁓—

At five P.M. there was one last surprise for the day, after she had cashed out, filed all the paperwork, and put her drawer back into the bank's vault. She said so long to Rhonda and to Amber, who was also cashing out, and tried not to look at Ellen Nickerson's office when she grabbed her purse and went out through the lobby, instead looking up at the framed photo of Larry Miles, who had wanted so much to get rid of Rhonda. And Rhonda was still here, and so was Jessica. And Larry Miles was not. So much for that.

She stopped still in the glassed-in foyer, which had two ATMs that were available at all hours, holding the door open for Amber, who was following her and reading something from her iPad, her thick purse over one shoulder.

"Thanks, Jessica," Amber said, pausing to tap on the iPad. "It's taking forever to load something. Damn Safari."

Jessica said, "Have you cleared the cache lately?"

"The what?"

Jessica took the iPad from Amber and with practiced ease went into the Develop menu and said, "Watch. Pull this down, click on Empty Caches. It clears up a lot of old temporary files the browser holds on to. Voila. Your browser should zip right along now."

Amber smiled and took her iPad back. Jessica saw Percy Prescott standing on the sidewalk, being talked to by a uniformed Warner police officer while Detective Doug Rafferty stood by, watching.

What the hell?

A blue-and-white Warner police cruiser was double-parked on the street, lights flashing, while downtown traffic slowly eddied its way around.

Jessica supposed she should go find out what was going on, maybe intervene on Percy's behalf. Her hand was on the door handle when she stopped herself. Why should she get involved?

Jessica had been feeling some regret and guilt over what she had told Detective Rafferty earlier, about Ted's absence and his gun ownership. But she also remembered how Percy hadn't cared much about the news of Sam Warner's death and how he had appeared at last night's memorial, drunk and apparently happy.

Was Percy being questioned, then? Or even arrested?

Maybe Detective Rafferty had already given up on interrogating Ted or doing anything else with Ted. Maybe the investigation had switched to looking at old high school acquaintances of Sam's, ones who still carried a grudge.

"Hey," Amber said, putting her iPad back into her purse. "What's going on?"

Jessica just pointed and didn't say a word. Amber looked past Jessica and said, "Well, shit. There you go. Glad to see him getting rousted."

"Amber, c'mon."

Amber slung her large brown purse over a shoulder, her earrings jingling. "Okay, so Sam and his buds gave Percy a hard time when he was in school. But that was a couple of years ago. Sam was a good guy.

Spent some time at our house with my brother, Jack. Percy should have manned up, gotten over it. Instead he brooded and bitched about it, and when Sam got killed, did he say he was sorry? Did he?"

Jessica said, "No, he didn't."

"And you saw him at the memorial service, right? Half in the bag and making jokes, and—oh, Jess, look, they're arresting him!"

Jessica turned her head, saw the police officer put his hand on Percy's shoulder, and then Detective Rafferty came up, took one arm and then another, and just like that, Percy was handcuffed.

Rafferty took Percy's right arm and went over to the parked cruiser and opened a rear door while the uniformed officer stopped traffic, allowing the detective to put Percy into the rear seat. The door was slammed shut. Rafferty and the officer briefly talked, and then the officer got into the cruiser. It sped off, heading to the police station where Jessica had been just a few hours ago.

Amber said, "Under arrest. Wow. Do you think he did it? Do you think he killed Sam?"

Jessica didn't say anything, just stepped over to where her coworker had just disappeared into police custody. And she hated herself for thinking this, but if Percy was in serious trouble, then the bank would cut him free, and Jessica would be safe here for some time to come.

A hateful thought, but a true one.

CHAPTER EIGHTEEN

In a pleasant surprise, Ted brought dinner home that night, and even though it was take-out pizza from Toni's—half plain cheese, half mushroom—the small part of her that refused to believe he was cheating on her appreciated the gesture. Earlier Emma and Craig had come home together, sharing a ride from Craig's friend Randy McMahon, who was dating Heather, a friend of Emma's. Randy's car was an old Volkswagen Jetta that belched smoke and nearly stalled out while pulling away, but it was nice to see Emma and Craig together.

Now the four of them were sitting around the kitchen table, sharing dinner. Seeing Ted laugh and joke with his son and Emma, Jessica couldn't believe the mixed feelings that were coursing through her. After all the nonsense of the past few days, it was a nice change of pace to have the four of them together, having dinner like a family should, especially a blended one like theirs.

But those feelings were poisoned by the two streams also flowing through her: Ted's betrayal and what she had said at the interview with Rafferty today. What had that been all about? Did she really want Ted to be a suspect in Sam Warner's murder, or was she just giving in to her anger by putting his name out there?

God, she wanted to stop thinking about it all. She wanted it to be a month from now, with all these problems and challenges in the rearview mirror.

Ted caught her eye. "Nice pizza, isn't it?"

"Delicious," Jessica said.

"It should be," he said, "I made it in an oven in my office basement."

Craig said, "As if, Dad."

"What, you don't believe me?" he asked, pretending to be shocked, and as he ate a slice, a blob of tomato sauce plopped right onto his dress shirt, which made Emma burst out laughing. When Ted tried to scoop up the tomato sauce, Jessica laughed as well.

Had she gone too far?

She took a bite of her own plain cheese slice.

Perhaps. Perhaps she had done that, in talking to the detective.

But Percy Prescott had been arrested. Maybe that meant that what she had said would be ignored. Jessica hoped so.

There was so much going on. So very much.

And Emma. The police thought she had been at a party at Sam Warner's Saturday night, not studying with her friend Bertie as she had told her mother. Jessica would have to talk to her about that. But not now. This brief moment of family peace was too precious to shatter.

—⁂—

Later that night, Craig Donovan was in bed, sheet and blanket pulled up to his waist, holding his iPhone in his hands, the glow of the screen illuminating the little tent he had made. It was late but he was texting with Mark Borman, one of the few friends he had at Warner High School.

> Craig: sup?
> Mark: not much
> Mark: but P Prescott is in trouble
> Craig: who?
> Mark: jeez—Percy Prescott—works with your mom
> Craig: not my mom
> Mark: lighten up bro she's a real MILF

Craig: oh plz

Mark: oh yeah, real MILF with big tits. bet u like seeing em

Craig: FU what happened w/ Percy?

Mark: got arrested

Craig: ???

Mark: don't know. but we can figure, eh.

Mark: u there?

Mark: u there?

Craig: yeah

Mark: also heard cops r looking into last Sat party at Sam's

Craig: rly?

Mark: guess its a shit show now

Mark: cops digging into who went

Craig: huh

Mark: didn't u go?

Craig: where?

Mark: didn't u go to party?

Mark: u there?

Mark: u there?

Craig: gotta go

He disconnected from his chat program, flopped back in bed, rubbed his face. God, this was getting so out of control.

He lifted his T-shirt up over his belly and chest. There wasn't a single hair there, but there was something else, a three-letter word that someone had scrawled there with a laundry marker last Saturday night, meaning it would stay there for a long, long time, enough for the rumors to start, the jokes in the classroom, the laughs as he walked by in the hallway.

FAG.

And he remembered Emma's promise, and he sat in his dark room and thought about his stepsister.

—m—

When Ted went into the bedroom that night, he was feeling all right, though knowing the guilt could come up at any moment and darken his spirit. And the truth was, the night had been going pretty well. Earlier today his partner, Ben Powell, had said that sometime soon Ted would be getting a nice brown paper grocery bag stuffed with hundred-dollar bills from Gus Spinelli, and that had put him in a good mood for the rest of the afternoon.

Okay, the story about him and Ben sharing burgers and beers had been so much bullshit—the truth was, he had been at Paula Fawkes's home, doing her on the living room couch, keeping his eyes closed so he didn't have to look at the framed photos of her husband in military gear on the wall—but Ben had reached out to Spinelli for financing and it was coming through.

Excellent.

Next up, get a rehearing at the zoning board in Concord, show them that he and Ben had the funds, get ground broken, start selling the lots, and pay back Spinelli quickly so the interest didn't start mounting.

"Hey," he whispered. "You awake, Jessica?"

No reply.

He stripped off his clothes in the dark—he always slept in his boxers—and slid into bed, and then the guilt came to him.

It had been a good day. He had been successful in supporting his family, he had brought home dinner, the kids and even Jessica had laughed and talked, and they were all here, under the roof of a home that had been in the Donovan family for more than a century and had belonged to his Uncle Don before his death.

That should have been enough. But no, he had to spoil it with the oldest story in business, humping the help. God, Paula was something else when they fucked, but, he hated to admit, the flirting, the heavy perfume, the teasing . . . today he realized it was all getting to be too much. It was like being hungry for a meal and only being offered cake, in the morning, afternoon, and evening. Too much sweetness, too much richness.

He lay there in bed, on his right side, thinking things through. He had met Paula's husband a couple of times at Chamber of Commerce functions. He was tall, well-built, with a shaved head and biceps that looked like he could crush walnuts with them, and a self-assured and nearly arrogant way about him, pronouncing to anyone near and far that he was a killer.

That simple. Not a killer in business, or real estate, or finance. No. The real deal, the type of killer who ended the day or night with the blood of his enemies upon him.

And here Ted was, banging the guy's wife.

Ted shuddered. He had glossed over it in the past, but now, in his quiet bedroom, with Jessica sleeping near him and the two kids safely in bed, he was scared out of his wits at what might happen if Paula's husband came back and found out what he had been doing. And what if he came home early, like on leave or something?

Ted shook his head. Nope, time to break it off, slowly and gradually. It wasn't worth it. A good hump and cum—to destroy his marriage. Hell, to put himself at risk from a combat soldier. Definitely not worth it.

He reached his hand over, gently stroked Jessica's hair. "You awake, Jess?"

Again no reply.

He shifted, reached over, kissed her hair, and whispered, "I love you, and I'm so sorry."

And then he rolled over and nearly instantly fell asleep.

—⁓—

In her bedroom Emma was curled over, iPhone in her hand, chatting with one of her friends from the track team, Kate Romer.

Kate: u know Percy Prescott
Emma: think so

Kate: u shld he works with yr mom
Emma: oh yeah
Kate: got arrested today
Emma: wht for???
Kate: dunno
Kate: bet it has to do w/ Sam's party
Emma: rly?
Kate: makes sense. u heard he tried to punch Sam
Kate: Sam kicked him in nuts
Kate: maybe he's a suspect?
Kate: hey how r u feeling
Emma: ok
Kate: I hear cops trying to track down who went
Kate: haven't talked to me yet
Emma: good
Kate: they talk to you?
Kate: Emma
Kate: Emma
Emma: wht?
Kate: the cops talk to u about the party?

Emma breathed in, breathed out. Just like she always did to calm things down before going out at a track meet, knowing in her heart of hearts that no one could pass her, no one could beat her, and most of all, no one could ever, ever catch her.

Emma: no
Emma: ttyl

Then she turned off her iPhone and rolled over and slowly curved herself in a tight ball, just thinking, remembering.

—∞—

Jessica had been awake the entire time when Ted had come in. She had pleaded being tired—after the day she had had, that was the truth—and Ted had wanted to stay up to watch some financial show on CNBC.

Before going to bed, though, she had spent a few minutes on the computer in the living room, checking out the website of the *Warner Daily News* to see if anything had been reported about Percy Prescott's arrest, but there had been nothing. So what was going on?

Jessica thought maybe she could talk to Percy during a break at work tomorrow if he showed up, but then she remembered that she had made other plans for tomorrow. Instead of being scared, she had an almost giddy sense of going into some kind of battle.

She would take care of the business with her nutty ex-sister-in-law. Jessica had no idea what kind of scheme or obsession Grace had with her over Bobby's death, but she would find out from that PI from Portland and take care of it.

Jessica listened in the dark as Ted got undressed. There was a pang of memory, thinking about the early years of their relationship, when she'd been so eager to have him climb in next to her and would roll over and kiss his chest, and how often that had led to some sweet lovemaking.

But Ted had changed. He stayed out later, worked harder during the week and weekends, until it seemed like five or six of her attempts at seduction had failed, with him whispering excuses like, "Not tonight. hon, I'm bushed. Hey, I just played eighteen holes with the planning board chairman, and my back is killing me. Next time, hon, I promise."

She had withdrawn. Hadn't tried again. And had waited.

Ted climbed into bed, and a sharp, insistent urge came to her to roll over right now and confront him with what she knew, what she suspected.

Are you fucking your office manager?

But she couldn't do it. Not now.

Tomorrow was going to be one hell of a day, and she had only so much courage to spare.

Jessica nearly jumped when Ted brushed her hair and whispered, "You awake, Jess?"

She stayed still.

He kissed her hair, and then whispered, "I love you, and I'm so sorry."

Ted rolled over, and she was surprised at how quickly her eyes grew moist.

Sorry? What was he sorry for?

But she knew. Deep inside, she knew.

He was sorry.

Did that mean he was breaking it off? Had it just been a one-time fling? Was it over?

Jessica wiped her eyes, listened to Ted's slow breathing.

All right. Maybe things could get back on track, things could work out. She'd handle that private investigator tomorrow. As for the bank scholarship, screw 'em. She would figure out a way to get that schooling, get a better job, be in a better position to support her family. All of her family, from Emma to Ted to, yes, even strange Craig.

She took a deep, satisfying breath. And maybe the police detective would overlook what she had said earlier. Percy Prescott had been arrested, and she couldn't imagine anything else that he could possibly be arrested for. So that meant he had to be a suspect in something. And the biggest something was Sam Warner's murder, and it was no secret what Percy thought about Sam.

So maybe the police wouldn't look at Ted. Wouldn't bother him. Would just leave them all alone.

But the next day the police did come.

CHAPTER NINETEEN

In the morning Emma and Craig had an early breakfast because even though it was a Saturday, they needed to get to the high school for some civic assembly that would give them both extra credit in their respective social studies classes. And the days of bankers' hours, of Monday through Friday, nine to five, were long gone, and Jessica was due to work both today and Sunday.

Jessica took a moment to watch Craig and Emma walk down to the sidewalk, where Craig's friend Randy had pulled up again in his green Volkswagen Jetta. After her two kids climbed in, the Jetta pulled out, stalled, and had to be restarted.

"God, now that's a shitbox," Ted said, standing next to her at the window, sipping from his second cup of coffee. "It's amazing it can even get to school and back. Why do our kids insist on riding in that piece of crap?"

Jessica said, "Did you ever take the bus to high school?"

"No," Ted said.

"It wasn't much fun. It always took too long, somebody was always fighting or throwing trash around. If somebody had a car and you could bum a ride, you took it."

"Well, I was lucky we lived close enough for me to walk," Ted said. "It was nice when it was sunny and warm, but it sucked when it rained or snowed."

"You poor boy," she said. "Did you walk a mile uphill both ways?"

"You know it," he said, giving her a quick kiss before walking back to the kitchen. He tasted of Ted, of coffee, and no, she thought, he didn't taste of anyone else. He didn't taste of Paula Fawkes.

Maybe it was over. He had said "I'm sorry" last night, hadn't he? So maybe it was over.

Should she bring it up? Ask him the question? Confront him in some way? Or just let it slide? Let him keep his secret, his shame? A sharp feeling came to her of wanting him to suffer in silence in the fear of her someday finding out.

Ted came out of the kitchen. "Off to work—got a possible showing in an hour. And I need to tell you something, Jess."

Something in her chest tightened up. Was this it?

There was a heavy knock at the door.

She and Ted both looked to the front. He looked at his watch.

"Who can that be?" he asked, surprised. "It's not even eight. Too early for Jehovah's Witnesses."

The knock repeated, just as heavy.

Jessica started, and Ted, perhaps feeling noble or being manly, pushed past her and opened the door. It squeaked, squeaked, squeaked as he pulled it open, and the cold feeling in her chest avalanched right down her body to her feet.

Detective Doug Rafferty was standing there, looking apologetic. A Warner police sergeant was standing behind him.

"Mr. Donovan?" Rafferty asked.

"Uh . . ." Ted was struck dumb. Something Jessica had never seen before.

Rafferty reached into his coat pocket, took out a folded-over piece of blue cardboard with a form inside. "Mr. Donovan, I have a search warrant here, signed by Middlesex County judge Julia Tucci."

"Uh . . ."

"Excuse me," Rafferty said, stepping forward. "This gives me the right to enter your home. Clark?"

Rafferty stepped into the entryway, the sergeant following him. Jessica had never seen the sergeant before in her life.

The detective unfolded the cardboard and handed it over to Ted, who took it in both of his hands. Rafferty said, "This warrant also allows me to search the premises for a twelve-gauge Model 870 Remington pump-action shotgun, serial number 1920716W, and to take it into my possession. Mr. Donovan, according to the Office of Public Safety's Firearms Records Bureau, you are the owner of said shotgun. Correct?"

Ted was looking at the search warrant, and Jessica just stood there, not allowing herself to think, or to act. This was her fault. This had to be her fault. How else? The police sergeant looked at her and she looked away. Any other time she would offer these visitors coffee or tea or orange juice, but God, this was so not like any other time.

"Yes," Ted replied, his voice faint. "Yes, I am."

"Thank you," Rafferty said. "Is this shotgun in your possession?"

"Yes."

"Do you have exclusive control of this weapon?"

"Ah . . . I guess so, yeah."

Silence for a moment. Traffic moved outside—regular traffic, people going on about their regular morning business, maybe just a handful of drivers spotting the unmarked police cruiser parked in front of their house, maybe those drivers wondering what might be going on at the Donovan house this morning.

Good God.

Rafferty broke the silence, his voice polite and level. "Mr. Donovan, there are two options available to us. One is that you don't say a word and refuse to cooperate, and Sergeant Stanley and I will go throughout your house, looking for the shotgun. Or you can cooperate, tell us where it is, let us have it, and then we can be on our way. Your choice."

Her husband looked up from the warrant as if he had just woken up from sleepwalking through the entire morning so far. Jessica caught his eye and he handed the search warrant over to her, but she couldn't read it.

Ted said, "Yes, of course. I'll give it to you. Hold on. It's in the closet."

He stepped back and Rafferty snapped, "No, please, don't move. Clark, open the closet, will you?"

The sergeant came forward, opened the closet door, and Jessica felt that slightest bit of shame of seeing her coats and Ted's coats and those of the kids hanging there, with shoes and boots tumbled on the floor. What a mess.

The sergeant pushed aside the coats and said, "Doug, we have a locked gun cabinet here."

Rafferty peered in. "So we do. Mr. Donovan, may I have the key?"

"Sure. Ah . . ." Ted reached into his left pants pocket and took out a jumble of keys, and his fingers shook as he went through them, desperately touching each key, as if by finding the right key in the right time, he'd earn the appreciation of the detective and the sergeant.

Jessica felt like she was going to start crying.

"Here," he said. "This is the key."

"Thank you," Rafferty said.

The detective put the keys on the floor—a mess, the hardwood really needed to be vacuumed and mopped—and then reached into his pocket and removed a thin pair of blue latex gloves. The snapping sound of him pulling the gloves over his hands seemed quite loud in the entryway.

Just like CSI, Jessica thought. *Just like those* Law & Order *repeats.*

Ted stepped closer to her, seeking reassurance or comfort. Jessica stepped away.

The detective ducked and unlocked the gun cabinet door, revealing what was inside: the shotgun and a hunting rifle with a scope and a leather sling. Bright cardboard boxes of ammunition were on the floor of the cabinet.

Rafferty gingerly removed the shotgun from the gun cabinet and held it up. He said to the sergeant, "Clark, will you read me the serial number?"

"Sure," the sergeant said. He had a little notebook with him and read off the numbers and letters, and Rafferty nodded.

"It's a match," he said. "Clark, will you write Mr. Donovan a receipt while I put this in the cruiser?"

Jessica swallowed hard, watching the detective walk out the open door, outside to Warner. She could imagine the rumors starting within just a few minutes: *Peggy saw the police take a shotgun from the Donovan house, the detective doing the Warner homicide investigation, oh, God, do you think, do you think, do you think . . .*

The sergeant wrote something in the notebook, tore out the sheet, handed it over to her husband. Ted folded it up and shoved it into his pocket.

Rafferty came back into the house, pulling the latex gloves off.

Ted cleared his throat. "Can you tell me what the hell this is all about?"

Rafferty said, "Mr. Donovan, does anybody besides you have access to that shotgun?"

"No, it's just me," Ted said. "What's going on?"

"Are there other keys to that cabinet?"

"No, I have the only one," he said. "What's going on?"

What's going on? Jessica thought. *Dear God, what is going on?*

"Mr. Donovan, have you used that shotgun recently?"

"Christ no, not for months, and that's it! Tell me why the hell you're here!"

Rafferty took the used gloves, glanced down at them for a moment, and put them in his pocket. "Mr. Donovan, we've seized your shotgun as part of our ongoing investigation into the murder of Sam Warner," he said. "I appreciate your cooperation."

"Wait, wait, wait," Jessica said, desperately wanting to know more. "Are you saying that Sam Warner was killed by a shotgun? Is that it?"

Rafferty said, "I'm sorry, I can't say anything more."

"But why me?" Ted asked. "Why did you come here? Did somebody give you a tip or some bullshit piece of information?"

Jessica felt like she was standing on the edge of a very tall cliff, with Detective Rafferty's hands on her shoulders, ready to shove.

But there was no shove.

"I'm afraid that's confidential," Rafferty said.

Ted clenched his fists. "Screw that! You'll be hearing from my lawyer within the hour!"

Rafferty nodded. "I look forward to it. In the meantime, Mr. Donovan, as a favor to me and the Warner Police Department, do stay in the area over the next few days, all right?"

Jessica's mouth was so dry she was surprised she could speak. "Why?" she asked. "Why should Ted do that?"

Rafferty started to the door. "Because, Mrs. Thornton, contrary to what your husband just said, based on what I just smelled and what I'm sure our forensics team will confirm, that shotgun has recently been fired."

—m—

The next twenty minutes or so were occupied by Ted pacing, Ted cursing, and Ted finally getting on the phone with his attorney, George Kahn. Ted spoke rapidly to George, and Jessica stood by, a hand on her husband's shoulder, while Ted went on and on, and then slowed down, and then said, "Uh-huh . . . uh-huh, okay, I appreciate it. Okay. Talk to you later."

Ted hung up the landline, went to the kitchen sink, ran some cold water, and splashed it and rubbed it on his face.

"What a goddamn mess," he said.

Jessica looked at the kitchen clock. She was due to be at work in ten minutes. Even though she had no intention of going to work.

"What did George say?" she asked.

"He said what I thought he'd say," Ted replied, voice still loud, full of anger and surprise. He tore off a sheet of paper towel, wiped his hands and face. "George is good at title work. At reviewing closing documents. At making presentations to the planning board."

Ted crumpled up the paper towel and threw it into the sink. Jessica hated it when he did that, but she kept her mouth shut.

"I need a criminal defense lawyer. Christ, what the hell do you think is going to happen to my business when that bit gets leaked out?"

"Does he have a name?"

"Yeah, some gal named Helen Wray. Has a practice over in Concord. George recommended her pretty highly, but damn—I can just imagine the billable hours. He's going to call her and set it all up. If I'm lucky, maybe I can see her today."

Jessica looked at the clock again. Just seven minutes left.

"Maybe it will all be wrapped up sooner than we think," she said. "There must be some mistake. I mean, you told him that you hadn't fired the shotgun in months. Months!"

Ted shook his head. "That's right. That doesn't make sense. And . . . shit." He had spotted the clock as well. "Can you believe it? I have an appointment in five minutes with some guy moving in from Ohio who wants to look at some houses, here and in Carlisle. Jesus fucking Christ, I can barely think straight, and now I'm supposed to show off a property, put in some enthusiasm, be upbeat. How the hell can I do that after what just happened?"

"Could you reschedule?"

"No," Ted said, walking out of the kitchen, heading to the front door. "No, I can't. Guy just flew into Boston yesterday, is staying at a motel out on Route 2. No way I'm going to dump him. I'll just have to plow through."

He shrugged his coat on and Jessica said, "Ted?"

"Yeah?"

"I . . . just so you know, having the cops stop by really upset me. I don't feel too good. I think I'm going to call in sick."

He gave her a look and said, "Shit, if I didn't have that appointment, I'd do the same thing, but I need a sale. I need a win, Jess, and I don't need being thought of as a suspect."

"I know."

He headed to the door and turned so quickly it surprised her.

"I need to ask you a question. Serious, question, straight up."

"Go ahead, Ted." She thought she knew what he was going to say, and she was right.

The voice was flat, deliberate. "Why didn't you ask me?"

"Ask you what?"

"Don't be silly," he said. "Why didn't you ask me if I killed that boy?"

Tears came to her eyes and she stepped forward, and he hugged her, and she kissed his cheek and said, "Because I knew you couldn't do such a thing. Honest."

After she saw Ted drive off, Jessica got to the phone and made a quick call to Warner Savings. Luckily it was Amber who answered the phone.

"Amber, I feel awful this morning. I don't know if it's something I ate or what, but I'm staying home today."

"Not a problem. I'll tell Ellen when she comes in. Anything else?"

Jessica remembered leaving the branch yesterday. "Percy—is he at work today?"

Amber lowered her voice. "Yeah, can you believe that?"

"Did he say anything about what we . . . what you and I saw yesterday?"

"Nope."

"Oh."

"Yeah," Amber said, "and he's in a mood, so I'm not going to ask him."

"Makes sense."

Amber said, "But tell you what, if he lightens up later, maybe I'll just mention that I left and saw him arguing with a cop out on the sidewalk. Maybe he'll let me know, and then I'll tell you tomorrow."

"Thanks, Amber, I appreciate that. I'm just curious, you know?"

"Sure," the younger teller said. "But you don't think he's a murder suspect, do you?"

Jessica said, "Amber, I have no idea what to think nowadays," and as she hung up the phone, that was the absolute truth.

CHAPTER TWENTY

After she got off the phone with Amber, Jessica waited a few minutes more—in case Ted came back because he had forgotten his briefcase or some file folder—and then she left the house, got into her Sentra, and started it up. The engine still sounded rough. Then she remembered that she had only a couple of days left before applying to Northern Essex Community College to take that management course.

Jessica backed out of the short driveway, thinking, *Well, what's the point now, with the scholarship disappearing at the bank?* But no, she would get to it. One way or another, she would make it work.

Jessica would make everything work.

—∞—

Twenty minutes later she was at the Warner Public Library, having taken a circuitous route. She didn't want to pass Ellen Nickerson at the local Dunkin' Donuts while she was supposed to be home sick.

There was parking at the back of the library, hidden from the street, and she sneaked in through the children's room, which was in the basement of the old building, one of the hundreds of Victorian-style libraries that had been donated more than a century ago by Andrew Carnegie.

Up on the first floor she went past the main desk, smiling and waving at two of the women working there, and walked to the far end, where a bank of public computer terminals were available for use by Warner residents. She dropped her purse on the floor, slid out the keypad from a spot underneath the long desk, opened Google, and started to work.

"Hey," came a voice, and she turned. It was Betsy Dummer, one of the assistant librarians and the mother of Patty Dummer, a track team member.

"Hey, Betsy, how goes it?" Jessica asked. Betsy was brunette, about her age, but she liked to dress to show off, wearing tight capri pants and sparkly sandals in the summer, tops that showed just maybe an inch more cleavage than was necessary, all in an attempt—or so Jessica thought—to try to shoot down any idea that she was a typical boring librarian.

"Not bad," Betsy said. "Terrible thing about Sam Warner, huh?"

"The worst," Jessica said.

"Paul says he hears the cops are making lots of progress, and I sure as hell hope so."

Jessica blanked for a moment, then remembered that Betsy's husband, Paul, was a captain at the Warner Fire Department.

"That'd be great," Jessica. "I agree."

Betsy nodded, and then said, "Oops, looks like there's a line forming at checkout. See you at the field next Saturday, okay?"

Next Saturday. Track meet. Of course.

"You bet."

Betsy said, "Good to see you again. Hope you get your computer problem at home fixed. I'd think with all the times you've come in here, Ted could get you both a new one."

"You'd think," Jessica said.

Jessica waited until Betsy got to the main desk, then went back to work. Thank God all she had up on the screen was the Google homepage.

She checked the time. Lots to do.

—⟋⟍—

At the Exit 5 Truck Stop on Route 128 in Avon, Gary Talbot had a booth to himself. It was 10:20 A.M. Ten more minutes to go.

On the drive down here from Portland, the traffic had been a bitch at the Maine tolls in York, despite its being morning, and then he had got caught up in the madness that struck Route 128 in the morning and late afternoon. The highway was a semicircular route surrounding Boston and its immediate suburbs, and by the time he pulled into the crowded parking lot he was sure that about a third of the population of Massachusetts had been driving on Route 128. The speed limit of 55 miles per hour was observed by no one, and quick lane changes and cutoffs seemed to be the rule of the day.

He sipped at his cup of coffee. It was 10:26 A.M.

In the nearly two-hour drive from Portland, Gary had worked and reworked in his mind what he was going to say to Jessica Thornton when she arrived, and what he would tell her about her former sister-in-law, Grace Thornton, and the woman's thoughts about her brother's death. Gary was pretty sure that Jessica was coming in here with her own plan, her own agenda, and, no offense to the woman, he planned to blow her plan out of the water within ten minutes of her getting here.

Which was now.

Through the miracles of the internet, he had seen two photos of Jessica Thornton online, both of her with her daughter and others at some track meet in Warner. The woman coming through the main door looked just like her: plain brown hair, plain brown eyes, light makeup, dressed in an ankle-length tan coat with flapping belt, black slacks. She was a good-looking woman, but it looked like she took the opportunity to wear dull clothes that didn't show off her body.

He stood up, held out his hand. "Mrs. Thornton, thanks so much for coming."

"Sure," she said, holding his hand just long enough to be polite, he guessed, and then she sat down.

"I bet your drive was better than mine," he said, trying to ease into things. "I always forget just how dangerous Massachusetts drivers can be."

"Some of us are proud of it," she said, and he couldn't tell if she was trying to make a joke. Her voice didn't seem to be in a joking mode.

Gary said, "Just before I pulled in, I passed one of those twelve-theater movie complexes, and can you believe it? Three of those theaters are playing the same movie. The new Tom Hanks movie—have you seen it?"

Jessica nodded, picked up a menu, put it down. "Yes. My husband and I saw it this past Saturday. I fell asleep during a good chunk of it. Please, I don't really want to be here, so can you get to the point? What the hell is Grace's problem, and why did she hire you?"

"It's about your husband's death."

"My first husband. Bobby."

"She has questions about it."

"What kind of questions? He died in a single-car accident, heading up I-95. Hit a deer, went off the road, hit a tree. State police found he had a blood alcohol content exceeding the legal limit. What is she up to?"

"Well, she thinks there are a few outstanding questions."

"Like what?"

A pudgy older waitress in a black uniform and with heavily tattooed forearms came over, and Gary said, "Please, a cup of coffee? Would you like some toast or a muffin, Jessica?"

And damn did Jessica give him a sharp look. "Coffee, that's all."

The waitress left and Jessica said, "All right, what kind of outstanding questions?"

"Before I get into that, I want you to know that I've done a fair amount of research into your husband, the accident, and you, Mrs. Thornton."

She gave him a blank stare.

He went on. "That's what I have to do, in my position, to make sure my client gets her money's worth."

Jessica remained silent. Her cup of coffee arrived. She tore two Equal packages and stirred the contents in, then pushed the cup aside as if she were waiting for it to cool.

"Mr. Talbot?"

"Yes?"

"Please excuse my language, but get to the fucking point."

Gary had been expecting a lot of possible reactions from this woman but hadn't anticipated this one, the one filled with hostility, with seemingly not a care in the world. Well, it was time to rock her world.

"I'll get to the point," he said. "But it's going to take a few minutes."

She glanced up at a wall clock over near the lunch counter. "Make it five, or I'm out of here."

"Very well," he said. "I know from my research that you and Mr. Thornton had a troubled relationship. The police were called to your home in Haverhill three times for domestic disturbances, and your husband even spent a night at the Haverhill Police Department before assault charges against him were reduced and eventually, as we say, 'swept.' He was also arrested twice on drunk-driving charges, and those violations were taken care of as well. The fact that your husband was prominent in the Haverhill community and that his car dealership gave substantial donations to the Haverhill Police Relief Association may have had a bearing on that."

Jessica picked up her coffee cup, took a sip, put it back down. "Go on."

"At one point," Gary said, "from what your ex-sister-in-law stated, you two were headed for a divorce. But Bobby—er, Mr. Thornton—claimed he would do whatever it took to keep your marriage intact. He went to counseling, he started attending AA meetings on a regular basis, and his sponsor said that for more than eighteen months he had kept perfect attendance and never once had a drink."

The woman made a point of looking again at the clock.

"Then came the night of his death. At first I thought Grace Thornton was . . . exaggerating what she had found. For all intents and purposes, it did seem to be an accident, although a sad one, involving drunk driving and your husband not being able to avoid that deer. But I did some more research, more digging, and found some discrepancies."

There.

Jessica Thornton looked like the booth seat had suddenly become magnetic, holding her into place.

"What kind of discrepancies?" she asked.

"About his drinking," he said. "I visited his old dealership and talked to six of his former employees, and every one of them said that Bobby Thornton had turned over a new leaf. He wanted to make amends, make your marriage work, and make sure that your daughter, Emily—"

"Emma," Jessica corrected. "My girl's name isn't Emily."

Gary nodded. "My apologies. Yes, Emma. He wanted to make sure that Emma was taken care of. He told his employees months earlier that he had removed every trace of alcohol from his residence. At lunch he no longer had a beer or two while eating with his fellow salesmen. He really had stopped drinking."

Jessica said, "So he had."

From an inside coat pocket, Gary took a folded sheet of paper, which he unfolded on the table.

"From my interviews with his employees and the accident report from the Maine State Police, I've come up with this timeline. On the date of the accident, he was traveling to Kennebunkport to a retirement party for a car dealership owner who had once worked with your husband. Do you remember?"

Jessica calmly took another sip of her coffee. "I remember everything about that night."

Gary said, "I'm sure you do. Well, the evening event in Maine was to begin at six thirty. He left work that day at four twenty and went straight home."

"Well, I'm not so sure about that," she said.

"I am, Mrs. Thornton. Three witnesses separately told me he left the dealership at four twenty. One of your former neighbors, a Thomas Laney, said he was trimming shrubbery next door when he saw your husband drive in. It was at four forty P.M."

She waited. Didn't say anything.

Gary said, "Don't you want to know how certain I am about the time?"

"I'm sure you'll tell me," she said.

That damn face was still blank and calm. An irrational anger started building inside him. He wanted to shake her up, make her stutter, tear up, anything to wipe away that calm suburban-mom exterior.

"Your former neighbor was using an electric hedge trimmer in front of his house when the power cord got stuck," Gary said, remembering his visit with the man, who was at least thirty years older than he. "This happened at about the time your husband came in, driving a dark-blue Mercury Grand Marquis with dealer plates. About ten minutes after your husband drove into your driveway, Mr. Laney made a mistake while untangling the power cord and cut three of his fingers."

Gary recalled how the old man recalled every detail of that day, and even made a point of showing him the white scar tissue on the three stumps on his right hand.

"Do you remember that?" he asked.

"No," she said.

Somewhere out in the kitchen area several plates crashed to the floor. The loud noise startled Gary, but apparently did nothing to the woman across from him.

"Well, you can understand that Mr. Laney remembers every detail. He remembers going back into the house, wrapping his hand in a dish-towel, and then dialing 911. And when the Haverhill Fire Department was leaving the scene with him in the rear of an ambulance, they nearly collided with Mr. Thornton as he was leaving the house. I checked with the fire department's records. It took some time, as you can imagine, and they verified that they left Mr. Laney's residence at five twenty."

Jessica seemed to make a point of looking up at the clock one more time, and Gary felt a sadistic pleasure in driving home the next point. This was one of the few pleasures of his job, confronting a reluctant or obstinate witness or interviewee with a hammer-hard recitation of facts that couldn't be challenged or disproved.

"Mrs. Thornton," he went on, feeling so cool and collected with having the evidence to back him up, as if some angel from his Catholic Youth Organization days were standing behind him, complete with sword.

"Your husband left your residence at five twenty P.M. The car accident in York that killed him took place at six P.M. As part of my investigation, I've traveled that route twice. Each time, it took exactly forty minutes."

He paused, letting her stew, but she didn't waste any time. "Meaning what?" she asked.

"Meaning that your husband was sober when he left the car dealership, and he came straight home. When he left your Haverhill residence and drove north to Maine, it took him exactly forty minutes—the time I have double-checked—to have a fatal car accident in York. The autopsy later showed that your deceased husband had a blood alcohol content level of zero point zero nine percent. The legal limit is zero point zero eight. Yet Mr. Thornton had no opportunity to consume any alcohol at the dealership, on his ride home to Haverhill, or on the trip north for that retirement party."

One more pause for effect.

"Mrs. Thornton, I just have to point this out," Gary said, carefully and deliberately choosing his words. "The only time and place that your husband could have consumed alcohol was at your home before he departed. And based on his Alcoholics Anonymous meetings, his vows to his coworkers and family members that he would never, ever drink again, there seems to be just one explanation for what happened that evening." Gary picked up his coffee cup. "Mrs. Thornton, somehow you got your husband drunk that night, and you're responsible—as Grace Thornton believes—for his death."

CHAPTER TWENTY-ONE

Jessica was quietly listening to the plain-looking man with the thin brown hair and the plain-looking suit sitting across from her at the truck stop, and when he started going on and on, like some high school lecturer intent on making a point, she knew where the story would end up.

No real surprise, she thought. Old secrets and old actions never really went away, and they always remained just out of reach, out of time, until they roared back and stood in front of you, demanding attention, ready to disrupt everything.

She gathered her strength, her thoughts. "That's one hell of an accusation."

He smiled at her, the self-confident and pleased smile of a man who thinks he knows it all, and who's also sure that he has this particular woman trapped. Like men everywhere.

"That's what the evidence points to," he said.

"Perhaps he had a bottle in his car," she said, wanting to draw this out. "Maybe that's how he got drunk."

"You know that no evidence of any alcoholic beverages was found in his car."

"Then maybe he tossed the bottle out before the accident," she said. "Mr. Talbot, it's clear he was drunk that night, isn't it? What's the confusion here?"

Talbot raised an eyebrow. "After his AA meetings? After telling coworkers and friends that he would never slip? That he would never,

ever do anything to threaten his marriage with you? That seems . . . improbable."

"It happens all the time," she said. "You've never heard of alcoholics falling off the wagon? Getting drunk because of one moment of weakness, one slip-up? I'm sure that's what happened."

The private investigator said, "Again, improbable, Mrs. Thornton. Oh, it could have happened. But I think there's another, more logical explanation. That in the forty minutes he was at home with you, you got your husband drunk. His sister tells me that he loved drinking orange juice, would have eight or ten glasses of juice a day, since he was convinced it kept him healthy and prevented him from having colds."

"That's what she said?"

Gary smiled. "And his primary-care physician back then, Maul. Oh, Bobby Thornton's records are still private, but I had a general conversation with the doctor about him and his physical health, and he was aware of his orange juice consumption. Plus I was able to get copies of your supermarket purchase receipts for a six-month period prior to the car accident. Astounding how much orange juice you purchased."

"You think I spiked his drinks?"

"Yes."

"With what?"

"Not gin or vodka. There's not enough alcohol by volume to do the job quickly enough. No, my guess is grain alcohol. The top seller is ninety-five percent alcohol by volume, and it's tasteless. Put enough in some OJ so it kicked in while he was driving north to Maine, such that he got woozy, or inattentive, hit the deer, and then went off the road and got killed. I mean, I can see you doing that, Mrs. Thornton, in an attempt to get him pulled over for drunk driving. That would give you leverage for an eventual divorce. Having him killed was indeed an accident."

She stared and stared at him, hoping to break his concentration or his mood, but Talbot matched her.

Jessica said, "Prove it."

And she quivered inside when he reached into his coat, took out a cell phone, and said, "If you insist." He looked pleased with himself. "When I went to your first husband's dealership, there were some there who remembered him well, were even still mourning him. And every one of them told me the same thing: that after his funeral, not once did you go back to the dealership. Not once. Eventually they boxed up his personal belongings and sent them to you."

Jessica's voice seemed very far away to her. "I didn't want to go there. Too many memories."

The private detective reached out, tapped at his cell phone. "I also learned a lot about Bobby Thornton, how driven he was to make sales. He'd even talk to potential customers while driving back and forth from work. He was so driven that he had actually put an app on his phone that would record his messages."

Not a single word, Jessica thought. *Don't say a single additional word.*

He picked up the phone. "I got hold of his call records from that night. Approximately five minutes before his fatal car accident, Bobby Thornton called home. What did he say to you?"

A memory: the caller ID flashing, her letting the phone ring and ring. "I must have been outside."

"Did he leave a message?"

"No," she said.

Delete, she recalled from that night. *Delete.*

"Interesting," Talbot said. "I suppose you don't have his cell phone from that night. Because whatever he told you would be recorded on that device. And we could both find out what he said when he called you."

"I don't know where his phone is," she said, which was true. It was at the bottom of the Warner River, but exactly where, she had no idea. No matter. The evidence was gone. *Relax,* she thought, *relax.*

"Oh, that's all right," he said, tapping his device. "Bobby Thornton had another app, one that automatically forwarded any call he made or received on his phone to a server back at the dealership, where it was recorded. And how fortunate that the folks there, who love him still, were able to dig it up for me."

The device was put back on the table, and Jessica felt a flash as her palms got moist, hearing that old cliche, a voice from the grave: *Hey, Jess, it's me. Something's wrong. Christ, I feel like I'm drunk as shit. I'm gonna pull over . . . I don't wanna get stopped by a cop. I'll call you again. Please come pick me up . . . Jesus, Jessica . . . Thanks.*

Talbot picked up the device, pressed another button. "Well," he said. "How about that?"

He watched her carefully, seeing the shocked look at hearing the voice of her dead husband, and then it was his turn to be surprised, when she proved to be much more than a housewife and bank teller.

"What do you want?" she asked.

Damn, he thought. *That was pretty quick.* He kept quiet.

Mrs. Thornton said, "Again, what do you want? You're an investigator, working for Grace. You're telling me all this evidence about what may or may not have happened some years ago. You've talked to witnesses whose memories might be a bit fuzzy. And you've got a recording of my dead husband saying something's wrong, he feels like he's drunk."

Gary said, "But this evidence—"

The insistent woman overran him. "All right, we've established that. You have the evidence. But why should I care? The only person who should care is your client, Grace Thornton. Why talk to me? What do you want?"

Gary hadn't thought that Jessica, a remarried, high-school-educated bank teller, would get to the heart of the matter so quickly, so he decided to reveal all.

"Good job," he said. "I do want something. And if I get what I need, then Grace doesn't see a word of what I've just told you."

"Excuse me for being direct," she said, "but why should I give a shit about what you do or don't tell Grace?"

Ah, here it goes, he thought. Something this woman could never have guessed.

"Because she's coming after you," he said, recalling the internet print-outs Grace had gathered about how to proceed, plans she hadn't told him about. "She wants to remove you as guardian of the trust for your daughter. Take control of the assets. Decide when and how they will be disbursed. From what I've learned, you can start withdrawing from the trust once Emma turns twenty-one, and when Emma turns thirty, the entire trust will be under her control. Any way you look at it, it would be a long, drawn-out mess if Grace took you to court."

"She can't do that," Jessica snapped, her eyes looking frightened. Gary so loved that look. *How does that feel, sweetheart?* he thought. *How does it feel?*

"If she can convince a judge, she can pretty much do anything she wants," he said. "And what she wants to do is go to court, saying you're unfit to be the guardian, with evidence that you had a hand in your former husband's death. Including your dead husband's voice saying that something was wrong, that he felt drunk and didn't know why. But you and I know why, don't we?"

"That's not enough proof!" she called out, and then she sat back, eyes flashing, as she realized how loud her voice had gotten.

Gary leaned over the booth's table. "That's all she has to do, Mrs. Thornton. Go before the judge with my interviews, my timeline, Bobby Thornton's voice, and present enough reasonable doubt that the trust and its guardianship will be taken out of your hands. Are you prepared for that, Mrs. Thornton? Are you? Your daughter is just fifteen or so, am I correct? You've probably been counting on that money to help pay off school loans after college graduation, or maybe as a nice nest egg once she leaves school. I mean, how much can you, a bank teller, and your husband, a failing real estate agent, save up for your daughter's college? Especially since your stepson will be college-bound before your daughter. And I know you've already spent your first husband's inheritance on track training for your daughter, along with other expenses."

Jessica stared at him, her eyes filled with anger and disbelief, and then she said again, "What do you want?"

Gary shrugged.

Payday.

"Twenty thousand dollars."

Jessica felt the acid taste of coffee nearly crawl up her throat after hearing what Grace had been planning by hiring this sleazy detective sitting across from her.

Twenty thousand dollars. Christ, she couldn't remember the last time she had two thousand dollars in her checking account. Twenty thousand!

She nearly felt like laughing at this absurd man. She said, "Twenty thousand dollars? Are you out of your mind? Make it two hundred thousand, two million. What makes you think I can get my hands on that kind of money?"

He said, "Your husband works in real estate. You work at a bank. Figure it out."

Figure it out. How she hated this man sitting so calmly in front of her. Weeks ago she hadn't even known him, had gone for months without thinking about Bobby and his death, and now . . . Damn Bobby Thornton and his drunken voice from years ago, now threatening everything.

"Or?"

"Or I tell your sister-in-law—"

"Former sister-in-law," she snapped at him, without even thinking. "I haven't seen her or spoken to her since Bobby's funeral."

"All right, your former sister-in-law," he said. "If I'm not paid by you, I'll tell Grace everything I've learned in a very detailed report, including a transcript of that recording. If I get paid, then I tell her there's nothing there. In fact, if I get paid within the next week, I'll encourage her to drop the entire matter. Won't twenty thousand dollars be a good payment to ensure that your daughter's trust fund remains under your control?"

Trapped, she thought. The whole matter of her daughter and that damn wrestler's death, the seizure of Ted's shotgun, and now this. But she hated to admit it, this man had a point. She had to do what was right to protect Emma.

Gary waited, tried to stay calm. Twenty thousand dollars would get him out of his hole, get him caught up on his overdue lease, give him breathing room, even allow him to take a vacation to Aruba this winter for the first time in his long and disappointing life. It all depended on this shaky-looking woman sitting in front of him. He restrained himself, not wanting to push her, not wanting to spook her.

She cleared her throat. "You must be licensed in Maine," she said. "Suppose I filed a complaint with the state, repeating what you just said to me?"

"You do that, it'll be a waste of time. You have no proof. And the moment you do that, I'll go straight to Grace Thornton and reveal everything. I'll also encourage her to take action. How does that sound?"

The woman looked trapped, a look that pleased him.

"It doesn't sound great," she said.

"I know."

Mrs. Thornton released a heavy sigh. "All right. I think I can do it. Within a week."

Success, he thought. Success.

But that feeling lasted just two seconds.

"But I can't possibly afford twenty thousand dollars," she said. "The best I can do is ten thousand."

He quickly shook his head. "What, you think this is some kind of bank negotiation, working out what kind of interest rate you can get for a business loan? It's twenty thousand dollars, Mrs. Thornton. Not ten."

She said, "It's going to be ten thousand. Or else."

"Or else what?"

"How much does Grace know about you?"

"Huh?" He didn't like this new direction. "Mrs. Thornton, I—"

"Come on, Mr. Talbot. Quick answer. How much does Grace know about you?"

"She knows enough to have hired me."

The woman suddenly smiled, as if she were the one springing the trap, not the other way around.

"Does she know that when you were a Maine state trooper, you were responsible for crippling the governor's son during a traffic stop?"

Just like that, the memory of the night came back to him, the realization that the drunk driver he had pulled over had the same last name as the governor, which explained why he had stepped out of the car, yelling, "Do you know who I am?" just before Gary could tell him to get back in the car, just before he could tell him to stop walking toward him, just before there was the blast of an air horn, the shuddering squeal of tractor-trailer brakes, and that deep, bone-crunching *thud* he could still hear in his dreams at night.

The woman before him no longer looked scared or trapped. The bitch looked happy. Looked smug.

That hadn't been the plan.

Jessica instantly felt better, seeing the surprised look on the PI's face.

"Ah . . ."

"You mean you didn't tell that to Grace? Hard-ass Grace? Judgmental Grace?"

Gary looked like he was trying to gather himself together. "I don't see how that matters."

"Oh, but I do," Jessica said, still enjoying the man's discomfort. "Even when I knew her back then, she was so faithfully on the straight and narrow that Bobby joked she could be used as a surveyor's tool on construction projects. She hated dirty jokes, got angry at seeing her mom read those naughty books like *Fifty Shades of Grey*, and when Bobby and I got married, even seeing the garter ceremony ticked her off. So what do you think she'd do if she found out you were the trooper responsible for putting the Maine governor's son in a wheelchair?"

"Ah . . ."

"The best I can do, and the best you can do, is ten thousand dollars. That's it. That's the deal. Take it or leave it, but do it now. I need to get back home."

"But—"

"If you take it, I can get you the money within the week. If not, then I'll call Grace and tell her all about you. Then she'll dump you. You won't get whatever fee you're expecting from her and you won't get any money from me. Your choice."

She waited.

Jessica had no idea where she was going to get ten thousand. But she wasn't going to let this private detective from Maine, this former state trooper, this *man*, take away what was rightfully hers.

Gary took a breath. "You think calling her will really have an impact?"

Jessica smiled. "Do you really want to gamble on that?"

His face seemed to reveal an internal struggle.

A few heavy moments passed.

"It was an accident," Gary said.

"I'm sure it was."

The man started off talking slowly, but then the words came out at a faster pace, as if he couldn't wait to explain his actions to someone new.

"It was one in the morning. On I-295, north of Falmouth. November night. The kid was driving an Audi. He drifted over to the right into the breakdown lane and then went back. That's it. No weaving, no sudden jerking left or right. I could have let him go. I could have."

Jessica didn't know what to say. She had half expected this PI in front of her to start arguing or fighting with her, but she hadn't expected this confession.

Gary felt like he was skidding on his ass after trying to cross an icy road. Now he had to get out of here with that ten thousand safely his. All right, most bills would be paid off and the planned Aruba trip would be postponed, but he knew Jessica was right. Grace Thornton was one customer who was tightly wrapped, and she owed him eight hundred bucks that he couldn't pass up, even with the ten thousand promised down the road.

"Do you see what I mean?" he asked.

The woman kept quiet. He should keep his mouth shut as well, but Gary felt compelled to tell all. Anything to keep her from calling Grace.

"I could have let him go, but I had a rep at Troop B, where I was stationed. A rep as a hardass, someone who didn't cut corners, who was aggressive as hell. So I made the stop, and the kid . . . the stupid kid wouldn't follow my commands. A few seconds, that's all it took, to put him in a wheelchair and kick me out of the state police."

Jessica gathered up her purse. "And how many seconds did it take for you to come up with this plan to extort me?"

Gary said, "It isn't extortion. It is—"

"Business? Understanding? Mr. Talbot, I'll call you in a week." She got out of the booth. "In the meantime, for what you were planning to do to my little girl, go fuck yourself."

—∞—

Outside, even with the smell of gasoline and diesel fuel and the heavy roar of traffic speeding by on Route 128, Jessica felt pretty damn good. The question of what her former sister-in-law was up to had been answered: Grace wanted revenge by prying Jessica away as the administrator of Emma's trust. Part of Jessica admired the sheer cold-blooded way Grace had approached her goal, by taking years to line up her case against Jessica.

So.

Ten thousand dollars? Where would she get that money?

Jessica was starting to have an idea of how she could—

Her iPhone rang. She dug it out of her purse, checked the incoming call. Warner Police Department.

What? Was Detective Rafferty calling about something to do with Sam Warner's murder? Or had something bad happened to Emma?

She dropped her purse on the dirty asphalt, slid a finger across the screen to answer the phone. "Hello?"

A shocked male voice answered her. "Jessica? Is that you? Jessica?"

It was Ted.

"Ted, what's up?"

And in the next three seconds, seeing the caller ID on her iPhone made terrible and awful sense.

"Jessica, I'm at the Warner police station," Ted said, his voice tight and strained.

"Ted . . ."

"Jess, I've been arrested."

And the next four words hammered her so hard she flinched.

"For Sam Warner's murder."

SAM WARNER'S STORY

Saturday Night

Even though he was in the middle of taking a shower that Saturday night, Sam could hear the music, the loud voices, the happy yells as his house party was getting under way. He ran his hands through his short black hair, wiped at his face, took a loofah and gave his back and other parts a good scrub. A while earlier he had gone mano a mano outside with a guy he went to school with, tossed him around with no difficulty, and it was good to wash the sweat and dirt from his skin. Pissy guy. Still having a grudge years later. *Grow up,* he thought.

Mum and Pop—my God, could those two have chosen stupider names to be called?—were out west at some numb cultural museum in North Adams and were spending the night with some equally numb friends. Sam, never one to pass up an opportunity, either here or in the wrestling circle, made sure tonight was in the works about five seconds after Mum and Pop told him about their plans.

He turned off the shower, wiped his face again, ran his hands across his upper arms and chest. Some good definition there, showing the results of workouts in his basement gym, and those muscles were going to open some good fucking doors in the months ahead. About a half-dozen colleges and universities were already offering him full scholarships, even though Pop could spring for tuition, room, and board without breaking a sweat. It was nice to be noticed.

He grinned. Fuck, it was good to be him.

—〰—

Later he came out from his bedroom dressed in Topsiders, chinos, and a WARNER WRESTLING polo shirt, and up on the second-floor landing was Brock Palmer, one of his best buds. He was dressed the same way. They slapped skin. Downstairs there was shouting, laughter; a door slammed. There was pounding at the door, swearing.

Sam said, "What the fuck was that?"

"Some guy came by to raise hell," Brock said.

"Another guy? What is this, a fucking convention? Who was it?"

Brock shrugged. "Dunno. Some dad was pissed about something. Wanted to get in. Hank asked him for his invite, the dad didn't have one, so Hank and Larry took care of it."

Sam headed to the stairs. "All right. Let's keep on eye on things, okay?"

"Got it, Cap," Brock said, and as always Sam got a tingle of joy hearing that title. Cap. Captain of the Warner High School Wrestling Team, and captain of everything he saw.

He went downstairs, saw the party was going well, Imagine Dragons playing hard from the living room speakers, some kids jumping and dancing in the center, some couples making out in chairs and on the couches, and nothing seemed to be a mess yet.

A girl he didn't know stumbled up to him, eyes glassy. Holding a red Solo cup, she threw him a hug, giving him a good squeeze with her free arm so he could feel her boobies. Then she kissed his cheek. "Oh, Sam, so glad I made it, so glad! What a great party!"

He slapped her on the butt, gently pushed her away. "Only great 'cause of girls like you!"

She laughed and stumbled back, and then fell on her ass on the plastic sheet covering the living room rug, and he maneuvered his way into the kitchen, pushing by his partygoers, his friends, his tribe.

Sam led his life by rules, from the food he ate to the workouts he maintained, and one rule was to run a great party without getting his ass in a sling. That in turn meant a lot of subrules. Like, nobody got in without an invite signed by him. No exceptions. No friends of friends, or neighbors, or anybody else who hadn't been vetted.

Another rule was no bottles or cans of booze on site. Solo cups were allowed, but that was because if trouble came, it was easy enough to dump the contents down toilets or sinks or out the windows. Beer and other booze was hidden either in cars or in the nearby town forest, named after one of his worthless ancestors. That way, if one of the neighbors in this high-priced development with three-acre lots and three-story homes ever called the cops, the only thing they'd find once they came up the four-hundred-foot driveway would be a group of happy and drunk teenagers with little evidence to arrest anyone.

Trash cans with plastic bags were placed on the first floor and in the furnished basement, and plastic sheets covered the pricy rugs that Mum had imported from Afghanistan or Kazakhstan or one of those other shithole "stans" out there. And when the party was done in a few hours, two members of the freshmen wrestling team would go through the house and clean everything up and get two free beers at the end as pay, as well as the email addresses of a couple of skanks who'd do a lot to get aboard with the wrestling team.

And if anybody bumped into something or made a mess or puked on the floor, Sam and a couple of his buds would tune him up and dump him in the woods.

In the kitchen now, with Kenny Blake and Larry Pond. He went up to Larry, caught his attention, and said, "So what the hell was going on there with that dad?"

Larry grinned. "Some guy came by, half in the bag, wanting to talk to you about the way you treat his boy."

"Let me guess, he was pissed."

"Yeah, and now he's even more pissed. We pushed him away and he fell into the drainage ditch just below the garage. Now he's wet and pissed."

Sam laughed along with Larry and Kenny. The kitchen was packed with laughing, happy, great kids, and they all looked to him as the one who got them together to have fun, get high or drunk, do some fooling around and maybe get laid, make great memories that you could look back on when you got to college and later.

Larry, next to the stainless steel refrigerator, gestured to him, leaned over, and said, "She's all set."

"My bedroom?"

"Oh, yeah."

"She ready?"

Larry gave him a wide smile. "Oh, shit, she's ready all right."

Sam slapped him on his muscular shoulder. "Great. You be a good boy, you'll get sloppy seconds."

He moved out of the kitchen, music still thumping along, and saw some kid from Concord dragging a puff. When the kid spotted Sam, he hauled ass outside and slammed the door behind him. Yeah, more rules. No smoking of anything in the house. Mum and Pop hated smoke like you wouldn't believe, and both had the noses of bloodhounds, able to trace even the smallest molecule of tobacco or weed.

There was another kid there, that goofy brainy Craig who had once helped him with his algebra and geometry homework, before he wanted more and before Sam got tired of the bleating little shit. Craig was sitting by himself in the corner, staring at his Solo cup, and Sam knew that if he had been built differently he would feel sorry for the weird shit.

He got to the stairs, where Brock was standing guard at the bottom.

YOU WILL NEVER KNOW

Brock sipped from his Solo cup. Two girls were sitting on the last stair, looking up at him with delight, until they caught Sam's eye and switched their loving gazes to him.

Brock said, "All set."

"Great." He gently pushed back the two girls and went upstairs.

Biggest rule of all: nobody except him got to be upstairs at this time of the night.

At his bedroom he opened the door and walked in. All the lights were off save one small one on his desk, which gave the bedroom a soft glow. There were framed photos of his victories up on the walls, along with shelves of trophies and other mementos, and photos of his team during the past two winning seasons. He worked hard to keep everything up there in its place, because Mum and Pop loved bringing their friends up here to show off what their special boy was accomplishing.

So what? That's not why he was here, to check out his "Look at Me" wall. Nope, he was looking at something else as his heart thumped right along and his hands got moist and his Johnson was tenting his slacks.

She was laid out on the bed, waiting for him.

"Fuck, yeah," he whispered.

He got his iPhone out, set it up on a little tripod, and then placed it on top of his bureau, right where he had earlier laid out a strip of masking tape to mark the perfect spot. He swiped on the Record button and then knelt on the bed.

Emma Thornton was pretty zoned out. How zoned?

He tugged at her ear, pulled at a lip, said, "Hey, Emma, you ready for a good time?"

She just sighed and moved around on his bed.

Yep, things were cool. One of his best buds, Barry Zahn, had a cousin who lived in one of the projects up in Lawrence, and that cousin had a source for good-quality roofies—not the shit that killed you or made you sleep for two days straight—and sprinkle some of that in a drink . . . well, this was what happened. Sweet little piece started

He moaned with pleasure, again making sure he wasn't blocking the shot.

Out and over her lips.

Breathing hard. His strong wrestling legs trembling with excitement.

"Sucky-sucky," he whispered again.

Her teeth were shut, so he stuck in a finger, forced her mouth open, got into position, and—

Somebody was yelling outside his room.

"Hey, you can't go up there!"

Sam turned his head.

More shouting.

Then the *thump-thump-thump* of someone running up the stairs. Turning the doorknob.

His finger slipped deeper into her mouth.

Emma coughed, choked, and then sat up and puked all over him.

CHAPTER TWENTY-TWO

O ut of the horror that had rampaged into Jessica's life during the last eighteen hours, the one saving grace that she had never expected had been a text sent to her phone from her usually ice-cold boss, Ellen Nickerson:

Just heard the news. Take tomorrow off. Nickerson, WSB

Now, this Sunday, she was in a small conference room in the law offices of Kahn, Trotter, and Pease, where George Kahn handled Ted's real estate business and where she was with Helen Wray, the criminal defense lawyer George had recommended when Detective Rafferty had come to the house to seize Ted's shotgun.

That shocking, unbelievable moment now seemed as innocent as attending a child's birthday party compared to what had happened to her and Ted.

Helen was about ten years older than Jessica, dressed fine and sharp in a dark red skirt-and-jacket suit, and Jessica wondered whether her brash and confident attitude came from birth, schooling, or training. Her hair was dark brown, swept back in a bun, and she had a set of what looked to be real small pearls around her tanned neck. She had a stack of paperwork on the polished wood of the desk, with a yellow legal pad nearby and what looked to be a fountain pen in her manicured right hand.

Helen said, "Okay, Jessica, let's get a few things out of the way, okay? First things first—how are you doing?"

Jessica had a tissue clasped hard in her folded hands underneath the table. "Awful," she said. "The phones were ringing last night, there were reporters knocking on the door, and shit, the Boston TV stations, they were doing live broadcasts in front of our house! At eleven o'clock last night! And this morning!"

Helen nodded. "Nosy little bastards, aren't they? Two kids were gunned down in Dorchester yesterday, and it merited two paragraphs in the *Boston Globe* and one sentence in the local TV news coverage last night. Sorry to say, this is what they call a sexy story. Wrestling team captain in a prestigious Massachusetts community is murdered and a local realtor is arrested."

Jessica felt her chin tremble. She just nodded.

Helen started scribbling. "Don't worry," she said. "After a day or two, they'll leave you alone until something new develops, there's a bail hearing, or some other spicy story comes up."

"Do you . . . do you think we have a chance?" Jessica asked, hating how weak her voice sounded.

"Oh, we've got lots of things going for us," Helen said. "Don't you worry." Then the lawyer stopped and stared at Jessica long and hard, without saying a word.

Jessica couldn't stand it. "Yes?" she asked.

Helen said, "Right from the start, you need to know that I'm going to be an advocate for your husband. I'm representing him. I'm not representing you. So I need to make it plain and simple: do you think you need an attorney as well, Mrs. Thornton?"

Jessica felt her stomach do a dive and flop. To throw up now, to be so frightened in front of this self-assured woman—what kind of message would *that* send?

"I . . . I . . ."

Helen said, "I want to make myself as clear as possible. If during my preparation for your husband's defense I come across evidence that is

167

exculpatory toward him and raises serious questions and concerns about you, Mrs. Thornton, I won't hesitate to use it. Again, Ted Donovan is my client. Not you."

Jessica nodded, took a deep, cleansing breath. "Okay. I see what you mean, Miss—"

"Call me Helen, please. We're going to be spending a lot of time with each other over the next weeks and months."

Her stomach seemed to be calming down. "Yes, Helen, thank you. No, I don't need an attorney. I see where you're coming from. I know you're here to help Ted, not me or anybody else."

The attorney smiled and Jessica felt even better. "Good. I can't tell you how many times I've had female clients who were willing to take the fall for something—usually drug cases—and when I found out their jerk boyfriends or husbands were really the ones involved, they screamed at me to leave their men alone. Can you believe that? So loyal to the guy who was willing to keep his mouth shut to see his woman go to jail." Helen shook her head, started scribbling. "Men."

Jessica said nothing, and Helen said, "I've gotten some information from the Warner Police Department, but not much. Eventually the county attorney will have to let me know what evidence they have against your husband for Sam Warner's death, but that'll be some time away."

"How much more time?"

Helen said, "Oh, for a case like this, I'd be surprised if we go to trial by October or November."

"October or November . . ." Jessica had the searing thought of Thanksgiving alone with Emma. And Craig.

Helen said, "Maybe even December. You're going to have to prepare yourself. But I'm in it for the long haul, okay?"

The lawyer gave her another bright smile. Jessica could only nod.

"I also need to get business taken care of before we start," she said. "I'll need a retainer of at least six thousand dollars to begin. My rate is three hundred dollars an hour."

"Did you say . . ." Jessica felt like she was going to slide right off this polished chair and fall under the table.

"I did," Helen said, "and I can tell I just shocked the crap out of you. I understand. Look, Jessica, I know your background, know what you and Ted have. Let's just leave the retainer for later, all right? I'll let you and Ted talk about what the two of you might do down the road to raise the money. For now, no worries now about paying up-front. Let's do our best to take care of Ted, and we'll worry about the bills later."

Jessica sat still, not knowing what to say.

Helen said, "Okay. Let's start, shall we?"

Jessica wished at this very moment she was back at Warner Savings Bank, with nothing more to worry about than ending the day, balancing out her cash drawer, and maybe catching an after-school meet to watch Emma win once more.

"Yes," she said. "Let's start."

Helen opened a file folder, started looking through copies of newspaper articles. "Not surprisingly, the Warner police and the Middlesex DA aren't giving me shit at this time," she said. "And it—"

"Wait," Jessica said, hoping to find any crumb of good news. "I thought they had to give any evidence they have over to you."

"Eventually, yes, Mrs. Thornton, but not for a while yet."

"Jessica."

"What? Oh, sure, if you'd like. Jessica. I wish real life was like Hollywood or TV, but justice can grind along at its own pace, and sometimes the alleged good guys aren't that good. Or aren't that competent."

She felt like she had just been put in her place. Jessica could only nod.

"All right," Helen said. "According to the newspapers and other media and the initial Warner police news release, Sam Warner was found murdered in the Warner Town Forest this past Wednesday morning." She looked up from the sheaf of papers. "Town of Warner, Sam Warner, Warner Town Forest—popular name around here, huh?"

"The Warner family were some of the first settlers here, back in the 1600s."

"Goodie for them," she said. "My family came over in steerage from Vilnius. So. Time of death was about twelve hours before he was discovered. And a local amateur astronomer said he thought he heard a gunshot at about ten P.M. on Tuesday evening. No other witnesses, no surveillance tape, and so far as we know, no drone footage showing your husband killing the boy."

Jessica's eyes welled up at hearing that last sentence.

"So we've got that going for us," Helen said. "But what they have is a lot of circumstantial evidence. Starting with Craig, your husband's son. I understand that he and Sam Warner got into some fights. So many that the assistant principal sent a note home to your husband, expressing the school's concern. Unfortunately, in some folks' minds, that's a motive. Your husband violently reacting to someone fighting with his son."

"Not really fights," Jessica said. "I mean, yes, there were things that happened, but I think they were more one-sided. Bullying."

Helen smiled. It wasn't a warm or pleasing smile. "Good. The wrestling captain was a bully. That's good to know. If this ever goes to trial, it'd be nice to let the jury know that the star athlete was also a star asshole. That'd go a ways toward undercutting the state's case."

Blaming the victim, Jessica thought—is that where we're at now?

The attorney went on. "The DA will probably use that as motive. And then there's the evidence. Not much of it, but there it is, and it's all coming down to your husband's shotgun."

Jessica shuddered. "I've never liked that in the house, never."

"What did Ted use it for?"

"Some hunting—duck, pheasant," she said. "Mostly up in New Hampshire. With clients or other realtors he was friendly with."

"Do you know what kind of shotgun it is?"

Jessica said, "Kind? There's a kind?"

Helen nodded, turned over another newspaper clipping. "Lots of kinds. Single-shot, pump-action, semiautomatic. And different sizes, called gauges. Ted owns a twelve-gauge Remington pump-action shotgun, which poses two problems for the state."

"What's that?"

Helen said, "What Ted told me and what the police haven't. So far."

"Huh?"

"Don't you remember?" Helen asked. "When Detective Rafferty seized the shotgun, he told you and Ted that it had been recently fired."

Jessica nodded, wiped at her eyes. "There . . . there was so much going on. Yes, now I remember. He said it smelled like the shotgun had been recently fired."

The attorney said, "That was just a sniff test, I'm sure. At this moment I can guarantee you that your husband's shotgun is at the state police forensics lab over in Maynard and they're running tests to confirm the detective's nostrils. They'll probably come up with a date range of when the shotgun was fired. It won't be good news if it's about the time the boy got shot. Then again . . ."

Somewhere nearby two people walked by, talking loudly, and Jessica had an urge to get up, open the door, and scream at them to *shut up, shut up, just shut the hell up!*

"Then again," Helen repeated, "the crime labs here in Massachusetts and the coroner's office haven't covered themselves in glory these past few years. Thousands of drug cases had to be tossed because of processing errors or outright fraud, and the coroners are usually overworked and underpaid, meaning they can't attract top staff. Not to mention the overtime and corruption scandals from the Mass. State Police. That will work in Ted's favor."

"You said there were two problems. What was the other one?"

Helen smiled. "Ah, this is going to be key. You see, whoever killed Sam used a shotgun, which meant he was hit by a number of shotgun pellets. That certainly wasn't good for Sam but is very good for your husband."

"Why?"

"Because if Sam had been hit by a bullet from a handgun or a rifle and the bullet was recovered and was in decent shape, forensics could tie it to a specific handgun or rifle."

"Meaning . . ."

"Don't you see?" Helen asked. "There's no way that forensics can link the pellets that killed Sam to your husband's shotgun. Even if they recovered five or ten or twenty pellets, there's no way to link them to your husband. Which leads to reasonable doubt, and that, Jessica, can lead to an acquittal."

She could only nod. What this lawyer knew, what she had learned, what she was capable of, and—

"Excuse me?" Jessica asked. "I didn't hear what you just said."

Helen smiled, and this time it felt like it had genuine warmth behind it. "Dear me, you have so much going on, that's entirely understandable. Now. Alibi time. I had a brief conversation with Ted before coming over here, and he told me that you could provide an alibi for him, at the time of the boy's murder."

"What time would that be?" she asked.

Helen paused for two seconds, and those two seconds seemed heavy indeed. She spoke clearly and slowly. "The preliminary information I managed to crowbar out of the Warner police is that the boy was murdered between six P.M. and midnight. Ted said that he was at home with you, beginning at six P.M. Is that true?"

True. What was truth, now?

Ted had been out that night, has not been with her, had not been with his son or stepdaughter. No, he had been out, and he wasn't out with his business partner Ben, like he claimed. He was out with that big-titted slut from the real estate office, and now he was asking his wife—*his wife!*—to provide him with an alibi to save him.

Those same damn talkers were now walking back again, out there in the hallway. *Just shut up!*

"Mrs. Thornton?"

She took a deep, bracing breath and said, "No, I can't."

Helen suddenly scowled. "What?"

"I said, I can't provide Ted with an alibi."

Helen looked like a cobra about to spit venom in Jessica's face.

"What the hell are you telling me, Mrs. Thornton?"

All right, Jessica thought. No more friendly first names.

"I'm telling you that I can't provide an alibi for Ted."

"Your husband told me that he told the police he was home with you that night, watching . . ." Helen flipped through some sheets of paper and said, "Ah, here. Yes. Ted said that he was watching one of the *Real Housewives* television shows on Bravo." She glared at Jessica.

Jessica felt fine.

Helen said, "Are you telling me that Ted lied to the police?"

"Yes, he did," Jessica said.

"And you . . ." Another frantic flipping through some papers. "You told the police, Detective Rafferty to be specific, that you could verify that Ted was with you all that evening. Is that a lie as well, Mrs. Thornton?"

"It is."

Helen placed both of her hands flat on the conference room table. "Mrs. Thornton, was your husband home that night?"

"No," Jessica said. "He got home at about eleven P.M."

Helen slowly shook her head. "Do you have any idea where he was?"

A cliche to be true, but, yes, he was in the arms of another woman. And am I going to bail him out? Am I going to help my cheating husband?

"No," Jessica said.

Partial Transcript of Recorded Conversation
Between Jessica Thornton and Theodore H. Donovan,
Inmate Number 4512283
Middlesex County Jail
Billerica, Massachusetts

INMATE: "You need what?"

GUEST: "Twelve thousand dollars, Ted. As soon as possible."

INMATE: "She didn't tell me that earlier! I can't believe she . . . "

[Cross talk]

GUEST: "Maybe it slipped her mind when she was asking questions about your—"

INMATE: "Jess, please, you know this is being recorded. All the goddamn signs say it."

[Pause]

INMATE: "Sorry. I . . . damn it, this is such a god-damn nightmare. The noise—I didn't sleep last night, I'm always on guard in case some shithead wants to pick a fight, the food is—"

GUEST: "Ted. The twelve thousand dollars."

INMATE: "Christ, Jessica, I don't think we even have a thousand in our checking account."

GUEST: "We don't."

INMATE: "The mortgage. A second mortgage might do it, but shit, who's going to approve a second mortgage with what's going on and—"

GUEST: "Nobody, that's who."

  [Cross-talk]

GUEST: "We need to go to Ben Powell. The money he's getting from—"

INMATE: "For God's sake, stop that! Don't talk anymore!"

  [Pause]

INMATE: "Jessica."

  [Pause]

INMATE: "Jessica."

  [Pause]

INMATE: "I'm sorry. We can't approach Ben."

GUEST: "Why not?"

INMATE: "Not here."

GUEST: "Ted."

INMATE: "Yes?"

GUEST: "If Attorney Wray doesn't get her retainer, that means she won't take the case. Which means a public defender."

INMATE: "Then okay, I'll get a public defender."

GUEST: "Ted."

INMATE: "Yes?"

GUEST: "Think it through. You get a public defender, you're announcing to Warner and the world that you don't have the money to hire an attorney. That means you're broke. You're out of money. Is that the message you want to get out there?

  [Pause]

GUEST: "Ted."

  [Pause]

GUEST: "Ted."

  [Pause]

INMATE: "All right. Get a hold of Ben. I . . . he was expecting me to meet with him. I'm sure he'll . . .

do what's right. Oh boy. They do let us make outgoing calls here. I'll do it."

GUEST: "Okay. Good."

INMATE: "Okay. When can you come back?"

GUEST: "I don't know. Attorney Wray was able to get me in here tonight on short notice by calling in some favors."

INMATE: "How's Craig?"

GUEST: "I think he's okay. He's over at the Bormans' for the night—and probably for the next few days."

INMATE: "Good."

GUEST: "All right."

INMATE: "I don't want him coming here. All right? I just don't."

GUEST: "Okay."

   [Pause]

GUEST: "Ted?"

INMATE: "Yes?"

GUEST: "Why didn't you ask about Emma?"

INMATE: "What?"

GUEST: "You asked about Craig, how he was doing. Why didn't you ask about Emma? Your stepdaughter?"

INMATE: "I . . . come on, Jessica. I've got so much going on and—"

   [Cross-talk]

GUEST: "All right, Ted, I need to leave."

INMATE: "Jessica."

GUEST: "Yes?"

INMATE: "You still believe, me right? That I didn't kill Sam Warner."

GUEST: "I'm sorry, Ted, I'm late. I've got to go."

   [Cross-talk]

CHAPTER TWENTY-THREE

After her visit with Ted at the Middlesex County Jail, Jessica entered her house, again pushing that damn squeaky door, and picked up the mail from the floor, which she had ignored yesterday during the chaos following Ted's arrest. At least no one from the news media was out there waiting for her, and it looked like Attorney Wray was right: eventually the press did go on to something else.

Good for them, she thought, and walked through the empty house, dropped her purse on the dining room table, and then threw the mail—a flyer from Hannaford's, a plea from Boston Children's Hospital, a checking account statement in her and Ted's name from her own place of business—across the room, making the pieces fly and scatter like baby chicks being kicked out of the nest.

Jessica looked back at that damn squeaky door. Remembered all the times Ted had promised to fix it. She went to the door leading to the cellar, opened it, went downstairs, grabbed a tool kit, and went back to the front door. She took out a screwdriver and pliers and went to work. It was good to have tools in her hands, to get something done. Jessica remembered the times back in high school, taking computers apart and putting them back together, sometimes fixing small things around the house.

A while later she put the tools away and tried working the door.

The damn thing still rubbed and squeaked. All that work had been for nothing.

She put both hands up to her face, took a deep sigh, wondered and waited, and then put the tool kit away, washed her hands and face, and went upstairs.

The door to Craig's room was closed. Big surprise.

The door to Emma's was slightly open and she walked in.

A mess, but why not? Emma was fifteen years old, had her entire future ready for her, from running track to having her mom get access to that trust fund when she turned twenty-one, to getting the whole thing when she turned thirty. All Jessica had to do was take care of her little girl.

She stepped over to the bed, kicked off her shoes, plopped herself down, and stretched out on the blanket, taking Emma's pillow and wrapping her arms around it, bringing it close to her chest. Taking in the scent of Emma brought back so many memories, just tumbling in, one right after another, including the night she had gotten the phone call from the Maine State Police that Bobby had died in York.

Long after the phone calls, the trip up to the Maine State Police barracks, coming home and relieving her neighbor—sweet old Mrs. Miller, a retiree from a tech firm out on Route 128—she had taken young Emma to bed with her, held her, whispered to her, brushed her hair. Emma had struggled and whined while in her mother's insistent arms but had fallen asleep, not knowing then that her daddy was dead, and in the new darkness Jessica had said, "I will always protect you, my little girl. Tonight, tomorrow, and forever. And you will never know what I've done for you."

Now, alone in her girl's room, she wondered how Emma was doing tonight.

—⁂—

Emma Thornton was at her friend Kate Romer's house and was enjoying her time until her phone tinged with an incoming text. Kate's parents, Doris and John, were loud, talking, arguing, laughing, and hugging each other in the crowded kitchen and living room. Kate's younger twin brothers, Paul and Peter, raced around, knocking things over, and Emma found the place fun and happy. Not like her own home, with Mom coming home from the bank, moaning about her sore feet, her stepdad Ted bitching about the soft real estate market, and Craig being Craig.

Which is why she swore when she saw the text she got on her iPhone:

need to see u RIGHT NOW

And she typed back

later

And in seconds,

NO!!! or I go to the cops NOW

She shook her head, let her fingers fly, and then went out to the kitchen, where Kate was drying the dinner dishes with her mom, laughing and flicking dishwater from her fingers, and Emma said, "Mrs. Romer? I need to go out for some fresh air."

Kate's mom, who was plump, florid-faced, wearing a flannel shirt and jeans, wiped her hands on a dish towel and touched Emma's cheek.

"Everything okay, sweetheart?"

Emma said, "I just need some fresh air. That's all."

Kate said, "I'll come along."

"No, that's okay," Emma said. "I just want a few minutes by myself."

Kate started to speak, but her mom gave her a soft glare, and that was that.

"Be safe, all right?"

Emma nodded.

Safe, sure.

Luckily the Romers lived near the Bormans, where Craig was hanging out with his equally weird pal Mark. Via text, he had agreed to meet her at the town common. The walk was quick enough. She walked with her head down and hair tucked up under a wool cap, hoping she wouldn't be noticed. Not that she had anything to be nervous about, but the fewer eyes on her, the better.

She went across the marked crosswalk to the common and over to the Minuteman statue and the bandstand, right where it seemed about half the town had gathered the other night for the sobfest over Sam's death.

Craig was leaning against the bandstand, hands in his coat pockets, knapsack on the grass before him. He was wearing a long denim coat that for some reason the geeks at high school had taken on as their uniform, not knowing that it made them better targets whenever they got in somebody's way.

"Hey," Emma said.

Craig said, "Don't fucking 'hey' me, Emma."

Emma said, "I'll say anything I want."

Craig stood there looking at his perfect stepsister, wondering why, with everything she had going for her—a free ticket to college, lots of friends, solid B-plus work at school, a trust fund her mother could tap when she turned twenty-one—she had to have this wicked crazy streak that nearly always got her into trouble. She was like one of those Hawaiian surfers you saw on ESPN, those hot-looking blondes in their red spandex two-pieces, riding on top of a wave so freakin' high, pushing it and pushing it, always just a few seconds away from tumbling into disaster, a wild-ass crazy grin on their faces. Emma was just like that, except in her case, if she was going to tumble, she was going to take Craig and Dad along with her.

Not going to happen.

He said, "My dad's in jail, and you're bitching to me about what you can say?"

"Stop being so dramatic," she said. "He's just been arrested, that's all."

"That's all!" he nearly yelled back at her. "You don't think that's enough?"

In a cool, controlled, and slightly contemptuous tone, she said, "He's been arrested. Where's the evidence?"

"The cops must know something."

"They know shit. They got your dad's shotgun, and they got evidence that his poor widdle son was being teased by the big bad wrestling team. That's all. In a few days he'll be out on bail, when his new lawyer gets him sprung."

"You don't know that."

"It makes sense. You know it does."

When Craig had first met Emma a few years back, when his dad had started dating Jessica, she had seemed impossibly beautiful and perfect, like one of those crystal-like dolls sold downtown at Warner Gifts and Collectibles. But now all he wanted to do was to punch that smug face, make her hurt like he was hurting.

"I don't know what makes sense," he finally said, blurting out the words he had been practicing to say for the last hour. "All I know is that I'm going to the cops tomorrow. Let them know what happened. I gotta protect my dad."

Emma stared at her idiot stepbrother and said, "You can't—and you won't—do that."

"Oh, yeah? Why not? You going to stop me?"

"You bet I am," she said. "You go, and our deal—it's done."

He shook his head. "Some fucking deal. You were never going to keep your end of it, were you?"

The thing was, Craig was right. She was never going to go through with it, but this wasn't the time or place to bring that up. Him going to the cops!

"Look, give it a day, okay?"

"What's a day going to do?"

She took a step toward him. "I'm over at Kate's, okay? And I heard her dad talking about a couple of cops coming into the hardware store. They were blabbing when they shouldn't have been blabbing, and they said the detective is also looking into the house party at Sam's last Saturday."

Craig looked like he was going to start bawling. "Ah, shit, no."

"Ah, shit, yes," she said, "but don't worry. It's not about me, and it's not about you. It's about something else that happened there."

"Like what?"

"Like somebody's dad came up to the house, drunk, pissed off, and he wanted to go in and meet up with Sam, and he got the shit beat out of him."

"I don't remember that."

"It's a big house, big yard. I don't remember that either."

And in a flash the fuzzy details of what she remembered from last Saturday night made her stomach whirl. *Enough,* she thought, *enough.*

Emma said, "I guess a couple of Sam's pals grabbed the guy before he could make a fuss, beat him up some, and dumped him in a drainage ditch."

"So?"

Emma was getting more and more exasperated with her older step-brother. "Don't you see? That's another suspect. A guy who came to the party telling everybody that he wanted to hurt Sam. The cops will start looking at him, and the case against your dad will go away."

Craig kept his mouth shut.

Emma saw her opportunity. "One more day," she said. "Maybe two. Don't go to the cops, Craig. It'll just . . . confuse things. Raise a lot of questions. Get you into trouble, me into trouble."

Craig nodded. Then he suddenly knelt down, lifted up his knapsack, and showed Emma what was inside.

Jesus Christ!

"Craig, I told you! I told you to get rid of it!"

"So I don't do everything you tell me," he said, zipping the bag shut, slinging it over his right shoulder. "And I tell you this—my dad gets out tomorrow, one way or another, or I'm going to the cops. No matter what. Okay?"

Craig wondered if he had gone too far, and then Emma sighed, pulled her blond hair free from the dark-pink wool cap, and let it fall over her shoulders.

"Craig . . . you're upset. I'm sorry," she said softly, stepping so close he could smell her fresh-soap scent, whatever it was that girls of her age wore on their skin or in the hair. "It's been so rough, and you've been a real man about it. And I know I owe you big-time. What I promised, to make it right for you, to help you? I intend to do it. In fact, I was just talking about you to Kate. She . . . she told me she would love to go out with you. She's just kinda shy."

Then her hands were on his jeans belt, and Craig's legs started trembling. He knew he was a geek, a nerd, someone to be teased at school, but my God, this was the first time a girl had ever taken hold of his belt. And started undoing it.

"You were very brave, getting me into that house party when everybody else on the track team was invited and I wasn't," she said, her voice just above a whisper. "I couldn't let that happen. Those bitches . . . they would eventually vote me out as team captain if they saw I was weak. And then, when . . . when . . ."

Craig saw her eyes seem to well up and heard her voice choke. "And when they roofied me and Sam was taking advantage of me, you manned up and came to rescue me."

The shaking in Craig's legs increased. How did any guy with a steady girlfriend get through the day, through school, knowing that at any time his girl could—and would!—touch him like this!

His belt was undone. Her soft hands were unzipping his jeans. The sound of the zipper being pulled down by a girl was the most wonderful thing he had ever heard in his life.

Emma's voice lowered some more. "And more brave . . . when Sam threatened to blackmail me with that video, you said you would help me. No matter how dangerous, you said you wouldn't let Sam hurt me. You said that . . . and I said I would reward you. Remember? Make it right after they hurt you. I told you I'd set you up with Kate. And Kate—you put a beer into her, Craig, and she'll do anything you like. Hear me? Anything you like."

Craig was humiliated and wanted to say something, but all he could do was let out a soft sigh. In this part of the bandstand they were hidden by a rectangular stone monument honoring Warner veterans, and by bushes and saplings.

Hidden. They were hidden.

Her hands were soft on his belly, and her hands moved down, down, down—

And Emma suddenly pulled up his T-shirt and said, "And if you screw this up, Craig, this"—and she slapped his belly where the humiliating FAG marking still was, no matter how many times he had scrubbed and scrubbed—"will be put on flyers and dropped all over the school. And Kate Romer will never go out with you. Got it?"

She stood up, wiped her hands on her jacket as if they were soiled, and strode away. Craig, sobbing, quickly zipped up his pants and fastened his belt with shaking hands.

—⁂—

Jessica slowly woke up, the bed shaking underneath her. She wondered where she was, and it was the scent that keyed her off that she was in Emma's room. She felt embarrassed, wondering what would happen if Emma came in, seeing that disappointed look on her face. She hated that look.

The shaking increased, and at first she wondered, *An earthquake?* But now there was the faint whistle of a freight train moving through Warner, and it was the old clapboards and beams of the house that were quivering from the passing train. Nothing more.

She lay awake in Emma's bed. Thought about earthquakes. It was strange, she knew, but there were times she wished she and Emma lived in California. There was something appealing to her about living in a place where natural events struck without warning. Landslides. Wildfires. Earthquakes. Here in Massachusetts, the danger came at you with plenty of warning. Hurricanes. Sleet storms. Heavy snow.

The shaking of the bed eased off.

But sometimes the warning provided opportunities.

She remembered.

—॥॥—

School had been canceled the day of a wet, heavy snowstorm that downed lots of trees in their Haverhill neighborhood. Mom worked for the tax assessor's office at City Hall, and Dad was a salesman for Hewlett-Packard out of Andover, and some months he made lots of sales, but lately the sales were starting to dry up. Once she had heard Dad, getting drunk and mean one night, tell Mom, "It's starting to fall apart. I don't know why, but HP's in trouble. Those fancy TV commercials and newspaper ads, they're all shit. We're gonna miss our projections and it's gonna be announced this month."

And there was more drinking, and some arguing, and some smacks she could hear in her bedroom, and in the morning, as always, Mom left with heavy foundation makeup on her swollen cheeks to try to hide the marks.

On that day Jessica Brown stayed home and hid in her bedroom while Mom went to work at City Hall and Dad called in to Andover and said he would work some leads from home. Which was all crap. On those days that Dad stayed home to "work leads," he worked on his thirst instead. He started in the morning with screwdrivers, then switched to shots of bourbon once the clock chimed noon, and he'd stretch out on the couch and watch movies on TV and doze, wake up, and drink some more.

But today was different. He was his usual angry self and looked out at their small, fenced-in backyard and said, "Jesus effin' Christ, look at what the Sinclairs' trees did to our yard."

Jessica thought it was funny that Dad would blame something not human like the trees, but she had long ago learned not to tease him. Out in the yard was a covered gas grill, a small stone patio, and a picnic table. At the very rear was the Sinclairs' house, with three large pine trees stretched above the stockade fence. The heavy snow overnight had broken off four large branches that were heavily draped over the picnic table.

"Fuck," Dad said, heading to get his boots and coat. "Guess I'm gonna clean up that mess, and you know what I'm gonna do?"

"What's that, Dad?" she asked, hoping he wouldn't ask her to go outside. It was warm and safe inside her bedroom, with a new Harry Potter book, and she dreaded the thought of having to go out in the cold, hauling branches with sticky sap, getting snow down her back and down her boots.

He laughed, but she had never liked her dad's laugh. It was fun on the surface, but underneath there was a lot of anger and hate.

"I'm gonna take those branches and toss 'em over the fence, dump 'em in his yard. Let him take care of it."

Dad went outside without asking for her help. She went up to her bedroom, sat on the bed, and dove into *Harry Potter and the Goblet of Fire*, and soon got lost into the details of a Triwizard Tournament being hosted by Hogwarts Academy.

Pages flipped by. Chapters. Big chunks flew by.

She looked at the digital clock and was stunned at how much time had passed. Where was Dad?

She put the book down on her bed, carefully crept downstairs. If Dad was back in the house, maybe he was snoring on the couch. If so, good; let him be. She could make herself lunch and go back up to her bedroom, not disturb him. It was never a good thing to disturb him.

The living room was empty. So was the kitchen. The bathroom. And with her parents' bedroom across from her own, she knew he wasn't there.

Jessica stood up on her tiptoes and looked out the kitchen window at the backyard. There was a shape in the snow, covered by a tree branch.

It was as cold as she had feared, and she slogged through the knee-deep snow to the rear of the yard. Dad was on his back, with a thick pine branch over his chest. His blue down coat was open, and his jeans were soaked through from the snow. One of his boots had slipped off. His bare foot was white and wrinkled.

Dad's eyes were wide with pain and his face was as gray as an old sock. He was breathing hard.

"Jess . . . Jess . . ."

"Dad."

He groaned, a deep sound she had never heard from him before. "I . . . my chest is hurting something awful. I think . . . I think . . . it might be my heart." Another deep groan. "Run back to the house, okay?" He bit his lower lip, his eyes filling with tears. "Call 911. I need an ambulance. Hurry!"

She turned and slogged through the snow back to the house.

Even as cold as it was, the sun was high up and the sky was clear, a very fresh blue.

Inside she kicked off her boots, tossed off her jacket, and went into the kitchen. The phone was on the near wall, next to the calendar and a little bulletin board that held thumbtacked doctor and dentist appointment cards along with that week's grocery list. A pencil dangled from a string tacked to the board.

She walked further into the kitchen. Looked out the window.

Dad was still.

Jessica made herself a peanut butter sandwich, poured a glass of milk, and sliced up a Granny Smith apple. Back upstairs in her bedroom, she read two more chapters, ate her lunch, and then went back downstairs and carefully washed her dishes and put them away.

What now?

She got dressed again and, very slowly and carefully, went out to where Dad was lying on his back, calling out, "Dad? Dad?"

No answer. His eyes were closed. His chest wasn't moving up and down. His face was a deeper shade of gray.

"Dad?"

Jessica turned and went back to the house, making sure her boots slid into the prints from before, and when she got into the house, she undressed in a mad scramble, tossing boots and coat aside, and then ran to the phone and dialed 911. By the time the Haverhill police operator answered, she had worked up a good head of tears and anguish.

"Please, I need an ambulance! I think my daddy is dead!"

—m—

Jessica finally got up from Emma's bed and went downstairs to grab something to eat, take a shower. As she puttered around in the kitchen, her biggest memory of her dad's funeral was of being hugged by Mom as her three aunts gathered around her, and Mom whispering into her ear. "Now," she said, "now we can have a safe life together. I think God helped us."

And Jessica just thought back then, as ever: *You will never know, Mom. You will never know.*

CHAPTER TWENTY-FOUR

On Monday morning Jessica made two phone calls, the first being to Warner Savings Bank. She chewed on her thumb, wondering who was going to answer and how convincing she could be in lying and saying that she was sick. The truth was, she didn't want to see anyone at work today. For the time being, she just wanted to stay home and vegetate.

"Warner Savings Bank," came a male voice. "How can I help you?"

Percy Prescott.

"Ah, hi, Percy, it's Jessica. I'm sorry, I won't be coming in today."

"Don't blame you," he said. "I'll let the Ice Queen know when she comes in. Anything else?"

Damn, that was a question. And her curiosity took control.

"Percy, everything okay with you?"

"Me?" A low laugh. "I guess so. You're probably asking about my encounter the other day with Warner's finest."

"Ah . . ." Now she wished she had kept her mouth shut. Jessica felt trapped.

Another laugh. "Don't worry. I was in a grumpy mood and that detective wanted to ask me lots of questions about something I didn't give a shit about. Eventually I said something to the effect that it was funny that one bunch of paid goons was trying to help out another bunch of goons—was there a union or something? The detective didn't like it and took me down to the station for the proverbial grilling."

"Percy, I—"

"It's all right," he said. "One of my uncles is a lawyer over in Concord, got me out in less than an hour. Pretty exciting stuff, don't you think?"

"But what were the cops asking you? Were they asking . . ."

She couldn't finish the sentence, but Percy did it for her. "Were they asking if I killed our little *Oberführer*? Not in so many words. But they did want to know if I was at a party at his parents' Saturday night, before he got his head removed. From what I heard, it was quite the raucous night, lots of fighting and screaming. Supposedly somebody who wasn't a student at Warner got tuned up by a couple of the stormtroopers after he showed up and threatened to kill Sam. The detective wanted to know if that had been me."

Jessica kept quiet. One simple phone call, just to call in sick, and it had turned into something else.

"You know what I said?" I said, *"Fuck you, prove it.* And right about then my uncle showed up."

"Oh, Percy. I mean—"

"Yeah, that was some party. Ask your daughter and stepson about it when you can. Hey, look, Rhonda's coming over here . . . Hold on, Jessica, Rhonda wants to talk to you."

She quickly disconnected the call. Closed her eyes quite tight. Remembering Emma telling her last Saturday night that she was going over to study with Bertie Woods.

Detective Rafferty had said that he thought Emma had been there, that there was a witness. But nothing definite. Yet Percy seemed to suggest otherwise.

She opened her eyes, started dialing another number just as her phone told her that a call was arriving from Warner Savings Bank. Jessica ignored it.

At his office in Portland, Gary Talbot was on his computer, trying to figure out if he could salvage something so he could do something fun after paying his bills—maybe he could make just a good-faith deposit on a couple of them—when his phone rang. He swung around in his chair, saw that it was a Maine number, picked it up, and smiled when he heard Sarah Sundance's voice, calling from the York County District Attorney's Office.

"Hey, Gary, how's life out in the private world treating you?" she asked.

"Like crap. Are you surprised?"

In his mind's eye, Gary was warmed at seeing her smile, but he didn't feel quite as warm when she said, "Well, that's what you get when you leave the government teat."

He didn't say anything for a moment, then replied, "I didn't leave of my own accord, Sarah. You know that."

"Yes, that's right. I'm sorry, Gary."

"It's okay."

It wasn't okay, and Sarah seemed to make up for it by saying, "I wanted to see how that Thornton case is playing out for you."

"Thanks again for passing it on," he said. "I'm afraid the guy's sister isn't going to be happy with me. Like you said, there's no there there."

Sarah said, "I hope you got some good billable hours out of it."

About $10,000 worth, he thought, and then he said, "I'm sorry, can you say that again?"

"I said, I'm glad you're upsetting the man's sister and not his widow. Whatshername. Jessica."

He slowly sat up straighter in his chair. "Why's that, Sarah?"

"I thought I had told you."

"If you did, I'm sorry, I forgot what you said about Jessica."

"Oh, I thought I'd do you an additional favor," she said. "So I did a quick background check on her, didn't find much in Haverhill or Warner. No big deal, right? But I did a wider search and found something that happened in Carlisle a few years back, involving both her and her daughter. Scary stuff."

"How scary?"

"This scary," Sarah said, and proceeded to tell him.

In a poorly painted and poorly ventilated room at the Middlesex County Jail, Ted Donovan stared for long seconds at his defense attorney, Helen Wray, not wanting to believe what she had just told him.

He just stared, then cleared his throat and said, "Paula Fawkes. Are you sure? Are you joking?"

Helen looked like a schoolteacher who was not amused. "No, I'm not joking. When I joke, I wiggle my ears. Did you see my ears move, Ted? So let me tell you again: Paula Fawkes told me that on the night the police say Sam Warner was murdered, you and she were not together."

"But we were!"

"That's not what she's telling me."

"But . . . are you sure you have the right date?"

The icy schoolteacher glare came right at him again, and Ted swallowed, told himself to calm the fuck down. But the truth was, it was hard to calm down, even if he had been in jail for not even two full days. But it had been a long two days, being in prison, even though technically it wasn't a prison. It was the Middlesex County House of Correction, and like everyone else behind bars here, Ted wore orange pants and an orange T-shirt that had MIDDLESEX HOC INMATE stenciled on the front.

But his short time here, with the constant noise, the awful food—cold and greasy—and sharing a cell with a young man with lots of tattoos and attitude, who seemed to take great pleasure in sitting on the open metal toilet at night and scratching his exposed crotch while shitting loudly—this short time was enough to make him want to sob with fear and disgust at how he had gotten here.

Helen was still staring. The only woman who was working on his behalf.

"That was stupid of me to say," he said. "I'm sorry, Helen. I just can't believe that Paula wouldn't back me up."

"Where were you that night?"

"Working late, in our office."

"Was anybody else there?"

"No," Ted said. "It was just the two of us."

"And what happened?"

"We had sandwiches, a couple of beers, and—"

Helen shook her head. "What then?"

"Ah . . ."

She said, "Ted, please don't screw with me. I'm doing my best to get you out of here, and I need to know the truth. Did you and this Paula Fawkes have sexual relations?"

Ashamed, face warm, Ted just nodded.

"In the office?"

"Yes."

"And what time did you get home to your wife?"

"Sometime after eleven P.M."

"And what did you tell Jessica?"

"I . . . I, ah, told her I had been out with my business partner. Ben Powell."

"So you lied."

"Yes."

"And when Detective Rafferty came to interview you and Jessica, you told him that you were home that evening."

"Yes."

"And you didn't tell him that you were out with Ben Powell."

"No."

"And you didn't tell him you were out with Paula Fawkes."

"No."

Even in the small room, Ted could hear loud voices outside, the clanging of barred doors being closed, a TV somewhere playing a Spanish-language channel. At this moment he would do or promise anything to get up and walk out with Helen Wray.

Helen said, "So, just to recap, as to your whereabouts the night police believe Sam Warner was murdered, you lied to your wife and lied to the police."

193

What else could he say? "Yes, that's right."

Helen pursed her lips. "Well, I hate to be the bearer of even worse news, but I've found out that your wife isn't going to cover for you either."

It was like the solid concrete and steel floor below was vibrating at some high frequency or speed, because he was having trouble hearing and now found it hard to find the right words. His mouth seized up. He had to chew his tongue.

"What, Jessica won't back me up?"

"That's right," she said. "I had a quick but fruitful discussion with Detective Rafferty. He had a one-on-one with your wife two days ago. Did you know that?"

He couldn't think. All he could do was automatically respond. "No, Helen, I did not know that."

"Well, as part of his interview, he asked Jessica to confirm your original statement, that you were home with her, watching some *Real Housewives* show on Bravo. She said she didn't know where you were but you weren't at home."

Oh, Jesus, he thought. *Oh, Jesus.*

"I . . . shit, well, why won't Paula Fawkes back me up then?

Helen quickly and crisply replied, "She says you weren't with her that night. In fact, more than that, Ted, she denies that the two of you ever had a relationship."

Ted felt the shame and humiliation of being dumped by a woman, even if it was one he had been having an affair with.

"But that's not true."

"Anyone ever see the two of you together? You have motel or hotel receipts that put you in the same place at the same time? Any surveillance video of you going down on her in some public venue?"

"No, but . . ."

Helen cocked her head. "Ted, are you really that dense? Really?"

"Huh?"

"Remind me again what Paula's husband does. And where he currently is."

Again the flush of shame. Now it came to him. How could he have been so stupid?

"Her husband's name is Antonio," Ted admitted. "He's a captain in the army."

Helen shook her head. "No, he's much more than that," she said. "He's a captain in special forces. Sometimes called the Green Berets. In other words, a stone-cold killer working on the behalf of the United States. How do you think he'd react if he came home and found out that his wife had been stepping out while he was risking his ass for hearth and home?"

"Not good," he said.

"Yeah, fine understatement there, Ted. Sorry to say, she's just looking out for herself. That's all. But any hopes of getting your butt out of here due to Paula's coming forth and providing an alibi is gone. And I know Jessica has told the Warner police that she can't provide an alibi either."

The orange shirt and pants he was wearing felt like they were something tattooed to his skin, something that would never, ever be removed.

"What now?"

He felt something cold start to grow in his gullet as he watched Helen gather up her notebook and pen, open up her leather shoulder bag. "I was hoping to get enough evidence right now to get this tossed before arraignment, but that's not going to happen."

His mouth had never been so dry. "Are you giving up?"

"God, no, of course not," she said. "It just means it's going to take longer than either of us want. The next thing will be an arraignment before a judge, where the charges will officially be read out to you. After that, a bail hearing. If we're very, very lucky, you might—and I emphasize the word 'might'—get out for a huge chunk of change and an ankle bracelet. But don't hold your breath."

Helen got up, and from the deep recesses of his mind Ted remembered some family event, when he had been very young, not even in school yet, and had seen his mother leaving without him, and he remembered his screams: *Mama, don't leave! Mama, don't leave!*

"And then?"

"Then we wait for a grand jury to indict you, and we prepare for trial."

She went up to the heavy metal door, knocked on it, and said, "Ready to leave," and per instructions, Ted remained seated. But as the door was unlocked, he said, "Helen, why haven't you asked me if I did it or not?"

Helen said, "Because right now it makes no difference to me."

The door was unlocked and she brushed past the uniformed Middlesex County jail officer. With Helen gone, the guard motioned, and Ted got up. A few minutes later—damn it, why hadn't he asked her about the retainer and why it had to be so big?—he was back in the general population and saw his cellmate standing with a group of his friends, laughing and talking in Spanish. His cellmate caught Ted's eye, gestured to his friends and to Ted, grabbed his crotch, and flicked his tongue at Ted. Everyone over there laughed at him.

Ted just walked away and kept on walking around and around the fixed seats and chairs, thinking of that shitty high school wrestling captain who had put him here.

—⁓—

Emma was in her friend Kate's bedroom on Monday afternoon, both of them on her bed watching *The Big Sick* on the TV, texting each other and their respective friends. They should have been clipping printed-out photos of Kate's grandfather for a school report, but Emma felt like just hanging and relaxing. Kate's mom had made them an afternoon snack of chocolate chip cookies, and Emma felt a bit heavy and bloated.

But she still felt comfortable. She wasn't sure if it was a sugar high or something like that. It was a nice treat, but she couldn't do it again for a while. Too much extra weight to carry out onto the track, which is why her friend always came in second to Emma at meets. Emma felt like telling Kate that if she'd just cut back on some of her desserts—and treats like homemade chocolate chip cookies—she might be able to cut a few seconds off her pace.

Kate said, "I think I got all the photos I need."

"Huh?" Emma said, not looking up from her iPhone.

"The photos of my granddad. The one who served in the navy. Our school report, remember?"

Emma nudged her friend in the side and said, "Yeah, I remember. And I remember you saying you'd help me with the words. And you haven't written a single one."

"Not true," Kate said. "I wrote Granddad's name and the name of his ship. The *Enterprise*. That's three words right there."

Then Kate's mom yelled up at them from downstairs. "Hey, you girls still up there?"

Kate leaned over her bed. "No, Ma, we ran away an hour ago to join the circus!"

Emma snickered, and Mrs. Romer said, "Ha, very funny, cupcake. Emma, your mom's here to see you!"

Kate turned to her. "You want me to come down with you?"

Emma swung off the bed, slipped her iPhone into her pocket. "Nah, it won't take long."

—⁓—

Jessica was pleased to see that Doris Romer was giving her and Emma some space in their deserted sunroom, just off the kitchen. She gave her girl a quick hug and kiss and said, "How are you doing, hon?"

Emma shrugged. "Okay, I guess. What's up?"

"I'm going to Billerica. To see your stepfather. Do you want to come along?"

It looked like Emma had just eaten something that was threatening to crawl up out of her gullet. "Do I have to?"

Jessica said. "Well, I just wanted to see if you wanted to join me."

Emma quickly shook her head. "I'm working on a school project with Kate. We're right in the middle of it and we don't have much more time to finish it."

"It's all right, I understand."

Jessica stepped forward, gave Emma another, longer hug, burying her face in her girl's pure blond hair. She kissed the top of her head and stepped away, tears suddenly forming in her eyes. "You want to come home tonight?"

Emma shook her head once again. "No, Mom," she said. "If it's okay with you, I'd rather stay here one more night, get the project done. Mrs. Romer will take us to school tomorrow. Besides, I'm scared to see those reporters again."

"They're gone, hon."

"But they might come back. Right?"

Jessica didn't feel like dragging this out. She had called her stepson earlier and he had given her a similar brisk, cold message, and she just wanted to get this day over.

"They might," she said. "Okay, you behave now, okay?"

Emma smiled and said, "I'll do my best, Mom."

She went out through the kitchen and Mrs. Romer came back again, her face lined with concern, and took Jessica's hands in hers. They were cold and chapped.

"Oh, Jessica, we're praying for you so much."

She could only nod her thanks.

—m—

Back upstairs, Emma jumped onto Kate's bed again and tried to steal her iPhone away from her, and Kate both laughed and shrieked as she backed away to the near wall.

"Knock it off!" Kate said, and Emma laughed again, dug out her own iPhone, and started looking to see what messages she might have missed while talking to Mom.

Emma sat up against the pillow and Kate said, "Everything okay?"

"Yep."

"What's up with your mom?"

"She's off to visit my stepdad in jail. Ugh."

"Ugh," Kate said. "You still okay?"

"Yep." Remembering something important, Emma said, "Ask you something?"

"Sure," her friend said.

"What do you think about Craig?"

"Your stepbro? Ick. No offense, I think he's a slug. A hairy slug."

Emma shrugged. "That's a good one."

Kate said, "Hey, you want to start working on that project now?"

Emma held her phone in her hands. Eight messages to reply to . . .

"Nah," she said. "What's the rush?"

CHAPTER TWENTY-FIVE

Jessica Thornton was surprised to find out that her visit with Ted was taking place in a more public setting. Instead of the thick glass windows, metal, phone receivers with thick cords, and signs that said ALL CONVERSATIONS SUBJECT TO RECORDING, they were in something called a public tier. This meant that Ted and the other inmates—she still couldn't get her head around using "Ted" and "inmate" in the same sentence—were seated on heavy plastic seats bolted to the concrete floor, in front of heavy plastic oval tables, also bolted down, with their visitors sitting across from them.

If her earlier visit to Ted had been surreal, this one was out deep in the twilight zone. Before her and to the left and to the right were about a dozen other inmates. Ted was the oldest and, as far as she could tell, the only Caucasian. On her side, again, Jessica was the oldest, and except for one woman at the far end, every other woman had a child or children with her. There was a heavy smell of sweat and disinfectant.

The kids did their best with dolls or other toys in their hands, but their wide eyes and questioning faces told the heartbreaking story of why they were in front of Daddy, unable to touch him or get a hug.

Jessica couldn't look at the kids and found it hard to look at her husband. The orange T-shirt and pants were worn and baggy, and Ted's skin had faded in color, as if he had been underground in a cave for a month. His face sagged more than usual, and his eyes flickered with fear as he looked around him.

"I'm in trouble," he said.

No shit, Sherlock, she thought. "I know, Ted."

"It's because I don't have an alibi for the night that kid got killed."

Jessica just looked away from him, up at the upper levels, where uniformed guards looked down.

"Why are we here?" Jessica asked. "The last visit we had to talk with phones, behind the glass."

His arms were stretched out in front of him. His hands were quivering. Ted saw that she was looking at them and quickly clasped them together.

"Jessica, I don't know. Something was wrong with the phone system—it wasn't working right, so we got dumped here. Which is good, because we've got things to talk about and this is a great opportunity. Jessica, I was counting on your alibi to help me—at least to raise questions in the judge's mind so I could get out on bail. But Helen Wray tells me that you're not going to stick up for me. In fact, she said that you later told Detective Rafferty that I lied about being home. Jess, how could you do that to me?"

Even in their roughest times, Jessica had always thought Ted was an attractive and rugged man, but now he was looking and sounding like a disappointed child.

"It was easy," she said. "Because it was the truth."

"Jess!"

She slightly shook her head. "Ted, that night—where were you?"

His eyes flicked back and forth again. "You know what I told you."

"That's what you said, but where were you, Ted? More to the point, who were you with?"

Jessica imagined that at this point Ted's face would turn a ruddy color from the shame and embarrassment, but, no, it retained the same pale look.

Like her dad, that frosty day in the backyard.

"I was out with Paula Fawkes."

There. The stab to the gut that she knew was always going to strike her, the only question being when and where. Over the past few days

201

there had been thoughts and suggestions of confronting him after dinner, or in the bedroom, or in the kitchen before the two of them went off to work. The thoughts had even gone as far to imagine the raised voices, the shouting, the screaming.

But never had she imagined that she would be so calm. Or that the confrontation would be held *here*, at a visiting area within the Middlesex County House of Correction.

"Did you fuck her before you got home?" she asked.

He held a hand up to his eyes, as if some bright overhead light had suddenly switched on.

"Jessica, please."

"Come on, Ted. Man up. Did you fuck her before you came home?"

Almost a whisper: "Yes."

"Okay, then," she said. "Now we're at the truth. That means I can't and won't lie for you, Ted. Do you understand?"

The barest of nods.

"Helen has made it quite clear that she's defending you. She's not defending me or our family. Just you. So if you need help with your alibi, go to your girlfriend."

"She's not my girlfriend."

A flare of anger unexpectedly roared through her. She leaned toward him and said, "Then your fuck buddy, or work whore, or whatever she is to you. Have her speak up for you."

"She won't," he said, speaking slowly, each syllable dragging through the shame. "She's told Helen that the two of us weren't . . . weren't even a couple."

Two words came to her, even though it made her slightly ill: poor Ted.

"Now I see what you meant," Jessica said, "when you said earlier that you're in trouble. You had two chances for an alibi the night Sam Warner was murdered and both of them don't exist."

Down the row of women and children, an infant in a bright pink onesie with a bow clipped to her fine hair started bawling, and her mother, also paying attention to two older girls, did her best to calm her down, jiggling the infant up and down on a thick leg. Her male companion held out two thickly tattooed arms and tried singing a lullaby in Spanish. A woman guard started over to their table.

Ted loudly exhaled. "That's why I've been thinking about telling Helen about the kids. What they were doing that night."

Where the hell did that come from? Jessica felt that if she had a knife in her hand right now, she would plunge it into Ted's chest.

"No," she said. "Don't even think that."

Ted opened his hands as he pleaded his case. "Look, you and I both know they were out that night. And that scavenger hunt story . . . C'mon, it was bullshit. We both know it was bullshit."

"How are you so sure?"

"Kids today—who the hell has the interest or time to do scavenger hunts? They'd rather sit on their asses at home and text each other, or play World of Warcraft or Candy Crush or something stupid like that. And we both saw what the tracking software said. They were both in the same area where Sam was shot."

"Their phones were there, at the murder scene," she said. "You can't say the kids were."

Ted's eyes widened. "Jesus Christ, Jessica, if someone comes to your teller window with a check made out to them for a half-million dollars and no ID, are you going to slide that money over, just like that? Don't be so gullible. You really think that the night Sam got murdered Emma and Craig went to the town common and hid their phones in plastic bags, and while they were out searching for old mailboxes and lawn furniture, some mysterious person took their phones, met up with Sam Warner, blew off his head, and then returned the phones? Really? Something weird went on that night, and we should tell the police it involved Craig and Emma."

Jessica reached down and grabbed her leather purse. "Ted, you do this, you'll be hurting Craig, not just Emma. Your son—he's the one who's had the fights with Sam Warner over the months. You tell the police that he might have been at the murder scene and you bring Emma into it."

He said, "If that gets me out of here . . . well, Jessica, I've got to think about it. I need to tell Helen what happened with their phones."

"But Craig—you'd do that to Craig?"

"He's a juvenile, Jessica," he said. "Once the word gets out about the bullying he put up with and—"

"No," she said, voice rising. "No. You will not do that. I forbid it, Ted. If it was just Craig, fine, I could give a shit about your whacked son. But not my daughter. I won't allow it. Not my daughter."

"I might not have a choice."

Jessica was on her feet. "You do have a choice, and you better make the right one. Leave my daughter out of this. Or else."

He stood up as well. "Or else what, Jessica? You threatening me?"

As she turned to walk out, Jessica said, "No. I'm promising you."

—m—

Craig saw the buildings and barbed wire fences of the Middlesex County House of Correction come into view late that Monday afternoon and started rubbing his hands on his pant legs, something he always did when he got nervous. Once he had tried to wear a rubber band around his wrist so he could snap it anytime the urge came over him, but he found he snapped it so much that the skin around his right wrist started turning red.

Ben Borman said, "You okay, Craig?"

"Yeah, I'm okay," he lied.

The drive had taken less than a half hour and he was surprised to see where they were. Craig had had the idea that a jail was in some scummy neighborhood with lots of rundown buildings and trashy streets, but for the past ten minutes they had been going past open farmland, stone walls, and nice houses. Even the jail looked kinda nice, if you ignored the barbed wire and fences. It was mostly brick and even had a white steeple. Ben Borman noted that and said, "Looks like a goddamn church, now, doesn't it?"

"I appreciate you bringing me here, Mr. Borman," Craig said, and this time he didn't lie. He did appreciate it. He knew that Jessica was also coming here today, but he didn't want to be with her while he visited Dad.

"Not a problem, kid. Glad I could help out. Mark, you stay in the truck, okay?"

Craig's bud Mark was sitting in the middle of the wide seat of the Ford F-150 pickup truck, and all the way down to North Billerica he'd been playing BattleBot IV on his iPhone while Craig just stared out the window.

Mark grunted and Craig got out, and so did Mr. Borman. He was about Craig's dad's age but was bulkier around the chest, had thick forearms and heavy hands, and his face was mostly hidden by a bushy black beard streaked with gray. He worked somewhere in Lawrence as a welder, did a lot of renovation work around his house, was an avid hunter, and he seemed amused by his geeky son. Mr. Borman had on dirty work boots, jeans, and a torn farmer's coat, but Craig thought the guy had smarts. Not like Dad, who could run numbers and make real estate deals, but last year, when a small freezer in their basement seemed to crap out, Dad had made a big deal of buying a new one and hauling the old one to the dump. By the time he had gotten the new freezer up and running, he found out the problem was an open circuit breaker. Mr. Borman was the kind of guy who wouldn't make that kind of mistake.

Craig followed him up a pathway that had signs that said VISITORS, and he found that his mouth tasted funny. He couldn't believe Dad was in here. Over the years Dad had taken him along—okay, dragged him along was a better word—to lots of different houses, trailers, and businesses, just to show Craig what it took to sell something. Craig thought Dad was trying to get him buzzed to join the real estate business at some point, but it sure did backfire. Meeting all those people? Trying to sell something? Getting shot down, day after day?

Nope. Just give him a computer and quiet time, and that's all Craig wanted from life. Well, except for one other thing.

"Here we go, kid," Mr. Borman said, opening the door, and they went into chaos.

There was a waiting area with scuffed and dirty chairs. The floor was scuffed, too. The place was practically full of women, young and old, and lots of kids. Besides feeling out of place as the youngest male in the waiting area, Craig felt really uncomfortable at being the only white kid in the room.

But he was pretty much ignored when Mr. Borman and he went up to a glass-enclosed area that looked like a bank drive-up station where a bored-looking young woman in a sheriff's uniform said, "Have you filled out your paperwork yet?"

"Ah, no," Mr. Borman said. "I just brought Craig here to see his father. Ted Donovan."

The woman said, "Do you know where the inmate is?"

Mr. Borman leaned in so he could speak better through the grille. There was a lot of noise coming from the women and children patiently waiting in the plastic chairs. "Wait, what? Has he been transferred somewhere?"

She looked both bored and exasperated. "No, I meant where is he in the facility? Do you know which tier he's in, or which pod? On Mondays we allow visitors in Pods A, C, and D, and in Dorm Two, Tiers A and B, along with J, K, and L."

Craig felt the familiar panic of not knowing something important, like being asked to write an English essay with only twenty minutes to get it done. Damn it, maybe he should have come with Jessica instead of saying no so quickly.

The woman added, "Has he just been placed here?"

Mr. Borman said, "Yes, just a couple of days ago."

The woman shook her head. "Well, he won't be in the work-release area. What's his name?"

Craig stepped forward. "Ted Donovan. He's my dad."

She stared at him. "And you want to see him?"

"Yes."

"How old are you?"

"Seventeen."

She looked to Mr. Borman. "Are you his legal guardian?"

He said, "No. He and my boy are friends."

The woman shook her head. "Sorry. Nobody under eighteen is allowed to visit an inmate unless accompanied by a parent or a legal guardian."

Craig couldn't stand it. "But I want to see my dad! Please!"

Again the head shake. "Sorry, those are the regulations. I don't make them. I'm sorry."

Mr. Borman said, "Oh, come on, this is the man's son. I'll be there with him. What could go wrong?"

The officer said, "I'd lose my job, that's what."

Craig said, "Can I give him a note? Please?"

She hesitated.

Mr. Borman backed him up. "C'mon. A note. We drove all the way down here from Warner. What's wrong with that?"

There was movement behind the barrier and a pen and a slip of paper appeared. "Make it quick. I shouldn't be doing this, so make it quick."

Mr. Borman said, "Thanks," but Craig was too busy thinking of what he could write to say a word to anyone.

One way or another, he was going to get his dad out.

GRECO-GUY: Hey. Anybody here? Anybody?

GRECO-GUY: Hello?

GRECO-GUY: Craig, you there?

HOPPERHERO: I'm here

GRECO-GUY: Weird handle

HOPPERHERO: Whatever. We got a deal?

GRECO-GUY: What, you didn't feel like chatting F2F? Or via email?

HOPPERHERO: Don't want to see you. And email can be easily tracked

GRECO-GUY: LOL. Afraid your loser dad will find out? Or the NSA? LOL

HOPPERHERO: We got a deal?

HOPPERHERO: We got a deal?

HOPPERHERO: Sam?

GRECO-GUY: Yeah, we got a deal. Same date and place

HOPPERHERO: No, I want to do it tomorrow night

GRECO-GUY: ? Why?

HOPPERHERO: Look, let's just get it done, okay?

GRECO-GUY: Okay. Tomorrow night. Time?

HOPPERHERO: Ten?

GRECO-GUY: Hah. Thought that'd be past your bedtime

HOPPERHERO: I've got to get her out there, too. Ten works for us

GRECO-GUY: Okay

HOPPERHERO: Okay

HOPPERHERO: Same place?

GRECO-GUY: Yah. Wooden footbridge, by Olson Trail

HOPPERHERO: Okay

HOPPERHERO: The deal tho. I need to make sure you know the deal

GRECO-GUY: Sure. Video of Emma. U give me 10 million bucks

HOPPERHERO: Not funny

GRECO-GUY: Yeah, but I'm laffing

HOPPERHERO: The deal

GRECO-GUY: Jesus Christ you fag. Yeah. Thumbdrive with Emma's video. I give it to u and she finishes the job

HOPPERHERO: Only if thumbdrive has the only copy of video

GRECO-GUY: What? U no trust me?

HOPPERHERO: Thumbdrive has only copy. Or deal is off

GRECO-GUY: Okay promise double-promise triple-promise

HOPPERHERO: Don't fuck with me, Sam. U know how good I am at computers. I can hack u and find it if you put it someplace else

GRECO-GUY: Ooh Im so fucking scared

HOPPERHERO: And then I'll hack your Pop and Mum. Screw with their investments. Let them know what I did and why I did it. Tell them what kind of good boy u really are

HOPPERHERO: U there?

HOPPERHERO: U there?

GRECO-GUY: Yah I'm here.

HOPPERHERO: We got a deal?

GRECO-GUY: Fuck u. We got a deal. Thumbdrive with video and your slut sister finishes the job.

HopperGuy: She's not my sister

GRECO-GUY: What?

HopperGuy: She's my stepsister asshole

HopperGuy HAS SIGNED OUT

Greco-Guy HAS SIGNED OUT

CHAPTER TWENTY-SIX

It was Tuesday morning, and once again Jessica had called in sick. She lucked out once more and spoke with Amber Brooks, who seemed all sympathy and good wishes, but Jessica hung up without a word when Amber said that Rhonda wanted to talk to her.

Dear Rhonda. There were at least ten or twelve messages on her iPhone and landline from Rhonda, but she wasn't going to let herself talk to Rhonda and go down a long series of conversations that could end up with something going awry. Rhonda was a sweetie, but years of experience dealing with all types of banking customers had left her with one suspicious attitude if she felt something was off. Jessica wasn't about to give her or anybody else that opportunity. As much as she cherished her old friend.

Now she was at Powell & Sons Contractors, in front of the old yellow two-story house that had been converted into offices in what passed for a rundown neighborhood in Warner. Jessica slowed down her Sentra. There was a dirt driveway to the right and she took it. At the rear of the house, she parked next to an overflowing green dumpster, near two pickup trucks, a dump truck, and some yellow piece of earth-moving machinery—an excavator, a digger, she didn't know the term—on a flatbed trailer. There was a row of distressed pine trees at the border and a fenced-in area holding various pieces of construction equipment, plus a thin-looking pit bull, who paced back and forth and barked at her.

Suddenly she thought, God, could Ted have called Ben Powell to screw things up? Would he do that? To get back at her?

No, she thought. Ted thought the money was going to pay for his defense. He wouldn't jeopardize that. Oh, no, she thought, he'd turn in his son and ruin Emma's life, all to get his ass out of jail, but he wouldn't think of stiffing his attorney, the one who was trying to save him.

The inside of the house was cramped, with cubicles and offices and a scarecrow-thin woman wearing a red jumper out front who was Ben Powell's wife, Monica. She picked up a phone from her cluttered desk and said, "Ben? Yeah, she's here." She hung up the phone, pointed down the corridor. "Last door on the left. Ben's waiting for you."

Jessica went down to the office, hearing phones ringing and people talking and smelling dirt and the scent of diesel fuel and asphalt. At the last door two large men in mud-splattered jeans, gray hoodies, and yellow work boots were standing in front of a metal desk where Ben Powell was rustling through a sheaf of papers. Jessica stood to one side and listened.

"You morons!" Powell said. "The address you were supposed to go to was 14 Forest Road, and you ended up at 14 Forest Lane."

The man on the left said, "Ben, look, the GPS, it took us there, and—"

Powell threw down the papers. "And if the GPS took you to Walden Pond, would you sink one of my dump trucks trying to drop a load of gravel in the center? Jesus. Thank God the property owner stopped you before you got too far on tearing down his garage. Christ. I've got insurance, but you better believe you guys are going to help pay for the deductible. Now, you two morons, get out of here."

The two men bumbled and stumbled out as if they were junior high boys being dismissed from the principal's office. Powell leaned to the side and said, "Jess? You there? Come on in."

Jessica went into the office, which contained bookcases filled with rolled-up blueprints and designs, filing cabinets, and toy models of construction equipment. She sat down and Powell said, "You doing okay, Jess?"

"Reasonable, I guess," she said.

Powell shook his head. He had on a blue button-down oxford shirt, sleeves rolled up over his beefy forearms, which bore faded tattoos of anchors and waves from his time in the Seabees.

"Jesus, Ted—I can't believe it."

"Neither can I," she said, wiping her eyes. "It's a real shock."

"And poor Sam Warner. And his parents. My boy Paul, he was on the wrestling team when Sam was just a freshman. Even back then, that Sam was a special kid. Everybody knew he'd go far, maybe even the goddamn Olympics if it all worked out. Hard to believe somebody wanted to kill him. Just a kid!"

Jessica nodded. "It is unbelievable, isn't it? I mean, in Warner, of all places."

Powell nodded. "How's your running girl?"

"Staying with friends for a couple of days," Jessica said. "The news media—TV, photographers, reporters—they're gone now but who knows if they'll come back or not. And the *Daily News*. Imagine seeing your spouse's photo on the front page. It's awful."

"And Craig?"

"Ah, he's staying with friends, too. I hope we can get them both back home in a day or two."

"And Ted?"

"He's holding up."

Powell's bushy eyebrows lifted up. "Really? When he called me at home on Sunday he seemed pretty rattled. He could barely get a sentence out without having to catch his breath."

Jessica said, "Well, I just saw him yesterday. He's got a good lawyer. She thinks the case against him is weak, and . . ."

She thought, *C'mon, c'mon, I've got to get back on the road and meet up with Gary Talbot, give him the payoff.* What's the holdup?

Powell spread both of his hands on the desktop. "Jess, I've done a lot of projects with Ted. He's a good guy. You don't need a contract with him, just a handshake."

Jessica kept quiet. What the hell?

"This Concord project—both of us were counting on it. It was a lifeline—no, it was a lifeboat. I know Ted was counting on the subdivision work to put his real estate agency back in the black, and me . . . Shit, Jess, we've been scraping around here and there, trying to get projects lined up to keep us afloat. The building business is barely moving, and we get undercut on lots of bids 'cause we don't have illegals working on our crews."

"Ben, please, I don't have much time." She checked the clock on Powell's desk. Christ, if she didn't get moving, and if traffic was heavy . . .

Powell said, "On Sunday I told Ted that yeah, I'd spot him the money he needs to pay for his lawyer. Christ, I should have been a JAG in the navy instead of building things, I'd be in a hell of a lot better shape. But I've slept on it, Jess. I'm sorry. I can't give you the money."

She kept it together. Breathed in. Breathed out. Time was slipping away. If she didn't show up to see Gary Talbot, how would he take it? As an insult? A broken promise? Would he go back to Portland and call Grace Thornton, tell her that yes, there was now solid evidence that her former sister-in-law had done things that had led to her brother being killed, even if it had been an accident?

And that trust fund—as a trustee, what would Grace Thornton do? Would she work on Emma's behalf? Or in her continued quest for revenge, would she ruin Jessica, ruin her daughter?

"That's quite a shock, Ben," she said, gently choosing the words. "I'm sure Ted is going to be very, very disappointed."

Powell nodded. "I'm sure. But things are tough all around. We've got to look out for our own interests, and my company . . . I hate to say this, Jess, but I'm not going to let this Concord subdivision project go belly-up because Ted's in jail. I might have to find another partner, and I'm still going to need the funds we received. Eventually I'll make it right for Ted, but right now, I don't see what else I can do."

Jessica said, "You could keep your promise to Ted, give me the twelve thousand dollars we need."

He stayed quiet.

She said, "You know what this means, don't you? Ted won't be able to afford his attorney, and she's already done great work for him. That means we might have to file for bankruptcy, get a public defender for Ted."

"I'm sorry, Jess, I can't do it. My hands are tied. I know you must be upset, and Ted, too, but I've got to do what I've got to do."

Emma. All for Emma.

"You know, Ben," Jessica said, "working at the bank, I get to know lots of people. The fire chief. The selectmen. The police chief. And Emmett Clark. You know who Emmett Clark is, don't you?"

Powell's face tightened, colored up. "The editor of the *Warner Daily News.*"

"That's right. I see him almost every week. A very nice fellow, but a tough journalist. I mean, he's a good customer of mine, very friendly, but that didn't stop him from putting Ted's photo on the front page. Am I right?"

"Jess—"

"And he's always looking for new stories. I mean, he always makes a joke when he comes in about wishing the bank would get robbed so he'd be guaranteed a nice front page the next day. He's old but still eager to find juicy news stories. So imagine how eager he'd be if he found out that a local contractor was getting money from Gus Spinelli, a mobster from Boston's North End. Money that would help scam the Concord zoning board to approve a controversial housing development. Do you think he'd like a story like that?"

The contractor who earlier had been chewing out construction workers twice his size seemed to have shrunk right before Jessica's hard gaze.

"Jess, please."

"Ben, you made a promise. Give me the money. Now. Or I'll call Emmett."

"Jess . . . you wouldn't dare."

She smiled. "Ben, try me."

—∞—

Same restaurant, same kind of day, and for all Gary Talbot knew, this was the same booth at the Exit 5 Truck Stop on Route 128 in Avon. But things today were different.

Before his conversation yesterday with Sarah Sundance about Jessica Thornton's arrest record in Carlisle, Gary had thought he had the bank-teller mom pegged. An overwhelmed, dull woman, grinding along in a teller's job, desperately trying to keep it all together so that her sacred trust fund would be preserved for her equally sacred high school daughter.

Now? Now he knew better. He felt like he had during his rookie year when he had pulled over a Chevy with New York license plates that had done a lane change just a tad too quickly and sloppily on a southbound lane on I-95 just outside Saco. He had pulled over the car and everything came back fine: license, registration, nothing in the system to raise any flags or warnings. Clean, no worries.

But yet . . . The driver had been Hispanic—at the time Gary had been too young and dumb to know whether the guy was Mexican, Puerto Rican, or Dominican—and he had been polite, but something had been going on there, behind those bright eyes and smiling face.

It was like feeling something changing in the air when you see thunderstorm clouds rise up in the distance. Something off, something wrong.

But it was late at night and Gary had no reason to hold the New York driver, so off he went.

And about a month later, and purely by accident, he saw a story in one of the New York tabloids that a trooper originally from New York liked to buy. On page four or five, there was the same guy, except it was a mug shot, and the story said that the guy was Cuban, a contract killer who had came down from Canada to wipe out the top tier of a drug gang in Queens.

—m—

Jessica Thornton strode into the restaurant with a striking air of confidence, carrying her leather purse in one hand, wearing the tan overcoat and black slacks.

Not the same woman who had come here the first time.

Yeah, Gary had the identical feeling from that early-summer evening as a rookie trooper. Something dangerous was now in the vicinity.

She slid into the booth and said, "I want to make this quick."

"Fair enough," he said.

She turned and looked into her purse, pulled out a thick business-sized envelope, slid it over the table. "Count it if you want, asshole. Ten thousand dollars."

Gary picked up the envelope, thought he'd feel a sense of success or accomplishment, but a voice suddenly started whispering to him about how far he had fallen since he had been a trooper with the Maine State Police. And Sarah Sundance, his friend from the York County Attorney General's Office—what would she think? And the rest of his buds in the troop?

He didn't feel great. He felt soiled.

But he still took the envelope and slipped it into the inside pocket of his suit jacket, sighing with pleasure at the thought of so many bills that were going to be paid over the next few days.

"All right, Mrs. Thornton, I don't need to count it."

"You trust me?"

"Probably not," Gary said. "But may I have a minute?" The smart thing would have been to walk out right now, but something about this calm-looking mom sitting across from him was bugging him, something he couldn't leave alone. And he wanted to make her uneasy as well, if only for a moment.

"Make it a quick minute," she said.

Gary said, "It's like this. I've done some additional research into the night your husband was killed."

"My first husband," she said. "You're wasting your minute. Go on."

He said, "I found out that the Maine State Police barracks in Alfred got a phone call that same night, maybe about fifteen minutes before the car accident. The anonymous caller said there was a drunk driver weaving in and out of traffic on I-95. The caller even got the make of the vehicle right, as well as the Massachusetts license plate."

The woman sitting across from him kept quiet. A waitress approached, but perhaps sensing the tension from them, that it was not a time to interrupt, turned around and headed to another row of booths.

"But the call came in too late," Gary went on. "Your drunk husband struck a deer, went off the road, hit a tree."

Jessica said, "Too bad."

"Yes, too bad," he said. "But I found out a few more things, going back and talking to his former employees. He was concerned that even with his being on the wagon, you might file for divorce. And that one screwup on his part might get a judge to be more sympathetic to your cause and that of your little girl."

"I think I told you last time, leave my little girl out of it."

"Almost done," Gary said. "So, here's something interesting. That anonymous phone call—it came from a public phone in Haverhill. Outside a 7-Eleven store. Less than two blocks from where you were living at the time. That's pretty amazing, I mean, that someone would know of your husband's drunken driving in Maine from a public phone in Massachusetts. And that this person would know who to call in Maine—I mean, the correct state police barracks and all."

Jessica stayed quiet, so he continued. "It's almost like someone called the Maine State Police wanting to have Bobby pulled over for drunk driving so that he'd have an OUI arrest in Maine, not in Massachusetts. Something his wife could take to a judge to say he couldn't be trusted around his daughter, something that would make the judge want to ensure a healthy alimony. Something I considered back when we first met. And now, after I dug around some more, it sounds like I was right."

She said, "That's . . . a possibility. But there's a big problem with your possibility, even with Bobby's last phone call."

"What's that?"

"You can't prove it," she said.

"You know I can't," he said. "But—"

"What? You wanted me to know that you might have figured something out? You wearing a wire for the Maine State Police? Good luck with that.

I didn't do it, and even if I did do it, there's no proof. Even with that call. Bobby felt drunk for some reason. Nothing else. No connection to me. But here's something for sure."

Gary said, "What's that?"

She nodded in his direction. "I've made your fucking payment. Now you go tell Grace there's nothing there about her brother's car accident, and she leaves me alone, leaves Emma alone, leaves you alone, and everyone else."

"You know I can't guarantee that."

"But you'll do your best, right?" she asked. "Or there will be consequences. I'll call Grace myself, tell her that you rooked her. I'll call whatever licensing agency you have in Maine to complain about what you've done to me. And that'll be just the beginning."

"The beginning of what?" he asked, knowing he was right on the edge of pushing her too hard.

The woman's face was sharp, hard. Not the face of a quiet housewife.

"You think you know what I'm capable of," she said. "Don't make me prove it again to you, Mr. Talbot. Accidents can still happen."

Then Jessica Thornton got up from the booth.

—⁓—

Jessica wanted to be out of this place as quickly as she could, but one last sentence from the son-of-a-bitch detective halted her just as she got up, her leather bag feeling light in her right hand.

"Like what you did in Carlisle, perhaps?" he asked.

That froze her. Sneaky bastard.

"The charges were dropped," she said, standing still. Other people in the restaurant were laughing, drinking coffee and juice, eating and being very happy and unconcerned. Jerks.

"They surely were," he said. "But you were lucky."

"No," she said, "they were lucky."

The private detective looked . . . concerned? Frightened? Whatever it was, it made her glad. She shifted her bag from one hand to the other.

Gary slowly nodded. "You—yes, you've been lucky. I don't know how, don't know why. But, Mrs. Thornton, I've had a fair bit of luck myself. So let's keep it at that, all right? I'll call your ex-husband's sister, tell her that there's nothing to her concerns. Then we're done. I won't contact you ever again. I'll even delete Bobby Thornton's recording."

Jessica said, "Good. And Mr. Talbot?"

"Yes?"

"Your luck sucks, or else you'd still be a Maine state trooper. Goodbye."

—◊—

Through the window, Gary watched the Thornton woman walk to her Sentra and thought, *Bitch.* Maybe he should have pushed for the twenty thousand instead of the ten thousand.

Maybe.

But now that he knew about what she had done in Carlisle, and with her young daughter right there next to her, well, it was probably for the best.

He reached down for his Galaxy phone, scrolled through until he found Grace Thornton's name and phone number, and started the call, knowing it would be a rotten call but also knowing that in just over an hour he'd be back in Maine, $10,000 richer, and he'd never see this truck stop, or that woman, ever again.

Some blackmailers liked to squeeze and squeeze, get as much green as possible. But not him. The woman was right. His luck probably did suck, but he was smart enough to leave well enough alone.

—◊—

At the Warner Public Library, Jessica sat in a chair before one of the public computer terminals, waiting for the damn thing to wake up and finally get working. These IBM clones were old, moved slowly, and some days it was as if the town library still depended on dial-up modems.

"Damn dinosaur," she whispered, wondering if Grace had gotten that phone call, the one Gary Talbot had promised. She remembered seeing a documentary a few years back about the nutty Frenchman who had walked on a wire between the two World Trade Towers in New York, back when they were still standing. Ted had said, "God, think how scary it must be, stepping out like that," and Jessica had said, "The first step is the easiest. The dangerous part is when you get closer to the other end, almost getting it done, and you slip or lose your nerve."

Yeah. Like right now.

Gary Talbot, Grace Thornton, and the ghost of Bobby Thornton were taken care of. In just a few more years Emma would be out of school, with a great nest egg to start whatever future she wanted. Now it was just Ted and the mess he had gotten himself into. What to do about that?

On the chair next to her was a discarded *Warner Daily News* from a couple of days ago, so to pass the long seconds waiting for the computer to finally come online, she picked it up, wincing at the big headline on the front page about Sam Warner's murder and the reprint of Ted's real estate advertisement photo. She flipped past the front page, went through the paper to her favorite page. The Warner police log.

Jessica started reading it, and then, about five seconds later, it wasn't her favorite page anymore.

> 11:14 P.M., Tuesday: Warner Police responded to Mast Road after a report of a car being abandoned. The VW Jetta was registered to Randolph McMahon of Warner. Police said a local driver nearby saw a blond woman and a tall man leave the vehicle and walk north. The vehicle was later towed.

Jessica dropped the paper.

Randy McMahon. Why did that name sound familiar?

Randy McMahon. A friend of Craig's. Who sometimes drove Craig and Emma to and from school.

The computer screen was no longer frozen. Jessica called up Google Maps, punched in "Mast Road, Warner," and although she knew what was going to appear, she had to see it for herself.

There. Mast Road ran right adjacent to the Warner Town Forest. And walking north . . . would lead you in a few minutes to a trailhead. And from there . . . right to the wooden bridge, right to the place where Sam Warner had been murdered.

She quickly closed the Google Maps page, not wanting anyone to see what she had up on the screen.

A band of steel seemed to be constricting her chest. Okay. No panicking. Grace Thornton was taken care of. Ted was . . . Ted could handle himself. She was sure of it. But Emma?

Jessica wasn't about to have Emma caught up in this mess, this horrid story. She could see the hungry and despicable reporters roaring back into Warner, finding another juicy piece of news to go with the story of the noble young wrestling team captain cut down in his youth, with his rich and suffering mom and dad being trotted out again before the cameras.

And Emma. Gifted, flawless, her running princess Emma . . . to be connected to this horror show? No.

But what to do?

What she had planned to do, and then . . . well, she'd figure it out. She always did.

Jessica started typing, cutting, pasting, and deleting, and felt that steel band start to loosen up. It would be all right

A few more minutes of work, and then she logged out of the library's computer system, picked up her purse, and went past the circulation desk and then right out onto the granite steps of the old building. Where she nearly ran into Rhonda Monroe.

Rhonda looked up at her, shocked, two hardcover books in her hand, big purse over her shoulder.

"Jessica," Rhonda finally stammered out. "You called in sick today. And why won't you return my calls?"

CHAPTER TWENTY-SEVEN

At Warner High School there was a five-minute gap between periods, and during the time before the last period of school that Tuesday, Craig Donovan hustled along the corridors, brushing past kids yammering or walking and texting, those hanging out around their lockers, with the buzz of laughter, loud talk, and the slamming of locker doors. He nodded a couple of times to kids he knew, but he had no time to see anyone except his bitch stepsister.

Craig turned a corner and there she was, holding court with her track friends. Damn it, just seeing her and three of her friends together, laughing and gossiping, made everything change for him. His face warmed, his skin seemed to tingle, his hands and feet swelled, making him stumbling and awkward.

Just turn around, a scared voice inside him said. *Just turn around.*

He almost did that, but no, not this time. Not this time!

He swallowed and took a large breath, pushed his way through, and said, "Emma, I need to talk to you."

Emma was laughing at something one of her friends had said and didn't look at him. "Later, Craig. I've got Algebra II in a few minutes."

"Now, Emma."

She turned to him, still smiling, her cold blue eyes looking at him, and Craig had a thought: *How can you go through life with such perfection? Long blond hair that's never tangled? Skin that never breaks out? Classmates who want to hang with you?*

Emma said, "Craig, I'm busy. Later."

Her three friends and fellow track team members—Gwen Tisdale, Blythe Cohen, Carol Niven—snickered and whispered, "Hey, it's the fag," and his feet felt like they were still swelling in his sneakers. He said, "Emma, I'm ducking out of social studies. I'm through. Just wanted to let you know."

That got her attention, and he felt a little thrill of satisfaction, seeing that cool and perfect face quickly wrinkle with concern.

"Girls," Emma said. "Give me a minute with my . . . brother, will you?"

As if they were connected as one, the giggling girls slipped away, and Emma stepped back against an alcove that held a water fountain.

"You shit, what the hell do you mean by that?" she demanded.

"You heard me," he said. "I'm through, I'm out of here." He turned, and she grabbed his arm.

Keep cool, Emma thought, *keep cool, you're in a race now, a race for keeps, and you can outrun this clown on any track, in any circumstance.* She grabbed his right arm and tugged him back. "No, don't go," she said.

He shook his arm free. "Nope, it's time. You promised and promised, and I got nothing. Nothing, Emma! I'm not gonna let my dad stay in jail."

She stepped closer to him, even smelled the sweat coming off his skin. "What are you saying, Craig?"

"What do you think? I'm going to the cops. Now."

Shit!

Emma switched gears, said, "Please don't, Craig. Please. It'll ruin everything."

"Everything? The hell with you. It'll get my dad out of jail, and you can do what you want. I don't care anymore. You promised me—promised me you'd set me up with Kate Romer, and nothing's happened, and—"

"Tonight," Emma blurted out, knowing she had to prevent this stinky moron from going to the police. The cops! "I'll handle it tonight. I promise. Name the place and time. I'll get Kate there with you. I promise."

She looked at him with a fearful face and slowly bit her lower lip, hoping, praying, part of her shuddering at knowing what she had just promised, knowing that she was lying to the sap, she would never, ever go through with it.

"No," he said. "You're a damn liar, Emma. I'm off to the cops."

"You can't!"

The asshole said, "I can, and I'm going right now, and you can't stop me."

"But I'll—"

Craig grinned, the happy look of a beat-down shit who finally has the upper hand, and said, "I know you're barely getting along in algebra. You can't afford to skip out, Emma. Can you?"

Emma was trying to think of something to say when his grin got wider. "Later," he said. "I don't know about you, but I'm going to have a great time with my dad tonight."

Craig walked away from Emma, staying focused, on track, even though she shouted something at him, and maybe he should have agreed, maybe this time she wasn't joking, but damn it, he was tired of being Charlie Brown to her Lucy holding the football. No more. Nope, no more. With Dad in jail, he was finally manning up, was finally going to do what he should have done days ago. He was going to the police, was going to confess all and get Dad out of jail.

—⁂—

Emma turned to the tile wall of the hallway, breathing hard.

All right. You can still win. Just keep it together.

The damn thing was, the asshole was right. She couldn't afford to skip Algebra II. Mr. Palmer was a real jerk, a real hard-on about attendance and marks, and he had warned her a couple of times that she was slipping.

She had worked with Mom to plot out her entire four years at Warner High School, classes and activities outlined for the next twenty-four months, and getting tangled up with Sam Warner's murder was not on the list. No!

She dug out her iPhone, saw that she had two minutes to get to her algebra class. Thank God it was just around the corner.

With her fingers shaking, Emma touched the small field for a number and brought the phone up to her ear, sticking a finger in her free ear.

It rang.

Rang.

For God's sake, answer. Answer!

———

Craig walked out into the cold afternoon sunlight, walking fast, each step taking him further away from the temptation and empty promises of his stepsister and closer to getting his dad out of jail.

Cripes, Dad wasn't perfect—he drank a bit too much, laughed hard at his own jokes, and was always dealing—but he did his best. He worked long hours, especially on weekends, and when Craig had mathalon competitions in the area, Dad always made it a point to show up and give him support. Some Saturday mornings he was the only parent there.

Craig looked around and saw Randy McMahon in the student parking lot, sitting on the hood of his Jetta shitbox, thumbing through his phone. He ran over and said, "Randy, please, I need a ride into town."

Randy looked up. He wore his red hair in a thick Mohawk and had small hoops in both of his ears.

"You got the hundred twenty bucks for the tow and storage fee?" he asked.

"No, not right now, but shit, I promised you I'd get you the money."

Randy shook his head, went back to his phone. "Give me the money, I'll drive you anywhere you need. If you don't have it, screw it."

"Randy, please."

"I ain't your bus service, especially when you dumped my car on Mast Road the other night. My parental units were some pissed, thinking I was out after curfew."

Craig felt like he was going to start bawling. He dropped his knapsack, pushed a hand into his pocket, pulled out some crumpled bills.

"Here," he said. "This is all I've got. It's yours. Please. I need to get into town."

Randy frowned, grabbed the bills, quickly counted it. "Nineteen bucks. C'mon, Craig, I—"

"It's an emergency, Randy, honest to Christ."

"Oh, come on."

"It's about my dad."

Randy paused, shoved the bills into his coat, slowly slid off the car. "What about your dad?"

"I need to go to the police station. Right away."

Randy said, "It's about your dad? For real?"

"Yeah," Craig said, feeling almost relieved at being able to tell someone what was going on. "I've got info that can get him out of jail."

"Well, shit, let's get to it," Randy said.

He went around to the driver's side and Craig got into the passenger's seat, brushing away crumpled McDonald's wrappers and empty Mountain Dew cans. He tossed his knapsack into the back and said, "Randy?"

"Yeah?" Randy said, pulling out his car keys.

"This being an emergency, can I have my nineteen dollars back?"

"You want to jog to the police station?"

"No," Craig said.

"Then shut up."

—⁂—

What to say, what to say, and then her iPhone chimed, and Jessica fumbled with her purse, saying, "Oh, Rhonda, give me a sec, will you? Please?"

"Jessica, what's going on?"

She looked at her iPhone screen, saw the incoming call was from Emma, and she knew the time, knew Emma had to be in class, so it had to be important. *Oh, no,* she thought. *Oh, no.*

She slid a thumb across the screen, turned away from Rhonda, and said, "Emma?"

Her little girl was crying. "Mom, I need your help. Oh, God, I need your help!"

—⁓—

Randy turned the key to the Jetta. It grumbled, started, and then died.

"Shit."

Craig said, "Oh, come on, Randy."

"Hey, I do what I can." He turned the key again. The engine sputtered, sputtered.

"Randy . . ."

"You want to walk? You want to call an Uber? Oh, yeah, you can't. You don't have enough money."

Craig looked back at the school, knowing Emma was right now doing something, but he wasn't sure what. All he knew was that his stepsister wasn't going to just stand there and not do a thing.

Randy murmured, "C'mon, *fräulein,* come to Papa, you know you want to." He turned the key, and the engine started right up with a burbling roar and stayed running. Randy grinned. "Unlike you, pal, I always have luck with the ladies."

"Fine," Craig said. "Just get me to the police station."

Randy backed the Jetta out and said, "You're not shitting me, are you? You really got big news about your dad?"

Craig remembered that night, walking and stumbling some on the trail, holding the shotgun, Emma beside him, prodding him and pushing him.

"Yeah," he said. "Really big news."

—⁓—

Emma started sobbing as she talked to her mother, her back turned so none of the other students could see what she was doing.

"Mom, Craig's gone crazy! I don't know what's wrong with him!"

"Emma, calm down, please, calm down. What's he doing?"

She kept sobbing. "He . . . he's going to the police. He thinks he can get his dad out of jail. I don't know what to do."

"Emma," came her Mom's sharp voice. "What do you mean, he's going to the police? How's he going to get his dad out of jail?"

She took a breath, let out of a series of sobs, not answering her mother until she was ready, and she said, "Oh, Mom, Craig is going to tell the police I killed Sam Warner! And he was there! And he thinks that'll get his dad out of jail! Mom, what are we going to do?"

Jessica stared at her feet, at the smooth stone worn down by thousands of library patrons over the years, in good times and bad, in sun or rain, in all kinds of weather, at all kinds of times. Like the time right now when you need to save your girl.

"Emma, calm down, calm down. Where's Craig? Where is he right now?"

"He . . . he said he's going to the police station."

"How's he getting there?"

"I don't know," her daughter said, sobbing. "He'll probably bum a ride from one of his friends. Mom, what—"

"Emma!" she said loudly. "I'll take care of it, all right? I'll take care of it. Look, where are you?"

"At school. Ready to go to class."

"All right," Jessica said, her free hand reaching for her car keys. "I'll take care of it, okay? Don't you worry about a thing. I'll take care of it, you go to class and let your mother take care of it."

The sobbing had died down to sniffles. "Oh, Mom . . ."

"I've got it," Jessica said, not really knowing what she was going to do but willing to lie to put her Emma at ease. "You just go to class and don't worry about a thing. Mom's got it."

Emma whispered. "I love you, Mom."

"I love you too, little girl. Make me proud."

Emma disconnected the call, put her iPhone away, and rubbed her eyes with a piece of tissue. She looked up at the hallway clock. A minute

S. A. PRENTISS

before algebra. Perfect. Mom would take care of it, and then it would be all right.

She joined the last straggle of students getting to class, took her seat right next to Carol Niven. Carol had her notebook out and glanced over and said, "Everything okay?"

Emma smiled and pulled her own notebook out. "Oh, things are just great."

—⁂—

Jessica put the phone back into her purse, quickly turned around, and nearly bumped into Rhonda.

Her friend's eyes were wide. "Jessica, what's going on?"

She made sure her purse strap was firmly over her shoulder. "Rhonda, I'm sorry, I need to run."

Jessica tried to brush past, and Rhonda said, "Hey, Jess, just a sec—how come you haven't returned any of my calls? I know you're under a lot of pressure. Please, I want to help. Anything I can do."

Even though Jessica knew she just had to get moving, had to do something about her stepson, had to protect Emma, she couldn't just dump Rhonda like this.

Tears were running down her cheeks, and she sobbed. "Rhonda . . . with Ted in jail, my kids—they're fighting. Craig . . . something's wrong with Craig and I've got to help him. Emma just called me and said he's run off from school." *Which was partially true*, a hard part of her thought.

Rhonda took her right hand, squeezed it. "Jessica, go, take care of things—and I'll cover for you back at work, all right? Don't worry about work. I'll help you with the Ice Queen. I promise."

Jessica kissed her friend on her cheek and then ran to her Sentra in the library parking lot.

230

CHAPTER TWENTY-EIGHT

Randy's Jetta bucked and gurgled as they headed into downtown Warner, but Craig thought that was just fine. He was on his way to the police station. Emma wasn't going to stop him. She could take all her promises to him and roll them up into a nice shiny ball and shove it up her cute ass, but Craig was through.

"Shit, Craig," Randy said. "The traffic sure does suck. We won't get there for probably another five minutes."

"That's okay," he said, crossing his arms. "Just get me there."

The thing was, Randy was right. The road was jammed with school buses coming in and parents joining a line to pick up their sons and daughters, not to mention the steady line of students who could depart at final period leaving. They came to the main entrance to the school, where a cop was directing traffic.

Randy said, "Hey, there's a cop over there. Why don't you talk to him?"

"Nope," Craig said. "I'm gonna talk to the detective handling the case. Somebody important. That cop, what's he going to do? He's going to tell me to stop bothering him and go to the police station. And that's what I'm going to do."

"Okay," Randy said, and then traffic started moving and they took a right onto Main Street.

Craig jumped when his phone started ringing. He grabbed it and looked at the screen. JESSICA, it said.

—w—

Jessica was stuck behind two patrons, gray-hairs both, who were driving their dull-looking GM sedans and who were taking their sweet goddamn time in leaving the library's parking lot. She slammed a hand on the steering wheel, grabbed her iPhone. It slipped out of her fingers and fell to the floor.

"Shit!"

Jessica bent down, fingers on the floor, until she got the phone and picked it up. The lead car was out of the parking lot. She slid through the touch screen, found the number for Craig, and gave it a push. She brought it up to her ear. It was ringing. Ringing. Ringing.

"C'mon, c'mon," she murmured. "Answer it, boy. Answer it!"

Jessica wasn't sure what she was going to say, but she knew that she had to say something. Ask Craig what was going on. Ask him what was sending him to the police station. What did he intend to say when he got there? Couldn't he just wait to talk to his stepmom? Couldn't they all work together as a family to get Ted out of jail?

The phone stopped ringing and Craig's voice answered.

—w—

Randy glanced over. "Who's calling?"

"My stepmom."

Ring. Ring. Ring.

Randy said, "Aren't you going to answer it?"

Ring.

Randy said, "Boy, you got some balls on you, Craig." He laughed. "My mom, if she doesn't get a pickup in the first three seconds, I get interrogated when I get home about why I didn't answer, where I was, and didn't I know I was disrespecting her."

Craig just watched the phone screen. There was a little tone as the call went to voicemail.

"No," he said. "I'm not going to answer it."

Randy laughed. "Boy, your mom is gonna be pissed!"

Craig looked out as the homes and buildings of Warner passed by. "Randy, she's not my mom."

—⁂—

Jessica heard Craig's voice and said, "Craig! It's me! What are you—" And she stopped. It was a waste. His voice had just been Craig's voicemail prompt, that's all.

"Craig!" she said. "Please listen. Don't go to the police, please. Talk to me! Tell me what's going on! We can work this out as a family. We can get your father out. Just don't go to the police right yet!"

A horn honked behind her. She looked up. The other GM sedan was gone. Now it was just her.

She drove out, briefly braked, and made a quick turn to the right. More horns honked as she cut it pretty damn close.

No matter.

She was moving fast.

To the police station. To get there before Craig.

—⁂—

Up ahead Craig made out the brick building that held both the police station and the fire department, and Randy said, "So, mind letting me know what you're going to tell the police?"

"That they got it wrong, that he didn't kill Sam Warner."

"Uh-huh. You know who did it?"

Craig kept quiet, his chest cold, filled with a feeling—a resolve, maybe?—that he was finally doing the right thing.

Randy said, "Okay, whatever. The guy was an asshole, so I'm not going to miss him. Still, if every guy who was an asshole in school got his head blown off by a shotgun, there wouldn't be many students around when prom season comes, you know what I mean?"

Craig said, "Right there. Don't bother going into the parking lot. You can drop me off in the front."

—⁓—

Jessica cursed again and again as she seemed to hit every red light. Was God punishing her? Finally, after all these years, had the hand of God come down to screw around with the traffic lights to prevent her from getting to the police station in time, to stop Craig from ruining it all?

Finally! The last light turned green and she tailgated the pickup truck in front of her, and there, there was the police station, and a Volkswagen Jetta pulling away from the sidewalk, and—

There! Craig was walking up the paved walkway to the front of the police station.

She pulled to the right of the pickup truck, forcing him into the middle of the narrow two-lane street. More horns were honking, but she didn't mind, she didn't care. All she cared about was *Emma, Emma, Emma.*

Jessica pulled the Sentra in front of a fire hydrant, jumped out, left the door open, and ran over to the grass in front of the station.

"Craig!" she yelled. "Craig!"

Her stepson hesitated, looked to the left and to the right.

"Craig!"

He finally turned around and looked right at her.

She waved. "Craig, please, wait!"

Jessica waited, heart racing so fast, like an outboard motor revving higher and higher. She waited. *Craig, oh Craig. Emma, oh Emma.*

She waved again.

Craig waved back. And then took three more steps, right into the police station.

—⁓—

It was the first time Craig had ever been inside the Warner police station. It took a few moments to get his bearings. To his right were two glass display cases, showing off trophies and black-and-white photos of Warner cops from years and years ago. In front was a wooden door with a sign saying VISITORS NEED TO SIGN IN and a smaller sign saying ALL CONVERSATIONS BEYOND THIS POINT MAY BE RECORDED. Over the door was a small CCTV camera, looking down at him and the scuffed tile.

"May" in this room sure was "will," he thought. There was a bulletin board with town notices and lost-and-found flyers and, to the left, a rectangular glass window with an opening below it.

He went over, bumping into one of the two light-orange plastic chairs set nearby, and he stood looking in. There were two desks, one empty, and an older woman with eyeglasses dangling from around her neck was furiously typing away on a computer keyboard.

Craig waited. He didn't feel good. His mom—his real mom—had always said as they drove by the brick building, "You be a good boy, Craig, or the police will take you and put you in there for a long, long time."

He thought, *I'm trying to be good, Mom. Honest I am.*

He brought up his right hand and tapped on the glass.

—m—

Jessica ran after Craig but gave up halfway across the small, well-tended lawn. Now what? She could burst into the lobby and try to convince him not to speak to Detective Rafferty, but what if he started yelling nonsense? The lobby and everyplace else was bugged, she remembered that.

And then? If Craig wouldn't listen, if she tried to pull him away, the door would open up, Detective Rafferty would come out, and—

No.

Jessica turned around, walked briskly back to her illegally parked Sentra.

No.

She got in her car, started it up, heard her phone chiming. Jessica took it out, saw RHONDA appear, and let it go to voicemail. Her dear friend. Wanting to help, eager to do what she could. Bless her.

Then she checked the time. School would be letting out soon. Emma didn't have any practice or meets today. She would go straight home. And between now and then, Jessica would come up with something. She had to.

Jessica eased her Sentra into traffic and started driving home.

—⁓—

The woman behind the glass looked up, startled.

Craig tried to smile, look relaxed, not in trouble.

The woman lifted a finger, as if to say, *C'mon, kid, give me another minute or two,* and then she went back to her typing.

Craig noticed his legs were shaking.

—⁓—

All the way home, different thoughts and options raced through Jessica's head. Call Detective Rafferty and plead her case that Craig was upset and would start talking nonsense. Call Detective Rafferty and tell him that she had new information on the case and would pass it along if he ignored what Craig was trying to tell him.

Or . . . find a public phone between here and home, make a quick anonymous call to the police station, tell them that the person who killed Sam Warner was someone with a grudge, someone who despised the young man, someone . . .

Someone like Percy Prescott.

It felt like a gift box inside of her mind had just opened up.

Sure. Percy. Already arrested by the police, known to hate Sam Warner, loudly telling people at the bank how much Sam and his wrestling buddies had mistreated him.

Percy.

—⚔—

Craig waited and waited. A police officer came in, the woman typing glanced up and pressed a buzzer system to open the door, and now he was alone again in the lobby.

With each passing moment, doubts started to grow. Was he doing the right thing? What would Emma and Jessica do? And most of all, would the police believe him? Would they?

Screw this, he thought, and he picked up his knapsack, turned, and—

"Yes?" The woman was standing behind the glass, speaking through a little round metal grille. "How can I help you?"

Craig just stared at her.

"Well?"

He said, "I was hoping—"

"You'll have to speak up louder, I'm sorry," she snapped at him.

He stepped closer to the glass. Smudged fingerprints were on the lower part of the glass.

"Uh, I'd like to speak to the detective who's handling the, uh, Sam Warner investigation."

Her eyes narrowed and she looked suspicious. "And who are you?"

"Craig Donovan," he said. "My dad, uh, is Ted Donovan, and I'd like to speak to the detective handling the case." He paused. "Please."

She said, "All right. That'd be Detective Rafferty. Take a seat. I'll see if he's free."

Craig's face was burning, and he sat down in the orange chair, lowered his head. *Dad,* he thought, *I'm doing this for you.*

—⚔—

Jessica pulled into the small driveway in front of her house.

Public phones? Damn it, there were none!

She remembered as a kid that every gas station, drugstore, 7-Eleven had a public pay phone outside, and of course she hadn't been paying attention these past years as they were all taken down. Now? She could buy a burner phone, but by the time she got that powered up, programmed, and paid for . . . no, she didn't have time.

Jessica got out of the Sentra, all her senses seeming to burn and tingle. What to do?

First things first: protect Emma. She should be home from school in about fifteen minutes, and Jessica would sit her down, have a frank talk with her, and then . . . well, leave. Pack a couple of bags, get out of Warner, see what she could find out from afar, either through watching the news at some motel room somewhere or by visiting another town's public library and using its open computers.

She unlocked the door, pushed her shoulder against it—shove, shove, shove—and the door squeaked open, and she looked down at the hardwood floor.

No mail. Odd.

She closed the door behind her, dropped her coat and purse on the chair nearby, walked into the dining room, and stopped.

Her husband was sitting at the dining room table, the day's mail at his elbow.

"Hello, Jessica," he said.

CHAPTER TWENTY-NINE

Craig snapped up straight when the civilian police employee said, "Craig? Craig Donovan?"

"Yes," he said, getting up and walking over to the glass.

The older woman said, "He's in a meeting. Once he gets out, I'll let him know you're waiting for him."

Craig nodded. "Okay, thanks."

And he went back to the empty chair.

Jessica had no memory of walking farther into the dining room.

Ted was home. Ted was sitting there, looking tired, wearing his usual real estate agent clothing of gray slacks and a button-down oxford shirt, but the slacks and shirt were wrinkled, stained. Ted's eyes were tired and haunted, and while she knew he had been in the county jail for only three nights, his pallor and expression made it look like he had been there for three years.

"Ted . . . are you . . . are you out on bail?"

A weary smile and a shake of the head. "No. I'm out."

"Out?"

"Charges dropped," he said. "I . . . ah, I just can't believe it."

Jessica watched as her husband started weeping.

And then there was a heavy knock on the door.

She went back to the front door, ashamed but glad to have her back to her crying husband. Jessica considered herself a feminist and a tough woman of the world—as much as she could be while living in Warner and working as a bank teller—but there was something so bone-deep wrong about watching your husband cry.

Tug, tug, tug at the door, not even bothering to wonder who might be there. Seeing Ted at the kitchen table was enough of a shock, but then the door ground open and she stepped back as Helen Wray, the attorney, said, "Hey, surprise! What a great day, am I right?"

Jessica backed away as Helen strode in with confidence, a heavy leather briefcase with a strap hanging from her shoulder. She was carrying what looked to be a bottle of . . . champagne? For real?

Helen said, "So after I got Ted out, I thought, *Hey, let's bring him home, and let's get a bottle of champagne to celebrate.*" She glanced at the label and said, "Shit. Looks like sparking wine from California, but so what? We've got a lot to celebrate."

The attorney brushed past her, and Jessica got the door shut, seeing a light-blue Mercedes-Benz parked next to her sad Sentra, and went back into the dining room. Ted was at least smiling now, as Helen went straight into the kitchen.

"Jessica, Ted, you folks have any champagne glasses around here? Do you?"

Jessica slowly sat down across from her husband. She called out, "Uh, no, no, we don't. There might be wineglasses in the upper cabinet, to the left of the kitchen sink."

"Okay, thanks, I'll be right in," Helen said.

Jessica looked at Ted. He still looked haunted.

He said, "The charges were dropped."

"Why?"

"Why? Because I didn't kill the kid, that's why," he said, voice sharp.

Jessica reached over, grasped his right hand. "No, no, no," she said. "I meant, well, how? How did it happen?"

Helen came back into the dining room holding three wineglasses by their stems, and Jessica felt a slight flush of shame that one of them didn't match the other two. Helen put the glasses down on the table and said, "It happened because of a screwup, that's how. A big screwup." She undid the foil around the top of the bottle, then the wire, and started twisting and twisting the white plastic cork.

Ted said, "Ah, yeah, there was a mistake. About Sam's time of death."

There was a *pop!* and the white plastic cork flew to the other side of the room, rattling to the hardwood floor, and Helen deftly poured the overflowing sparkling wine into each of the glasses.

"Ted," Helen said, "a mistake is when you list a property for two hundred thousand dollars and the seller really wanted to list it for two hundred ten. That's a mistake. Screwing up the time of death—guaranteed this'll be on the front page of the *Globe* and *Herald* tomorrow."

"How?" Jessica said, not daring to reach over to pick up a glass. "What happened?"

Helen pulled a chair away from the table and said with pride, "I nearly predicted it, didn't I? Law enforcement and forensics have had a couple of rough years here in the Bay State. Thousands of drug cases have been tossed out because the forensics tech was making shit up. Other drug cases were tossed because another forensics tech was in love with an assistant DA and was faking evidence to get in his good graces. And don't get me started with the state police and how some troopers have been padding their payroll and expense accounts over the years and brooming away cases because some judge's kid or wife got caught."

Ted repeated, "Forensics got the time of Sam's death wrong."

Jessica's voice was nearly a whisper. "How?"

Helen reached over, pulled a laptop out of her leather briefcase, lifted the cover, and powered it up. "The Office of the Chief Medical Examiner investigates cause and time of death in violent crimes and assists small departments like Warner. Nearest office to Warner is Boston, but when Sam's body was discovered, nobody was available. It got bumped over to the regional office in Sandwich, and the lead folks were on some sort of boondoggle trip to DC, so it was a new kid who did the initial exam."

Jessica hadn't even sipped from the sparkling wine and she already felt drunk. Not the happy, loose-limbed, relaxed kind of drunk, but the kind of drunk when you put your hand out to touch a table and the table feels like carpeting and the room is canted and voices echo and re-echo.

"And being a new kid, and under pressure, he screwed up," Helen said. "Based on core temperature, rigor mortis, and lividity, Sam Warner was murdered between six and eleven P.M. last Monday. *Not* last Tuesday. But the kid"—Helen laughed—"he put the wrong date down in his hurry and was too scared to correct his mistake."

"How could something that simple happen?" Jessica asked, still bewildered at how quickly everything was unfolding in front of her, as if a stage magician had suddenly halted his act and was now busily pulling apart props and displays to show the secrets hidden in plain sight.

"Because politicians around here don't learn," Helen said. "Look, the National Association of Medical Examiners recommends that forensic examiners not take on more than two hundred and fifty cases per year. Two hundred and fifty. You know what the number is in Massachusetts? A few years ago they were performing nearly four hundred and fifty, and the numbers were getting worse. It's a wonder there aren't more screwups like this."

Jessica said, "But Sam's parents—"

Helen was tapping on the computer screen. "Sam told them he was going to spend the night at a friend's house. And they weren't concerned too much when he didn't return on Tuesday. And the school—well, I guess Sam was such a precious child, stuff like recording his absences weren't a priority."

Ted swallowed. "And Monday night . . ."

"Oh, God," Jessica said. "The Chamber of Commerce event."

With triumph in her voice, Helen said, "That's right! You and your family were at the Chamber event, and who was the MC at the podium all night long? This guy!" She spun the laptop around, and there was a YouTube video put up by the Warner Chamber of Commerce, and standing at the podium was a relaxed, happy, and joking Ted Donovan. Helen said, "Your man was there from five P.M. to nearly midnight, being the happy master of ceremonies."

Helen pressed a key on her laptop, and through the tiny speakers Jessica heard applause and laughter and the little echoing voice of Ted saying, "Okay, okay, simmer down, guys and girls, we got a lot of ground to cover," and there was more happy, joyous laughter, and Jessica thought, all that laughter, all those happy people, and Sam Warner was either dead or on his way to be killed.

Helen grinned and picked up a wineglass, and so did Ted, and so did Jessica, and the happy attorney said, "Here's to incompetence, and to videotape!"

Ted smiled more widely and repeated the phrase, and Jessica joined in, but all the time, while sipping the sparkling white wine, she thought, *Craig.* What was Craig saying to the police at this moment?

—m—

Craig Donovan got up again from the orange plastic chair. His legs felt as if little ants were crawling up and down inside the skin, making him jumpy, twitchy.

What was taking the detective so long?

He tried to pass the dragging time by looking at the dusty glass display cases. Old police badges. Whistles. Civil Defense helmets and armbands. Black-and-white photos, most curling around the edges, showing policemen from long ago, even way back when they wore those funny tall helmets like the cops in London. Some faded color prints showing various years of past police departments, everyone looking so serious, so plain, the color prints fading into yellow. Lots of fading away, until nothing was left but these stupid little souvenirs.

"Young man?"

Craig turned. The woman at the window seemed just a bit more cheerful. "Detective Rafferty will be here in a few minutes."

—⁂—

Jessica said, "What now?"

"Ah, yes, what now," Helen said. "Right now, Ted, you take the rest of the day off, and go right back to work tomorrow morning like nothing ever happened." She laughed for a moment. "You know, you might even see a jump in business. Potential and curious customers coming by to see what's what."

Jessica said, "But isn't there other evidence? Like the guy who said he heard a gunshot? And the police thinking Ted's shotgun had recently been fired?"

Helen turned to her, an amused smile on her carefully made-up face. "What? You looking to put Ted back in the county lockup?"

"No, no, I just don't want . . . I mean, this is such great news. I don't want the Warner police coming back and trying to arrest Ted again."

Helen shook her head, started to shut down her computer. "Not going to happen. First of all, having the time of death be wrong like this is going to make the police very, very concerned and careful. Not to mention the Middlesex County DA. And trust me, if all they have is the sound of a gunshot and Ted's shotgun, I would relish cross-examining whatever witnesses they could dig up. A sound of gunfire? Nice. Did you see who fired the gun? No? Oh, and are you sure it was a gunshot and not something else? A car backfiring? A tractor-trailer truck accidentally dropping a piece of equipment? A boiler somewhere blowing up?"

Jessica looked on in awe as Helen kept on talking, reciting facts, questions, and assertions, and she wished she could have gone to the same schools and had the same breaks as this attorney had. How differently her life could have turned out!

"And then there's the recently fired shotgun. Dear me, after the medical examiner's office screwed up the time of death, about as basic a piece of evidence as you can have, I would love, love to cross-examine the forensics crew determining when the shotgun was fired," Helen said, taking a good swig of the sparkling wine. "Your smell determined it had been fired recently," she went on in the voice of a determined cross-examiner. "Is that measurable? How does your sense of smell compare to others? And you said that powder residue also suggested it had been recently fired. Suggested? Is a suggestion measurable? Can you give the jury an exact time when this firearm was discharged? You can't? Tell me, is there any way to determine if the shotgun pellets that killed young Sam Warner came from Mr. Donovan's shotgun? Oh, you can't do that? Well, at least can you tell me how many shotguns there are in Middlesex County? Oh, that many? All right, witness dismissed."

Another healthy swig and her glass was empty. She slapped it down on the dining room table. "Nope, for you, Ted, and your family, it's over."

Ted's eyes were filling up again, and Jessica knew it was wrong to feel this, but *for God's sake,* she was thinking, *Ted, keep it together. Don't start crying in front of me and your lawyer.*

"But in other cases . . . I mean, the cops might back off, but they'll keep you under surveillance, dig around—look for other evidence."

Helen picked up her computer and slipped it into her bulging leather briefcase. "What, you think this is an episode of *CSI Warner*? That show *48 Hours*? Or *Dateline*? Ted, it's done. Over. And besides, the cops have found other evidence and are chasing it down as we speak. By this time tomorrow the cops are going to have at least a dozen other suspects."

Ted said, "How? What's going on?"

Helen got up, slung her bag over her shoulder. "A friend of mine in the DA's office passed this along. Investigators seized Sam Warner's computer, based on a couple of tips they received. It seems the star of the wrestling team, the perfect child of his parents, the wonderful athlete and scholar, was a rapist."

Jessica felt as if those last words were punching her in the gut. Ted stared at her and she stared right back at him.

Helen went on. "On his computer there are about a dozen videos of him with teenage girls, the girls either drunk or roofied. All of them were recorded in his bedroom. And this past Saturday, just before he got killed two days later, some father went to a party at the Warner house, tried to get in and confront the little creep."

Ted said, "Do they know who he was?"

"Nope. But with that and those recordings, a whole lot of parents in Warner have motive. So relax."

A moment passed. Helen looked at the two of them and said, "Hey, you haven't even taken a sip of your California bubbly. Aren't you happy? Aren't you proud of your attorney? Welcome home, Ted!"

A long, long second passed. Jessica nodded, decided to play the part that was hers. She picked up the wineglass, looked right at her husband, and parroted the words: "Welcome home, Ted."

—w—

Craig stood up quickly and got his right foot tangled in his knapsack's straps as the door leading into the lobby unexpectedly swung open. The same police detective who had come by their house the other day stood in the door, looking angry, tired . . . confused? His striped shirt was wrinkled, and his red tie was undone at the collar. A police ID was dangling off a blue-and-white lanyard from his neck.

"I'm Detective Rafferty," he said, not moving from the open doorway. "You're Craig Donovan, right?"

Craig got his foot untangled, grabbed his knapsack, stood up. "Yes, yes sir, I'd like to talk to you about my father, Ted Donovan."

The detective shook his head. "Go home, kid."

A spark of anger flared within him. Jesus Christ, why did adults always have to prove they knew everything, were so superior, were so smart? Craig started to talk, but the detective held up his hand, cutting him off.

"Go home, kid. Your dad's there, waiting for you."

And before Craig could say anything more, the detective walked back into the police station, letting the heavy door slam shut behind him.

CHAPTER THIRTY

Ted had never been one for taking long, hot showers, especially after growing up in a crowded apartment building on the other side of Warner where Mom and Dad kept strict watch on the utilities, but tonight he was breaking his old habit and was still in the shower nearly fifteen minutes after he began, scrubbing and rescrubbing, working desperately not only to get the scent of the Middlesex County HOC cell block off his skin and out of his hair, but Jesus, he wanted to get that stink off him down to the skin level—fuck, the molecular level. Before getting into the shower he had attacked his fingernails and his mouth, cutting the nails down to the base, then brushing his teeth, flossing—he never flossed, but he took some of Jessica's—and then brushing his teeth again and rinsing twice from a bottle of Listerine. Now he stood directly under the blasting shower head, knowing that this initial wash would take care of the surface stink and memories, but it would be a long while before he could move on from those humiliating days in prison.

He switched off the shower, got out, dried off, and then started whispering to himself, as he always did before closing on a major deal or meeting with a deep-pocketed client. "It's gonna be all right," he whispered, rubbing and rubbing. "You were there for less than four days. Some guys get arrested by mistake and they're locked up for four years or four decades. You'll bounce back, get to the office tomorrow morning, walk in like you own the fucking world."

Ted finished with the towel and glanced down at his clothes, picked up his pants, took out a folded slip of paper with Craig's handwriting on it:

> Dad,
> Don't worry, I'm going to get you out.
> Craig

Tears welled up in his eyes again. His boy—his teenage nerd, thinking he could do the magical and release him from the county jail.

Nope, it was the Commonwealth of Massachusetts's incompetence that got him out.

He put the note on the vanity, then went to ball up his clothes and toss them down the laundry chute.

No.

He stopped.

No. Those clothes—he wouldn't let Jessica wash them. He would never again wear those slacks, shirt, hell, even the socks and underwear. Those were the clothes he had been wearing when he had been arrested, processed, and then transported to Billerica, home of the county jail. Nope. Those clothes were going out in the trash.

He took a fresh towel, wrapped it around his waist, stepped out onto the second-floor landing.

The doors to Emma's room and Craig's room were both closed. His throat thickened as he remembered the previous hours, when all of them had been downstairs together, finally celebrating with take-out Chinese food from Szechuan Taste, after Craig had burst into the house and given him a long, long hug, sobbing into his shoulder, and then Emma had come home and for the first time ever—ever!—had screamed out, "Daddy!" and had nearly jumped into his arms.

It had been a good time, the first time of their new life, their new family.

Ted went downstairs to the bedroom. The room was dark, barely lit by a nightlight in the corner. By touch he opened a bureau drawer and removed a fresh pair of shorts, and then he dropped the towel on the floor.

He could tell Jessica was in bed. But she hadn't said a word.

He gently closed the door to the bedroom and slipped between the crisp, clean sheets, nothing like the smelly old bedding he had endured at the county jail.

He didn't say a word. Neither did Jessica.

Well.

"You awake?"

"Yes." Her voice was calm, even.

"Can we talk?"

"Sure."

He slipped his hand along the side, finding her arm, wrist, and then hand. He clasped her hand, looking to receive a signal. Drawing back was a very bad sign. Not clasping in return was a bad sign. A gentle clasp was just above neutral, on its way to being a good sign.

That's what he was now receiving.

Ted sighed and said, "If I live for another forty or fifty years, I still won't be able to say I'm sorry enough times for what I did. It was wrong, it was stupid. Hold on, that's not right." He nodded to himself in the dark bedroom. "I was wrong, I was stupid, I was weak. Paula—she tempted me. I was at a low point, with what was going on with the business, and I gave in to temptation. It was nothing more than that. I don't even like her that much, Jessica. And you know what? First thing tomorrow, I'm going to find a way to fire her. I don't want her around the office anymore. She'll be a distraction, a memory, something I don't want there."

He waited for a bit, to allow Jessica to say something. Lord knows he had pissed her off so many times in the past, interrupting her or assuming he knew what she was going to say in a conversation. *Don't ever assume,* she would say sharply to him.

Ted said, "Jessica, we're in a bad place now. I know that. I put us here. And it's too soon for forgiveness, I know that. I don't deserve it, not now.

But I'll work for us, I'll fight for us. And if you think counseling will help, absolutely, let's do it."

He waited again.

"Ted?"

"Yes?" And now his heart was really hammering along, because right now his love for Jessica had come back to him, and he didn't want her to leave him, didn't want a divorce, and there were things that needed to be addressed and settled, but now, after being freed from prison and getting back to his life, he really wanted to grow old with her. He wanted this blended family of theirs to thrive. He waited, and said, "Jessica?"

"Ted, don't fire her right away. That'll just piss her off, give her a reason to file a complaint with some town or government agency. Wait a while, until she does something that gives you an excuse to fire her for cause. All right?"

"Sure, Jess, yes, that makes sense."

"But . . . I never want to hear her name ever again."

"Absolutely."

"And beginning tomorrow, you'll never, ever lie to me about who you're seeing or where you're going. You've destroyed my trust in you, Ted, and it's going to take some time to repair it."

He squeezed her hand, and to his joy, she squeezed back.

"Yes, of course. No more lying, no more secrets. You can call me anytime you want—anytime. I'll even FaceTime you to show you that I'm where I said I'd be."

"Well, maybe not that far," she said, and the tone of her voice was so open and light that Ted couldn't believe this was going so well.

"Whatever you say, Jess. Whatever you say."

"Good."

"But I need to know something."

Ted thought, *What? Jesus, I've already told you everything.*

"Sure, Jess. Go ahead."

He thought he felt her take a deep breath, and she said, "The night the kids went missing. Before we left the house. We were both searching, and I heard the closet door opening and closing. I knew your coat wasn't in there. So why did you open the closet?"

He didn't want to tell her, but he had just made a promise to her, just seconds ago, and as rough as it was going to be, he was going to keep his promise.

"I'm embarrassed to tell you."

"I think we're both beyond that, Ted."

He was glad that both of them were in the darkness, for he didn't want to see her face, or her to see his, with the next few words.

"I . . . like I said, I had come back from the office. From . . . well, I was there with . . . her." *God, so fucking humiliating.* "And when I left, she stuffed something in my coat. A souvenir, she said. And when we were looking through the house, I checked my coat. It was a pair of her panties."

Jessica didn't say anything.

"I panicked. I didn't know what to do. So when you were upstairs and I was downstairs, I took them and tossed them into the closet. And when I got back before you, I cut them up and flushed them down the toilet."

Again, not a word from Jessica. He waited.

She finally and slowly said, "Thanks for telling me the truth, Ted."

"Thanks, Jess," he said, and he was thrilled again when she squeezed his hand back, and he said, "About that night. I guess the kids were telling the truth about the scavenger hunt, right?"

His wife said, "I always knew they were telling the truth."

"Yeah, but now it makes sense. They were out there wandering around in the rain, trying to find what was on the list, and maybe somebody took their phones. As a prank. Like one more thing to find at the end. And they were going to dump them in the town forest. And when they went up the path, they found Sam's body. Got scared. Went back, put the phones where they were, and didn't tell the cops."

"I can't believe they wouldn't tell the police."

Ted said, "If you were out past curfew and found something like that, would you tell the police? Or go home and figure someone else would find the body?"

Jessica said, "That does make sense. It's awful, but it does make sense."

Ted felt pretty good now, answering Jessica's questions, confessing what he had done, and man, maybe he shouldn't bring this up right now, but things were really looking up, and Ted thought, *Well, strike while the goddamn iron is hot*—whatever that means—and he said, "Can I ask you a question, hon?"

Her soft hand was still in his.

"Of course."

Ted said, "Hon, where did the twelve thousand dollars go?"

CHAPTER THIRTY-ONE

All the lights were off in her bedroom and Emma was under the covers, playing solitaire on her iPhone. She left only a bit of the blankets open to let in some air, and she was happy and content to let her fingers fly across the screen and move around the little playing cards. She was in charge of this game—she enjoyed being in charge of everything—and the best part of solitaire was that when she got stuck, she could just stop the game and start over again.

And she loved it. Good ol' Mom had saved her again, and Emma was so happy that things were finally straightening out. She had even done her part, coming home from school, wondering what was going on, wondering if Mom had stopped Craig in time, and when she saw Mom and Ted at the dining room table, with Craig hugging his father, she had played along, even calling Ted "Daddy," which seemed to please him.

A good night. But still . . . Precautions had to be taken.

Craig had threatened a lot of things, had said some nasty things. She wasn't sure what he would do next. Lots of times over the past few months he had told her that Mom was one tightly wound and nutty woman. Even though Mom did everything she could to protect Emma and her future.

But could she ever trust Craig?

Earlier she had taken her desk chair and had shoved it under the doorknob, even after locking the door. She wasn't going to take any more chances.

Emma went back to her solitaire game.

Still in control.

—◊—

In his bedroom Craig was stretched out on his bed, trying very hard to read a graphic novel about Thor and not doing a good job of it. His head seemed to be spinning from all that had gone on earlier today, leading up to hugging his dad and realizing he was home, was back, and was safe, and then the laughter and joy of being with Dad, eating take-out Chinese, and now . . . In bed. Alone. Thinking things through.

Emma looked happy, Dad looked happy, and Jessica looked happy. He knew even he looked happy. There had been laughter, and toasts, and Dad had said how he was going to get up early tomorrow and go to work, and Jessica had rubbed his shoulders, and Emma had called him "Daddy," which nearly turned Craig's stomach.

How could they all be fooled?

There were still questions and promises that needed to be addressed, needed to be resolved.

He put the colorful book down on the bed, raised up his T-shirt. FAG. He could easily make out the letters, even though they were upside down and were finally fading away.

FAG.

Craig lowered the T-shirt.

Yeah. Promises had to be kept, rumors and jokes had to be stopped.

He picked up the graphic novel and tried to start reading again.

—◊—

Jessica thought, *Well, here we go.*

"Why do you ask, Ted?"

"Why . . . I mean, well, I talked a bit to Helen when she drove me out of Billerica, and I talked about how happy I was, and we talked about her fee and how I had arranged for you to give her a twelve-thousand-dollar retainer, and she said you haven't given her any money."

"That's right," Jessica said, holding hands with her husband, resting in the darkness, feeling very full and alive. "I didn't give her a dime. But still, I can't imagine her final bill will be that much."

"But Jess. The money. Where did it go?"

"I've spent it."

"Spent it? Where?"

"On something important."

"Like what?"

With each passing minute Jessica could feel Ted's body tightening up as he seemingly couldn't believe what she was telling him.

"Ted, forget it."

"Forget it? How in hell do you expect me to forget where twelve thousand dollars have gone?

She squeezed his hand. "Just like you expect me to forget Paula Fawkes."

His hand was still in hers. Part of Jessica was surprised.

"That's different," he finally said.

"Maybe, but that's the way it's going to be."

"Jessica, that's a lot of money. What do I tell Ben Powell?"

"Anything you want."

"Jessica, I—"

"Ted."

"Yes?" he asked.

"This is what happened," she said. "And what's going to happen."

He paused. It was still so very dark in the bedroom.

"I'm sorry, I don't understand what you're saying, Jess."

She said, "Do you remember the Saturday night before all this started?"

"Jesus, Jess. Yeah, okay. We went to the movies. The new Tom Hanks film."

"Right. Which show did we go to?"

"The . . . the second evening show."

"What time did it start?"

"What time? Jesus, Jess, what does this have to do with anything?"

She squeezed his hand hard, as hard as possible in the darkness. "We've been together for a long time. You know I don't like the late showings. I always fall asleep. So when we went to the movies, after dinner at Giovanni's—where you insisted we split a bottle of wine—I was practically asleep during the previews. And at some time during the show you left."

Ted said, "I know. I was there."

"And what did you tell me?"

"I . . . I saw that you were dozing, so I went out to get some popcorn. I ran into Mr. LeBlanc. An old client of mine."

"I know that's what you said. And I know what I saw. I heard you leave. I waited a couple of minutes, then I went out to the lobby. You weren't there. I went back to the movie. I waited. I waited nearly a half-hour. And then you came back. Breathing hard. With muddy feet. I know you had muddy feet, because your shoes were covered with mud when we got home."

Ted stayed quiet.

Jessica said, "I didn't know where you were. Or what you were doing. But I'm pretty sure where you went. You went to Sam Warner's house. Somehow you found out about that party. You knew Sam's parents were gone. What were you thinking—hoping to get revenge? Push him around? Hurt him?"

She wondered what he was thinking. What he would say. What he could possibly say.

His hand was still in hers. She felt like he had surrendered.

He sighed. "I had heard of the party. I knew about Sam bullying Craig. I had a lot to drink that night, and when you were dozing, I thought, shit, the Warner house was a five-minute drive from there. Just five minutes, and five minutes to scare him and tell him to leave Craig alone, and then I'd be back."

"You didn't see him, did you?"

"No. A couple of his wrestling friends pushed me around. I was . . . humiliated. And so I went back to the theater."

In the darkness Jessica nodded, even though she knew Ted couldn't see the gesture. "Did any of the boys recognize you?"

"I don't think so."

"So there's no evidence that you were there."

"Not that I know of."

Now, Jessica thought, *now. Seal the deal.*

"I'll never talk again about Paula Fawkes, and you'll never ask me about the money. And Ted, if you ever do talk to me about the money, the police will get a tip that you were at the Warner house two nights before Sam was murdered, threatening him. And how long before they reopen the case against you?"

Ted shifted, and whispered, "Why, Jess? Why are you doing this?"

Jessica said, "Because I can."

Ted felt Jessica's hand slip away, and he wished now he had kept his mouth shut, had never raised the subject of the money. What was going to happen next? How could he ever—

Jessica rolled over and kissed his cheek, his lips, and then tongued his ear, and her hand worked across his chest, lightly scraping his skin, flicking his nipples, and she threw off the sheets and blanket, and in the dim light he realized what she was wearing, and he was stunned that he was getting erect.

She had on what she once jokingly called her "please jump me" lingerie, a silky black thing with straps, cutouts, and lace that she had worn the night of their first wedding anniversary. It really looked good on Jess, and he got harder, thinking of Paula Fawkes, who wore such slutty stuff all the time, but he couldn't remember the last time his wife had taken this out. There was something just so deeply arousing in seeing his wife wearing something so hot instead of her usual dull stuff.

He kissed her and kissed her, deep and hard and raw, and he squeezed her breasts, flicked her erect nipples, gave them the attention he knew she loved, and, like performing an old familiar dance, he slipped into the routine of hot lovemaking that they hadn't done for a very, very long time. And then . . .

She pushed him.

What?

He had taken off his shorts and was starting to roll her over, but Jessica pushed him again, on his shoulder, more insistently, and she whispered, "You just lie back."

So he did. Not an unusual position but not typical for them. Jessica straddled him and he slid in with no difficulty, just moaning with pleasure, and he decided he didn't care what position they were using.

—⁓—

Later Ted was gently sleeping and Jessica was on her side, her back to his back, her legs clenched together. Eventually she would have to get up to clean herself and get rid of this ridiculous Victoria's Secret knockoff, but she was still enjoying the afterglow of one intense orgasm. Considering everything that had gone on today, she was surprised at how quickly and how deeply it had rippled through her, but she knew why.

There were lots of names for what a couple did together, from sport screwing to lovemaking to comfort sex, or even angry screwing. But this was the first time Jessica had done a deal fuck, to ensure that Ted kept his mouth shut from tonight on, and she had enjoyed riding her husband, being on top of him and sealing the deal.

Ted kept on sleeping. Jessica stayed awake for a while, smiling with the glow of satisfaction.

SAM WARNER'S STORY

Last Monday Night

When he was a kid, the thought of walking alone at night through the Warner Town Forest would have scared him shitless, but Sam Warner was going along a quiet trail in the dark, alone and feeling badass and happy. And why shouldn't he be happy? Another party at his house last Saturday had gone off great, even though Percy Prescott had stopped by, some dad from somewhere had tried to barge in and had gotten himself tuned up, Emma had puked over his dick, and Craig had gotten pushed around some. Still. Tonight was going to make it all right.

He walked along with confidence on the narrow dirt trail, not feeling scared at all, like little Sammie would have been back in the day. But ever since he had slid into puberty and picked up wrestling, there was nothing to be scared about. Ever. And even if there was a bit of pussy inside him, good ol' Mum had done her part to make things less scary in the woods. Up ahead on the trail was a small lamp set to the side, letting off a glow of light. Most of the trail was lit like this, even though about half of the lamps weren't working. Another one of Mum's special projects to improve Warner. She and some dimwit committee had spent months working on ways to "improve" the town forest, and someone had come up with the idea to put in lighting so the place would be more "inclusive" and "welcoming."

That had kept her and her idiot chatty friends busy for a year, debating lighting options, pricing, finding out if the lights were "green" or not and whether they came from a company that was environmentally conscious, blah-blah-blah. In the end they picked these lights, which were solar-powered, and one day Sam overheard Pop telling one of his golfing buddies that "the silly bitches didn't even realize that most of the lights wouldn't work because they were in the middle of the woods."

He passed one of the lights and smashed it with one good kick.

He checked his iPhone. About five minutes to go. He put the iPhone back into his coat pocket, right next to the thumb drive of him and Emma. At first Sam thought about giving Craig a drive with a video showing him giving Craig the finger and saying, "Fuck you, fag!" but he decided that wouldn't be the safe thing to do. Better to give him the drive with the video, and only the video, and make sure he erased the original.

Craig was a wimp, but there was something scary about his computer skills, and Sam didn't want the bitch hacking his computer and screwing things up or, even worse, going after Mum and Pop and having his dense parents start questioning why their computers were getting screwed up.

Besides, he had at least a half dozen similar videos—without the puking over his Johnson, thank you very much—hidden in a folder on his computer, so it wasn't like he didn't have enough whack-off material to last him for a while.

The narrow trail descended, and he could hear the tinkling of water from the forest stream in front of him.

Nope, he'd do what Craig asked and then wait. Maybe a month, maybe next year, maybe after graduation, but one day Sam would get his revenge, settle up accounts. That's how he rolled.

Last year a wrestler from Methuen had made a point of pinning him to the mat and whispering in his ear, "Take this, honey," before letting off a real stinky fart. Yeah. Lots of laughs, but last month there had been a rematch, and Sam had managed to pin the joker down and say, "Honey, right back at ya," and later the guy had gotten to his gear and found someone had smeared dog shit over his civvy clothes.

Revenge could take a long time, but it was so satisfying.

There. The little wooden bridge.

"Craig?" he called out. "You out here?"

Nothing.

He checked the time again. Right on time. So where was Craig?

"Hey, girlfriend, you here?"

Still no answer.

He walked up and down the little bridge, maybe ten feet or so in length, letting his strong hands feel the railings. This bridge had been built by Pop and at least was still standing. Pop was proud of the Warner name, and while Mum was out trying to save the world, Pop was at his own meetings, trying to "improve" Warner. He was so goddamn proud of the Warner name that he spent lots of money putting plaques around town, tracing his family's genealogy, and he even flew to the UK—with Mum, leaving Sam behind—to go to the Brit town his ancestors supposedly came from.

"Craig?"

Big freakin' deal. Sam wished that ol' man Warner back in England had stayed put. Maybe by the time Sam came along, the Warners would have been earls or dukes or something like that instead of being the boring stiffs Mum and Pop were, and—

Footsteps. Coming up the trail.

He peered down the other side of the bridge. Now he wished Mum and her girlfriends had done a better job of putting in the lights.

"Craig?"

The footsteps came closer and then stopped.

"Craig?"

Sam walked a bit along the bridge, then stopped at the near side. Screw that. He wasn't begging for anything.

"Craig, you there? You better not be alone, you know what I mean?"

261

S. A. PRENTISS

Footsteps on the bridge.

"Craig?"

Something else came to him just as a bright light struck his face, causing him to close his eyes, hold up his hand, and he was about to shout back, protest, say *something*, when her voice shouted: "Rapist!" and another light suddenly flared—much brighter, harsher, and louder.

282

CHAPTER THIRTY-TWO

T wo weeks had passed, and it was five minutes to closing at Warner Savings Bank on this Friday, and Jessica couldn't believe how contented she was. It had been a busy week, with lots of good stuff happening at the bank. Outside it was a sunny, perfect day in downtown Warner, and soon she'd be leaving to attend a meet where Emma was competing.

She was cashing out her drawer, preparing a deposit, getting the paperwork together, as the new girl, Stacy Kiln, struggled next to her.

"I don't know," Stacy said, shaking her head. "I don't know if I'll ever get used to this."

"Oh, you will, don't worry about it," Jessica said.

At the next teller station, Rhonda gave her a slight smile. It was usually Rhonda's job to train new tellers—a task she hated—but Jessica wanted to repay her friend for helping her out during the earlier weeks when it seemed like everything she had worked and sweated for was about to collapse, so she had volunteered to train Stacy. Boy, had that made Rhonda happy.

Percy was over at his drive-up station, and he gave her a little wave, and she smiled back at him, and she tried to think if she was feeling guilty or not about how close she had come to turning him in—even with no evidence—but decided that it was too much work.

It all came down to one thing. Love. Especially a mother's love for her daughter.

"Jessica?"

Standing in the lobby, just on the other side of her NEXT TELLER PLEASE sign, was Ellen Nickerson, the branch manager.

"Hi, Ellen," she said. "What's up?"

"When you get your drawer put away, do you have a minute?"

Jessica nodded. "Sure, but if you don't mind, it has to be quick. I'm going to my daughter's cross-country meet and it starts in less than a half hour."

"It'll be quick, I promise."

Jessica grabbed her drawer and said to Stacy, "Tomorrow, get in a few minutes early, and I'll show you some little teller tricks I've learned over the years to get through the day faster."

Stacy had flaming red hair from a bottle and a rough complexion, and her revealing clothes were cut for someone about twenty pounds lighter, but she was like a scared puppy, and with her station next to Jessica, Stacy had latched on to Jessica as if she were an all-knowing mama who would look out for her.

"Gosh, thanks, Jessica," she said, "I owe you so much, you have no idea. Honest." Jessica then walked to the vault. She unlocked the cage door, got in, put her drawer into the vault, closed it, and spun the dial, and then Rhonda came in, carrying her own drawer.

"How's the new girl working out?" Rhonda asked.

"Lousy, but she'll turn out okay," Jessica said.

Her friend said, "Hey, can I ask you something?"

"Sure, but the Ice Queen needs to see me. What is it?"

Rhonda's face flushed and she looked away for a moment, as if she were embarrassed—or scared?—to say what was on her mind.

She said, "Look . . . just curiosity, that's all. But when we were at the town common for Sam Warner's service, we were talking about Larry Miles. And how he died when he was rock climbing."

It was like a seam in the vault had suddenly opened, blowing cold air on the back of her neck. "Sure. I remember."

"Well . . ."

Jessica said, "Rhonda, please. Ellen wants to see me."

"It's just this," Rhonda said, her voice a bit shaky. "You said something about him dying because his crampons fell apart. But I didn't know that. It wasn't in the news how he died. They just said it was a climbing accident. How did you know?"

Jessica stared at her oldest and best friend, one who had stuck with her while Ted was accused of murder, who had helped her when she was calling in sick two weeks back. And what she really, really wanted to say was this: *That man wanted to fire you. He wanted to hurt you and your family. And I wasn't going to let that happen. And one day when he was in Boston for a staff meeting, I went into his office where he kept his climbing gear and with a few twists of a screwdriver I did what had to be done.*

But she shrugged. "Oh, Ted probably told me. You know how he has friends in the police."

Rhonda reluctantly nodded. "Probably."

Jessica touched Rhonda's hand. "Now, I really have to go."

—⁂—

In her office, Ellen was looking as sharp and as managerial as ever, wearing a bright yellow dress-and-jacket combo that looked pretty good on her, all things considered. She motioned for Jessica to take a seat and Jessica did so.

Ellen managed a smile. "How's everything at home?"

"Couldn't be better," she said, which was true.

"Glad to hear it. I can't imagine the pressures you and your family went through, with Ted being falsely arrested like that. Thank God you can put it behind you. Ted doing all right?"

Jessica said, "It's funny—his lawyer told him that with the news of his being innocent coming out, his real estate business might take a jump. And you know what? She was right. This week's been the best week he's had in almost a year, and the Concord zoning board has approved a development he and his partner have been working on for months."

Ellen said, "Well, I'm happy to tell you that the good news is still coming your way."

"How's that, Ellen?"

She turned her computer screen around to give Jessica a look and said, "You've successfully upsold four customers in the past two weeks, one who has nearly a million dollars in combined deposits and assets. Even if you were to stop right now, which I don't think you will, you'll be the lead this month among all the tellers. That's very good news, Jessica."

She couldn't help but smile at Ellen and think, *Yes, three weeks ago you were looking to fire my ass.* "Thank you," Jessica said.

"No, I thank you, and the bank thanks you," Ellen said. "Which brings me to another happy topic. Since you've shown such a commitment, I've made some phone calls, tugged in a few favors, and it looks like I can get you that scholarship for your community college courses. How does that sound?"

Jessica smiled. "That sounds wonderful, Ellen. Let me think about it."

Ellen looked shocked. "Think about it? Really? But when I told you that the funds were gone, you—"

Jessica stood up, recalling the $12,000 she had gotten from Ted's partner and how $10,000 of it had ended up with Gary Talbot to quiet her bitch ex-sister-in-law. She had kept $2,000 to pay for her upcoming education.

"I think I can cover it myself," she said, thinking, *Sweetie, I don't need your sympathy.* "Now, really, I've got to go."

—⁂—

It was cold and blustery on the Warner playing fields, but Jessica didn't mind. Her coat was buttoned up tight and her hands were in her pockets while she waited, waited for her Emma to emerge from the woods. The stands were nearly empty and there were just a few parents here. She didn't recognize any of them, which meant that they had to be from the other school running today, Lowell.

Coach John Webber was standing by himself, watching and waiting with the clipboard, and Jessica thought of her Emma running in the woods over there, hopefully taking the lead, hopefully scoring a win today, one more win, which would get her to statewide competition sooner than expected and make more colleges aware of her skills.

What a wonderful day.

And then after college, Jessica would have that trust fund to use in any way she saw fit, so career opportunities that Jessica had never had at her daughter's age would be open for Emma, a golden future for her golden girl, and a satisfied voice inside whispered, *You did it, you did it all for Emma. You did it.*

And a young man's voice shattered her bliss and stillness. "Hello, Mom."

She quickly turned. It was her stepson, Craig. And this was the first time—ever!—he had called her "Mom."

He looked at her with a firm, hard gaze, no joy or affection there.

What was wrong? What did he know?

Jessica found her voice. "Hi, Craig," she said. "What's up?"

—⁂—

In the woods next to her high school, Emma Thornton once again had the smooth trail to herself, a familiar and welcome feeling. She had outpaced her own track team and the poor runners from Lowell, and all that was ahead for her was the finish line and another victory. But as she kept her breath even and steady, kept her pace strong and regular, she was thinking about her idiot stepbrother and what he had said to her just a few minutes ago, right before the track meet started, leaving her with no time to call Mom.

"I'm going to see your nutty mom later," he had said, "and I'm telling her every . . . single . . . bit."

And all Emma could say was, "She's not nutty!" and Craig had laughed and said, "Frankie Aikens—his dad is good friends with Bruce Fortner, from Carlisle, and he told me everything that your mom did back then. Everything."

Her feet pounded with satisfaction on the dirt path. Just a few minutes more and she'd emerge into sunlight, and she would win again. But what of Craig? And what of Carlisle?

Emma didn't want to, but she remembered.

—◦◦◦—

Three years ago, in her eighth-grade school year, it had become clear that Emma had the talent, strength, and grace to be a track star. She had started running for Warner Regional Junior High and in a matter of months had shattered all the track records for her class and was on her way to breaking a few more statewide.

There wasn't much of a coaching staff at the junior high, so Mom, who had done some track in high school, had offered to run with her and train with her as much as possible during the week and on weekends. That meant Mom juggling her work schedule at the bank and pressing Emma to run when Emma would rather just sit home and play games or text with her friends, but with each new win and new ribbon or trophy, Emma had begun to love running with Mom.

Until that day in Carlisle, the next town over from Warner, an easy run from their home.

It was a sunny Saturday afternoon, late spring, with lots of birds chirping. She and her Mom were running on a country road near the Warner River and had the one-lane road to themselves, just keeping up a pace, running by some of the old stone walls and rare open farmland in this part of town. The road didn't get much traffic, but on this afternoon a light-blue Toyota Camry had slowed down and then sped up after passing them, the horn honking a couple of times.

Mom was next to her. "You know them?" she asked.

"Um, no, Mom, none of my friends are old enough to drive yet. You know that."

"Okay."

Three minutes later the car came back, heading toward them, slowing down. Two men were in the front, the windows were down, and each guy leaned out and whistled at them. They looked to be in their twenties or so, and each had a thin beard, and each was grinning as they went by.

"Nice ass, Mom!" the passenger yelled.

Mom whispered something under her breath and said, "Just ignore them, Emma. Ignore them."

"Okay, Mom," she said.

But the car returned again in a few minutes and slowed down so that it seemed to be pacing them. Mom reached into a small fanny pack that had a water bottle and her cell phone and said, "Shit, no coverage out here. Can you believe it?"

Emma said, "Who were you going to call? Stepdad Ted?"

"No, the cops."

"Mom!" she protested. "It's okay."

But a few more feet passed in their running, and it didn't feel okay, because over the low sound of the motor she could hear the men's voices in bits and pieces:

". . . look at Mom's ass . . ."

". . . shit, daughter looks fucking fine, too . . ."

". . . Mom's got better tits . . ."

". . . daughter more fun . . ."

Up ahead was a dirt driveway. A new home was being built in the woods, and dumped at the side of the road were some lumber, shingles, and lengths of pipe. Mom stopped at the new driveway, grabbed a length of metal pipe, and ran back to the car.

"Hey!" the driver yelled.

"Leave my daughter alone!" Mom shouted. She swung the pipe and caught the driver right in the face, and his back arched up and he screamed. It was the first time Emma had ever heard a man scream. Again and again the pipe came down on the man's face and head, each time Mom shouting, "Leave my daughter alone!"

The passenger desperately got his window up, but Mom went to that side of the car, broke the side window with the pipe, and started pounding him as well. More screams from inside the car.

More yelling from Mom: "Leave my daughter alone!"

Emma just stood there, not moving, catching her breath as another car stopped. Two women got out. A cell-phone call was made, and the police came. After spending some time at the police station, she and her mother had been driven home by a Carlisle detective driving an unmarked cruiser. Her stepdad had been at a charity golf tournament, and her stepbrother was off with his moody friends. Mom sat her down and said, "Our secret, all right?"

And a while later Mom whispered to her one day that no charges were going to be filed, because the driver of the car had been on probation and his father didn't want anything to show up in the legal system, so that had been that.

Except that Emma never ran with her mother again.

—⁓—

Slap, slap, slap. Her feet on the trail.

Run, run, run. Quick glance back. All alone. Perfect.

Breathe, breathe, breathe.

Up ahead the trail broke free of the woods, offered a quick glimpse of the playing fields, and then swung back into the trees.

There. Nearly empty playing field, there was Mom, and—

Oh, shit.

Craig was talking to Mom and was now pointing at her. He was doing what he had threatened to do.

Oh, Mom, she thought, swinging back into the woods. *Protect me.*

CHAPTER THIRTY-THREE

Craig liked seeing his stepmom like this, a bit shook up. He couldn't remember the last time he had called her "Mom," if ever, and now was the time to get things settled.

"What's up?" he said. "This is what's up, Jessica. It's time for you to know some facts, okay?"

Her voice was soft. "What kind of facts, Craig?"

He had to laugh. This was going to be fine. Months and years of frustration were about to come right out and slap his pretty stepmom right in the face. Yeah, she was pretty, and maybe she was a MILF after all, but this was going to be all right.

Craig calmly said, "Your precious, pampered track star, your golden girl who can do no wrong, is one mean cold-blooded bitch."

"Craig, I'm not going to let you—"

"Oh, you're going to let me, Jessica, or I'm going to the police."

That seemed to knock her back on her heels. "The police? What for?"

"To tell them the truth about Emma—and everything else."

Jessica turned her head and looked at the school. The wind had come up, disturbing her hair, and she had a memory of a Greek mythology class and a drawing of the evil Medusa.

Like mother, like daughter.

"What truth is that, Craig?"

"Truth? Here's the truth. Me and Emma, we went over to Sam Warner's house Saturday night. Your sweet precious innocent little girl knew

I'd done math homework for Sam, and she wanted me to introduce her. Seems like some of her teammates had been invited to this special party and she couldn't stand being left out. She also wanted a chance to see if she could hook up with the captain of the wrestling team. Pretty basic, huh? But Sam had other ideas. I was there and found out he had her taken up to his bedroom after a few drinks. So I did the noble older brother thing, tried to go up and get her out of there, and this is what I got for being brave and looking out for your perfect daughter."

Craig slowly lifted his jacket and T-shirt, showing his stepmom the fading letters on his belly. FAG.

Jessica gave it a good long look. He lowered his coat and shirt.

"Emma barfed all over Sam. He was pissed, and as I got her out of there, after they whacked me around some, he told me that Emma had better come back sometime later to finish the job or he'd make her life hell at school."

"How?" Jessica asked.

"Go figure it out," Craig said, nearly shaking his head at how stupid she was. "You want to know why Emma was in her bedroom all day Sunday? She was still coming down off the drinking and the roofie. I told her what Sam was threatening to do, and then she came up with a plan."

Craig stopped talking. Waited. Jessica just stood there as if she were carved out of rock or some tough gray wood.

She shook her head. "What was the plan, Craig?"

"Pretty simple. When I went in to grab Emma, I saw that Sam was recording what was going on. I told Emma later. The plan was for me to reach out to Sam, ask him for a copy of the video, and then we'd make a trade—the video on a thumb drive, and then Emma would suck him off. Sam wouldn't pass the video around, and Emma wouldn't get the treatment."

Jessica said, "Oh, no."

Craig laughed. "Man, you really don't know the half of it, do you, Jessica? That was only part of the deal. Emma wanted something else."

"What's that?"

"She wanted Sam dead."

Jessica gazed at the nearly empty stands and thought, how could she have been so stupid? The wrestling team hadn't been up there to support their fellow athletes, as she had assumed. No, they had been up there on a scouting mission, seeking out fresh meat.

"I don't believe you, Craig," she said.

"I don't care if you do or don't," her stepson replied. "But it's the truth. And there's more."

Craig now knew what it must have been like to be Sam Warner, feeling on top of things, good and stable, and most of all, being in charge. Jessica was no longer his stepmom, complaining about toilet seats being left up or socks not going down the laundry chute. Nope. This adult woman, twice his age, now belonged to him. It felt great. No wonder Sam Warner had smiled all the fucking time.

Craig said, "Emma came to me with her plan, her deal. The two of us would meet Sam in the town woods, Sam would hand over the thumb drive, and then I'd . . . I'd shoot him."

"You? How?"

"Thanks to Mark Borman's dad. He's a gun nut. Belongs to the NRA and the Gun Owners Action League. I took a shotgun from his collection that you can break down and put in a knapsack. So I had that with me, and when Emma was going to go up to Sam and take care of him, I was going to kill him."

There was a rumble of thunder. "That was going to happen Tuesday night, with us sneaking out of the house. We borrowed Randy McMahon's Jetta, but the piece of crap died on us. I wanted to turn back, but Emma insisted we keep on going, even if we had to walk. We got on the trail, and—"

Jessica said, "You found Sam Warner. Dead."

"Yep."

"So, no scavenger hunt?"

Craig laughed. "I told Emma that you'd believe that story 'cause you wanted to, and that Dad would be suspicious. But it worked, didn't it? So we came back home the long way and soaking wet."

"Some story."

"Yeah, but it's not the end. One more thing, Jessica, one more thing, and if it doesn't get settled, I'm going to the cops in the next fifteen minutes. And then their investigation is going to include Emma, and the whole world will know about it. Know about the real Emma Thornton, not the made-up running doll."

Jessica tried to bring back that sense she had had a few minutes ago of being on this track field, happy that at last things were being settled and were on the right path, and now this . . . boy. This creature, this demon, had come up to spoil everything.

"Go on," she said. "Tell me."

Craig thought, *Well, now we're getting somewhere.* He said, "Emma promised me something to go out there and shoot Sam. She said, 'We get out there and go home and Sam Warner is dead, I'll take care of you.' That was the promise."

"Really?" she asked. "You were going to kill a fellow student because of a promise my daughter gave you?"

Lots of old memories came to him—of Sam bumping his books away, shoving him into lockers, tripping him in the cafeteria. He hated that his eyes were tearing up, but he said, "Once Emma got me going, I didn't mind. Thing was, I wanted to kill the shit. I really did. And when we got there, he was dead, and then Emma, she backed out on the deal."

His stepmother said, "A deal? What kind of deal?"

Craig couldn't believe how happy he felt, telling his nutty stepmother the following sentence. "Jessica, the deal was, Emma said she was going to take care of me if Sam Warner ended up dead. Sam's dead. And Emma hasn't taken care of me."

"Craig—"

"Yeah," he said. "In exchange for seeing the captain of the wrestling team dead, your precious sweet innocent golden child was going to pimp out one of her friends. Kate Romer. She told me that Kate would go out with me and suck me off. And your bitch daughter didn't come through. Stupid me, I believed her."

Jessica looked like she had just been slapped in the face. "That's the truth?" she managed to say.

He nodded. "The truth. And if I don't get taken care of . . . well, I'm going to the cops. Christ, I don't know what the cops will say or do, but I'm sure that Emma's name will be out there. She'll be humiliated, embarrassed. Hell, for all I know, maybe she did shoot the asshole."

"But Craig . . ."

He lifted his shirt again. FAG. Kept it up.

He said, "It's one thing if a guy or girl comes out gay. So what? But it's another if people think you're a fag and you're not. Kids in school are already talking. And so I need to prove that I'm not a fag, to shut them up."

His stepmom's face looked frozen, like one of those Botoxed house-wives she liked to watch so much on Bravo.

"So you don't want students to think you're gay. You'd force your sister to have one of her friends perform oral sex on you, is that it? And then tell your friends later what happened?"

Craig lowered his shirt. "She promised. I wouldn't be forcing her at all. And she's not my sister. So yeah, that doesn't count." He reached into his coat pocket, took out a thumb drive, made a twirling motion with his hand in front of Jessica's eyes. "Here's the video of your little girl with Sam's cock in her mouth, before she got sick, that I hacked from Sam's laptop. So yeah, that's the truth. And in addition to going to the cops, I'll email this to every student and teacher at Warner High School. Just to get even. For everything, including my dad getting arrested."

Jessica just stared at him. Her look should have scared him, but it didn't.

"So, what's it going to be?" he asked. "Mom?"

CHAPTER THIRTY-FOUR

Jessica just stood there, looking at this foul child that her dearly beloved husband had spawned, and she just repeated the last two words. "The truth," she said.

Craig smiled, still holding up the thumb drive. "That's right."

And Jessica just stared, and thought, *The truth. Here's the truth.*

I've never once trusted you, young man, ever since we joined our families together. And I know what you thought about me, how you thought I was just a simple bank teller, and you never suspected that I had twenty more years' experience than you working with computers.

From day one, after we moved in, I've been monitoring your internet activity, your search results, your email, using a public terminal at the town library, and, trust me, young man, librarians won't give up anything without a search warrant.

So I knew about the party—and I admit that knowing that Emma was attracted to that lunk still disappoints me—and I know what happened that night. And the video I saw you viewing Tuesday night when I came into your room? What, you don't think a mother recognizes her own daughter?

But Sam had already been dead for nearly a day when I saw that video.

I had texted with him earlier in an encrypted chatroom, pretending to be you—although I almost gave it away by using the name of my favorite computer hero, Grace Hopper, as an avatar—and set up an appointment to kill him.

Very simple, of course. Because I had made a spare key to the gun cabinet a week after we moved in, just in case I needed to defend Emma and myself if there was a break-in. And on that crowded Chamber of Commerce night,

276

do you think anybody really missed me when I drove out to the Warner Town Forest and blew off that rapist's head? Do you?

And when the little shit came down that bridge over the stream, I said one thing to him, to make sure his last bit of consciousness on earth would be to think that his victim had paid him back.

"Rapist!"

So that's the truth.

Which you will never know.

Aloud, Jessica said, "Can I trust you, Craig? Can I trust that the video of Emma and Sam—that it only exists on that thumb drive?"

There was the briefest hesitation, and he said, "Sure."

She said, "You're lying, but that's understandable. All right. You know I'll do anything, anything at all, to protect Emma. But it begins with you handing over that thumb drive, showing me your computer's hard drive, and promising that the video doesn't exist anywhere else."

"Why should I do that?"

"Because," Jessica said, holding out her hand, "I will make it right for you. But only if you give me that thumb drive, right now. No hesitation."

She waited, wondering how he would react, and a little voice inside cried out *Yes!* when the drive was slowly placed in her hand. Jessica closed her hand around it and slipped it into her left-hand coat pocket, where it nestled next to the drive she had taken from Sam's body that blessed night.

"Okay," she said, and she rubbed at her shoulder where it had ached for days after she shot that rapist.

And then, finally emerging out of the woods into the errant sunlight from overhead, where the sun had just broken through the overcast skies, here came her Emma, running alone, running safe, ready again to cross the finish line on her way to a safe, happy, and productive future, doing everything that her mother could never have done.

Craig said, "Now what?"

She took a breath. "There's a new girl at work. Maybe two years older than you. Stacy Kiln. She'll do anything I ask her to do, so I'll set the two of you up. This week. How does that sound?"

277

He hesitated. "That . . . that sounds okay. But, I mean . . ."

"You want to know if she'll do it for you? Give you oral sex? So your friends know you're not a fag?"

Craig nodded.

"I promise, I'll take care of you."

Jessica turned away from her stepson, looked out to the playing fields. Her child, her pride, her Emma, was coming right to her, smiling so widely, so happy, so safe, so ready to go on and on.

"You mean that?" Craig asked, nearly whispering.

"Oh, yes, Craig," Jessica said, meaning every word. "I'll take care of you."